Mammy's Boy

MAMMY'S BOY

DOMINI HIGHSMITH

BANTAM PRESS

LONDON · NEW YORK · TORONTO · SYDNEY · AUCKLAND

TRANSWORLD PUBLISHERS LTD
61-63 Uxbridge Road, London W5 5SA

TRANSWORLD PUBLISHERS (AUSTRALIA) PTY LTD
15-23 Helles Avenue, Moorebank, NSW 2170

TRANSWORLD PUBLISHERS (NZ) LTD
Cnr Moselle and Waipareira Aves,
Henderson, Auckland

Published 1991 by Bantam Press
a division of Transworld Publishers Ltd
Copyright © Domini Highsmith 1991

Extracts from 'As Time Goes By' and 'That's My Desire' reproduced by
kind permission of Redwood Music Limited. Extracts from 'Your Feets
Too Big' by Ada Benson and Fred Fisher, © 1936, Morley Music Co. Inc.,
USA, reproduced by kind permission of Francis Day and Hunter Ltd/EMI
Music Publishing Ltd, London WC2H 0EA.

The right of Domini Highsmith to be identified as author of this work
has been asserted in accordance with sections 77 and 78 of the Copyright
Designs and Patents Act 1988.

British Library Cataloguing in Publication Data
Highsmith, Domini, 1942–
Mammy's boy
I. Title
823.914

ISBN 0-593-02211-4

Typeset in 11/12pt Century Schoolbook by
Chippendale Type Ltd, Otley, West Yorkshire.
Printed in Great Britain by
Biddles Ltd, Guildford and King's Lynn

for Tony

and for Duke and Melodie

ONE

Frankie's face began to twitch with anxiety. He screwed his eyes tightly closed and prayed silently:

'Please, God, don't let them see me. Don't let anyone see me.'

Frankie was nine years old and not always as brave as he would like to be. Right now he was really scared because it seemed to him that all hell had been turned loose in his mam's kitchen. Women were screaming and men were yelling. It was just like one of those saloon-bar riots in the cowboy films, where everything got smashed up and windows were broken and bodies were tossed about all over the place, only this one was for real. He had very nearly walked right into it. Only at the very last moment had he leaped for cover, when the kitchen door suddenly burst open as he approached and a ferment of brawling people erupted into the back yard.

Now he huddled in a crouch beneath a mound of filthy tarpaulin in the uppermost corner of the yard, his heart thumping in his chest as he witnessed the growing bedlam of disorder taking place only a short distance from his hiding place. What made matters worse was the fact that he should never have been there at all. He was supposed to stay to school dinners, but Mr Sunderland had sent him home for not bringing any money, because boys who were allowed to eat without paying then felt free to ignore all the rules and forget their dinner money willy-nilly. Mr Sunderland was the school's headmaster, and he was well-acquainted with the disgraceful liberties taken by grubby little boys who thought they could pull the wool over teacher's eyes and sit down to dine for free.

'The school meals service is not a charitable institution,' Sir had reminded him that very morning, emphasizing the words with pursed lips and a wagging, chalk-and-ink-stained forefinger. 'Nor can our school kitchens be run on credit simply because lazy-minded individuals like yourself refuse to obey the rules. Pull your socks up, boy. Get it through your thick head that here at St Andrew's Primary School, Listerhills, we pay up prompt on Monday morning or we go home for dinners the *whole week*.'

'Yes, sir,' Frankie had said, acutely embarrassed and wishing he had remembered to ask for his money on Sunday afternoon, before the party started. He had only himself to blame for his predicament. It was entirely his own fault for not planning things properly.

Trudging homeward at noon with his stomach painfully empty, he had wondered how it would feel to be one of the free-dinner kids who paid for their food in taunts and jibes instead of hard cash, but who ate well every day and always seemed to be first in the queue for seconds of meat and potato pie or rhubarb tart or treacle sponge pudding and custard.

It was a long walk from his school on Listerhills Road to the very top of Thorpe Street, where a rough, steep track led down the side of Brooke Parker's Chemicals Ltd to the rear gates of Old Ashfield. He hadn't dared take the short cut along Dead Man's Alley and across the Mucky Beck, even though it would have saved a lot of time and brought him out below the terraced gardens at the front of the house, from where he might have slipped indoors unobserved. His last experience of that eerie, deserted alley had proved near-fatal and left him with a fear of drowning and a renewed horror of being eaten alive by sewer rats. He could still recall how his best leather shoes had been sucked by the current into that dark tunnel mouth, and sometimes he could still taste the nauseating slime that had to be hosed from him while he shivered in an old tin bath outside in the yard.

'Look out! Stop him, someone! Stop that lunatic before he chokes the life out of her!'

Frankie's entire body suddenly jerked with a nervous start as the metal dustbins stacked outside the tool-shed were tipped over with a resounding crash. Their contents were immediately claimed by dozens of scuffling feet and freely distributed about the yard. By now the barking of the tethered Great Dane could scarcely be heard above the din of hysterical human voices. What had begun as an untidy skirmish had rapidly deteriorated into bloody warfare involving such weapons as pots, pans, sticks, empty buckets and anything else that came to hand. Several screeching women managed to detach themselves from the brawl's nucleus and stagger back to the house, there to be greeted by yells of abuse and threats of violence from those already inside. There must have been twenty or more people involved in the battle, all of them shouting and bawling at the tops of their voices and lashing out with fists and feet at anyone within reach.

Frankie was desperately worried about his mam. He had not dared wake her to ask for his dinner money that morning, and for all he knew she was still locked in her ground-floor room, a helpless maiden in distress trapped behind wooden shutters while the survivors of last night's party fought a pitched battle through her home. He didn't want to think of her with the big Irishman, so he hoped she was all alone and then felt horribly guilty because that would leave her unprotected and frightened. Added to his concern was the humiliation of knowing there was nothing he could do to help her. He was simply not big enough. Nor did he possess the kind of courage it would take to wade manfully into the mêlée and fight his way to her assistance. It was the same old story. He never quite managed to come up to scratch. He was seldom any *real* use to his mam at all.

'*You lousy, two-timing swine! I'll teach you to go Tom-catting around the minute my back's turned.*'

Someone shrieked a stream of obscenities and hurled a flat-iron through the kitchen window. It shattered the glass in all directions and missed the Great Dane's head by inches, sending the already agitated animal into a frenzy of leaps and howls. A black woman in a tight green dress appeared briefly at the kitchen window before making a dash for the back door. As she reached the yard a huge, pink-palmed hand appeared as if from nowhere, grabbed her halo of frizzy hair and dragged her, kicking and screaming, back into the house. Seconds later she broke free and, still screaming at the top of her voice, rushed upstairs, flung open one of the back bedroom windows and proceeded to toss out whatever came to hand. She had managed to dispose of a whole stack of newspapers, the flock filling out of a slashed mattress, two badly stained sheets, the contents of a chamber-pot and several items of underwear before she was grabbed from behind by a fat, screeching blonde wearing nothing but a short cotton vest that barely reached her navel. For a while the two figures lunged and lurched at the bedroom window, arms flailing and fists flying, the blond woman's bouncing breasts and vast, quivering buttocks dominating the spectacle.

'Oh, *Jesus!*' Frankie muttered, watching with sickly fascination through a rip in the tarpaulin.

'Oh, sweet *Jesus!*'

Then an upstairs door slammed and a man he had never seen before arrived on the scene to bring the squabble to an abrupt end. He did so by grabbing the coloured woman by the hair and punching the blonde full in the face, sending her sprawling, bloodied and senseless, across the bed.

In a safe corner of the sloping, irregularly paved yard, nine-year-old Frankie had squeezed himself into the narrow gap between a pig-swill bin and a broken wheelbarrow, both of which were partially concealed by old tarpaulin sheets that stank of dried turkey entrails. He could see bright droplets of saliva spraying from Nader's mouth as she strained at her chain and barked and barked as if demented, pausing only occasionally to savage a portion of mattress flock or a scrap of clothing in sheer frustration. Through the shattered kitchen window came the sounds of breaking crockery and angry, yelling voices.

'She's nothing but a bloody whore,' a woman shrilled.

'Oh yeah?' taunted another. 'And just listen to the greasy old chip-pan calling the kettle grimy-arse.'

'If you ask me, *all* women are whores,' a man bellowed in complaint. 'And there's not one of 'em worth more than ten bob with her knickers off.'

'And you should know that better than anyone,' a woman screamed in reply. 'Only a ten-bob turn who doesn't care what she catches would be interested in *your* doodah.'

'Watch your mouth, woman. There's many a chick around here showing an interest . . . a lot more chicks than the likes of *you* could count.'

'Yeah, that's only because you'll put the damn thing anywhere, you dirty *dip-stick!*'

The crude gibe was followed by a loud slap and a cry of pain. At that moment wails and moans began to issue from upstairs as the big blonde in the tiny vest came to her senses to find her nose and mouth bleeding and her face swollen. Somewhere in the house several men were quarrelling. A woman sobbed hysterically. There were crashes and bangs and a number of more ominous, less identifiable sounds. Above the bedlam of sobs and yells, a wireless tuned to *Worker's Playtime* played at its highest volume and Wilfred Pickles encouraged a captive audience to sing along with Mabel at the piano:

'*It's a long way to Tipperary, it's a long way to go.*'

Frankie muttered the words of the song in time with the voices on the wireless.

11

'It's a long way to Tipperary, to the sweetest girl I know.'

He dared to stretch out his cramped legs, first making sure his feet could not be seen protruding from the folds of the tarpaulin. Then he rubbed his nose vigorously with the back of his hand to ease an itch deep inside his nostrils. The fine feather-dust trapped beneath the tarpaulin was making him want to sneeze, while the smell of turkey entrails was beginning to settle on his stomach and leave an unpleasant taste in the back of his throat. He remembered being horribly sick on the bus to Leeds, when one of his aunties took him out for the day and bought him chocolate and fizzy pop to eat on the journey. At the time he had been convinced she was trying to poison him, and who could he blame for that but himself? He had been warned a thousand times never to let *anything* pass his lips that came from his three aunties or their mother, his Nanny Fanny. They were all liars who were not to be trusted. They only *pretended* to be fond of him. In secret they were so jealous that they hated him. They only bought him all those chocolates and toffees and cakes and ice-cream so that his strong white teeth would be ruined, and one of these days they would poison him to death because they were wicked, vindictive women who would do anything at all to make Frankie's mam unhappy. And she had been right. His mam had known all along that his auntie would try to poison him on the bus to Leeds.

'And it just serves you right for being a disobedient little fool,' she had told him. 'Doesn't this *prove* they're trying to poison you? It's your own silly fault, Frankie. I warned you, but you chose not to listen to me. I *told* you never to trust them. Didn't I tell you? Didn't I warn you about them at least a thousand times? Well, didn't I? Didn't I?'

His mam had sounded very angry, but all the time she was saying these things she had smiled and nodded her head as if it was all right for him to be feeling so ill and miserable. And even now there were times, especially when

12

he was *very* hungry, when he found himself forgetting the proof and the warnings and just enjoying the things his aunties and his nanny bought for him. So far he had been lucky because he was still alive, even though he was halfway convinced that he risked certain death with every mouthful they made him eat. Sometimes, though, he wondered if his being sick that day on the Leeds bus had really been his auntie's fault at all. He *always* felt sick on buses. The smells of petrol and oil and hot exhaust fumes seemed to gather in his stomach and at the back of his throat, just as the stench of the tarpaulin was doing now, and sooner or later he would have to throw up in order to get rid of it.

'It's a long, long way to Tipperary,' he muttered, trying to focus his thoughts away from the prospect of being sick. 'But my heart's right there.'

He was hungry. There would be lots of food left over from last night's party; cold meat, cheese and pastries, and sandwiches gone hard and curly at the edges, if only he could find a way of getting into the kitchen and helping himself. He leaned forward and peered out through the gap in the tarpaulin. The yard was clear now except for one man who appeared to have fallen asleep with his back against an up-turned dustbin, and two women offering tearful comfort to each other just outside the kitchen door. The commotion inside was moving away, perhaps along the hallway towards the main door at the front of the house. It looked as if Frankie was not to be trapped for the rest of the day in his hot, smelly hidey-hole, after all. The coast was almost clear for him to make a dash for the kitchen, grab something to eat and get back to school in time for the bell for afternoon lessons.

He was on the verge of creeping out to investigate further when a tall figure, clad in a short fur coat and clutching a zebra-skin handbag, appeared in the open doorway and began to tip-toe furtively up the sloping yard. This was

Blossom, the lanky black woman from Howard Street who painted her toe-nails and fingernails the same vibrant blood-red as her lips and laughed all the time around a mouthful of enormous white teeth. Frankie had heard them say that Blossom packed her brassieres with handkerchiefs and lumps of cotton wool to make her breasts so big and round, but he knew that wasn't so. He had seen them with his own eyes, naked and without any kind of padding to make them bigger. He had looked through the keyhole to see what she was doing in the bedroom with Detective Norman Parkinson, and that was how he knew for a fact that Blossom's breasts were coal black like the rest of her, and had purply-brown nipples that stuck out like little door-knobs, and were just as fat and just as round with all her clothes taken off.

The wireless was still playing and Nader was barking so ferociously that Frankie did not hear the click as the yard gate opened. Blossom had ducked down into a low crouch in order to pass beneath the kitchen window without being seen. With her skirt hitched up over her thighs and her knees wide open, her knickers were an unexpected flash of bright white against the shiny blackness of her skin. She was still bent double, teetering precariously on her high heels, when a strong masculine voice bellowed from a point only a few feet from where Frankie was hidden:

'What in hell's name is going on here?'

Frankie stiffened, then drew his limbs close to his body and screwed his eyes tightly shut, willing himself to become invisible. In his father's tone of voice he detected the simmering anger that at any moment might become a volcanic burst of fury.

Blossom cursed softly and hauled herself upright, stretching to her full height of more than six feet including high-heeled shoes and distinctive mop of frizzy, coal-black, candy-floss hair.

14

'Go in and see for yourself,' she said sulkily. 'I've had enough of this. I'm going home. And you don't have to worry about Her Highness. Nobody's seen hide nor hair of her since last night.'

'So what's the score here?' Buddie drawled menacingly. He jerked his head in the direction of the house, taking in at a glance the litter-strewn yard with its overturned dustbins and shattered window. 'What's the problem?'

'How the hell should I know?' Blossom snapped. Her voice had risen in pitch in order to compete with the ferocious barking of the dog. 'It has nothing to do with me. Things just got a bit out of hand, that's all.'

Buddie glowered angrily. He seemed such a tall, impressive man, standing on the top step with his legs wide apart and a fist clenched on each hip. Big boots, denim pants and a red chequered shirt with rolled-up sleeves gave him the look of a rugged North American cowboy. Beneath his wide-brimmed Stetson hat his hair was black and wiry, and his sun-browned face, its upper lip darkened by a neat ebony moustache, was more strikingly handsome in real life than ever it was in the paintings done of him at the Bradford School of Art.

Frankie squinted at his father through a fist-sized hole in that section of the tarpaulin covering the wheelbarrow. He watched him descend the five stone steps from gate to yard, his impressive stature diminishing in size with every stride until he stood beside the black woman with the rim of his Stetson hat on a level with her chin. Buddie was a big, big man packed into a powerful but shorter-than-average frame. Almost everyone he met towered above him, and yet everything about Buddie was so much larger-than-life: his Fats Waller voice with its clear American accent, his sudden explosions of bellowing laughter, his fabulous jewellery, his fearsome, hair-trigger temper. Even the solid brass buckle on his belt was by far the biggest, heaviest, shiniest brass buckle Frankie had ever seen in his life.

15

'Down, Nader! Quit your damn barking! *Down* I say!'

The large, toffee-coloured Great Dane shrank from its master's voice just long enough to draw breath before continuing its tirade of frenzied barking. The blond woman in the back bedroom, still wearing nothing but her skimpy vest, dropped a bloodied towel from the open window and slumped against the frame, wailing and nursing her bruised face. The yard was a shambles of discarded kitchen utensils, ripped clothes, broken glass, mattress stuffing and excrement from the shattered chamber-pot.

'Get back in the house, Blossom,' Buddie ordered, grinding the words through clenched teeth.

She looked down at him from her greater height, her eyes narrowed as she peered along the short, flat bridge of her nose. She folded her arms across her body and shook her head until her earrings danced and her breasts wobbled.

'Not me,' she declared. 'I'm going home.'

Buddie grabbed her elbow and began to march her back the way she had come.

'Back inside,' he growled. 'You'll leave when I say so and not before. Quiet, Nader! For Christ's sake shut up, you stupid animal!'

At the kitchen door he gave Blossom a shove that sent her tottering inside, turned abruptly and strode across the yard to silence the Great Dane with one practised blow from his steel-capped right boot. With a high-pitched yelp Nader lurched backwards against the wall and then collapsed on her bed of old sacks like a felled oak. Frankie winced at the sickening force of the kick. His face began to twitch with anxiety and he hardly dared breathe lest his hiding place be discovered and he, too, fell within the boundaries of that awesome rage. He found it difficult to understand why the dog was so stupid. Even its predecessor, the vicious Rosie, had eventually learned the folly of provoking her master beyond a certain point. Buddie prided himself on being the undisputed master of his own animals, and he was not

16

a man to coax or cajole them into obedience. He always maintained that the worst tempered dog in the whole world could be brought neatly into line once it made the association between bad behaviour and a boot in the ribs.

'Don't let him see me. Please, don't let him see me,' Frankie prayed without moving his lips. 'I'm not here. I'm not. Don't let him see me.'

The prayer was little more than a confused jumble of words inside his head, but the unspoken chanting worked like a genuine magic charm. As the dog collapsed, its deafening barks reduced to a series of shallow gasping sounds, the now furious Buddie stamped away to kick open the kitchen door with sufficient force to send it clattering back on its hinges. There was a sudden brief silence, then the door slammed shut behind him and the hubbub inside the house took on a new intensity. Everyone began shouting at once and fresh quarrels broke out as blame for all the trouble and damage was shifted this way and that amongst those present. Frankie did not wait to discover the outcome of his father's arrival on the battlefield. At the first opportunity he crept from beneath the tarpaulin and, scuttling on all fours like a startled crab, made a dash for the gate. Once outside he turned sharp left and moved away stealthily, hugging the wall for cover and terrified lest he be spotted and hauled indoors to give account of himself to his parents.

Frankie's home was at the centre of a row of three stone-built dwellings; a big, dark, draughty house of countless rooms and incalculable secrets, all crammed like a sandwich-filling between its long-derelict neighbours. Frankie had learned that it was originally built by a rich local mill-owner more than a hundred years ago, in the days when the hills and hollows of Great Horton offered wonderful views and fresh, clean air that only the very wealthy could afford to own. The house had been designed with long, steeply terraced gardens at

17

the front, formal gardens to each side and many acres of natural woodland to give it extra privacy. In those days a stream had run right through the valley to mark the lower edge of the property, a clear, fresh-water stream where Quaker people came to paddle and to enjoy their summer picnics. Then somebody with more money than sense had put up all the dirty mills and factories to spoil the views. Hundreds of workers and their families had come to the area, and within a short time their sewage and rubbish and industrial waste had transformed the Quakers' pretty West Brook into the rat-infested Mucky Beck. Now there were rows of steep cobbled streets on the opposite hillside, all flanked by pokey little houses with smoking chimneys and outside lavatories and no hot water taps. Frankie had once written a long composition about the history of Old Ashfield. Mrs Greenwood said it was very good and gave him eight out of ten and a gold star and a pat on the head for his efforts. The only reason she did not pin it up on the classroom wall was because the handwriting was poor and there were too many black smudges on the paper from his inky fingers. He was secretly very proud of his composition, his first real, grown-up essay. Even if it *was* true that only he and Mrs Greenwood were able to decipher his dreadful handwriting, he could still be proud of his special mention and his high marks and his first-time-ever gold star.

He had reached the boarded-up kitchen window of the end house when a voice called out from a point high above his head:

'Hey, Frankie, how's your mam?'

'Nice party, kid. Bet you were ogling the big blonde's tits and arse, eh? Like 'em nice and fleshy, do you?'

'Hey, forget the fat blonde. Tell us about your mam, Frankie.'

He stopped dead in his tracks. He was on the littered rear driveway where the turkeys were housed in untidy makeshift pens and two of the goats were tethered on a patch of grass between a pile of scrap iron and a rusting pig-swill boiler. The drive was completely enclosed on its far side by the blank, windowless rear wall of Brooke Parker's. A soaring, roughly-finished wall rose to the much higher level of the factory's lorry park, nearly forty feet of sturdy red brick that usually ensured the privacy of Old Ashfield and its occupants. Now three young workmen were sitting astride the wall, smoking cigarettes and grinning from their lofty vantage point. Frankie guessed that they had seen everything, especially the half-dressed women fighting at the open bedroom window. He felt his cheeks grow hot with humiliation. It shamed him to have his home and family gaped at like freaks in a side-show.

'What's the matter, Frankie? Cat got your tongue, eh? Cat got your tongue?'

They exchanged nudges and whispered comments he was not meant to hear but which caused them all to slap their thighs and roar with ribald laughter.

'Hey, how's your mam, Frankie?'

More laughter. He had seen the men up there before, and he knew they must have parked their lorry very close to the wall so they wouldn't be seen by the bosses when they climbed up to spy on innocent people and throw their empty cigarette packets down into the turkey-pens and ask Frankie questions about his mam. He hated the Brooke Parker men. They were forever teasing him and making him feel ashamed of what they wanted to do to his mam. On impulse he balled his hands into fists and stiffened the first two fingers of each hand into a double V-sign. Then he stuck out his tongue and jabbed his fingers vigorously in the air a number of times, aiming the insult upwards at their grinning faces. He could not be certain of the impact his obscene gesture had on them, but just doing it made him feel better. He was chuckling to himself as he broke into a sprint, reached the end of the dirt drive and vanished around the side of the derelict house.

TWO

For a long time he stood with his back against the wall and his hands thrust deep into his pockets. There was a long safety-pin clipped into the waistband of his pants, holding the fabric in a bulky pucker that was supposed to tighten the elastic and keep his pants up. It did not work very well, because each time he put the smallest pressure on his pockets he could feel his pants slipping further and further down over his hips. He would have bet anyone a tanner to a poke in the eye that he could take his pants right off without unfastening a single button.

When at last he dared to look back the way he had come, he saw that two of the Brooke Parker men had jumped down from the wall into the factory lorry park and were now out of sight. The third, a cocky chap with light brown hair and a laugh that made even the most innocent comment seem dirty, took a final draw on his cigarette and flicked the stub into the air. It made a wide, red-tipped arc before dropping through an opening in the lean-to roof on one side of the turkey-pen. Frankie's eyes widened and he held his breath. A split-second later there was an unholy uproar as a scorched bird began to squawk and jump about in alarm. One by one its companions followed suit. The knock-on effect was incredible. Soon the entire enclosure, into which the birds were packed shoulder-to-shoulder with barely an inch of space between, was heaving at the very seams. Within minutes of the lighted cigarette-end finding its target, no less than eighty-seven spooked turkeys were stamping and screeching and flapping about in mindless panic. Clearly satisfied with the end result of his handiwork, the grinning Brooke Parker man dropped nimbly out of sight on the other side of the wall. His parting taunt was yelled at the top of his voice and reached Frankie's ears above the din of turkey noise:

'How's your mam then, Frankie?'

'Oh, bugger off,' the boy muttered, and stabbed a few more V-signs in the general direction of the lorry park, just for good measure. Then he stepped out for a better view round the angled corner of the house. Clouds of feathers and stale, dried bird droppings were gusting into the air. Turkey heads, wings, tails and feet protruded from every gap in the structure, which was little more than a hotchpotch of planks and old doors and sheets of rusting corrugated tin all battened down with ropes and weighted here and there with broken house-bricks. It was chaos and confusion only loosely confined. Quite clearly, the worst was yet to come.

Thoughts tumbled through Frankie's mind at a confusing rate. He knew he should run back and warn Buddie that the birds were about to break free, but that would mean passing the turkey-pen on his way to the gate, and at that moment he could envisage nothing worse than finding himself caught in the open when the stampede began. Besides, there was trouble in the house and Buddie was already in a rotten mood and everyone knew that Frankie should have been eating his dinner at Grange Road School canteen instead of sneaking around Old Ashfield where he was not meant to be. If he told on the Brooke Parker man who threw down the lighted cigarette-end he would also land himself in serious trouble for making double V-signs and sticking his tongue out at an adult. Even as he managed to talk himself out of raising the alarm, the first of the turkeys made its bid for freedom by launching itself from the pen and flapping off in an ungainly rush, heading for the chicken runs in the farthest corner of the grounds.

21

'Oh, hell,' Frankie muttered under his breath. 'Oh, bloody hell . . . bloody *hell!'*

He sighed deeply and turned to make his way along the side of the house. It was not his fault. He was not to blame for all this trouble. He was just an innocent bystander who had not done anything wrong and did not want to be around when Buddie saw what was happening to his turkeys. All Frankie wanted was to grab something to eat and get back to school as quickly as possible. If he did not eat now, while he had the chance, his belly would growl all afternoon and the other kids would snigger and poke fun at him until Sir made him stand on a chair in a corner with his hands on his head for deliberately disrupting the rest of the class.

'You are a stupid boy,' Mr Sunderland had reminded him that very morning. 'You are a poor reader, your spelling leaves a great deal to be desired, your handwriting is disgraceful and your marks in arithmetic are usually the lowest in the class.'

'Yes, sir, but please, sir, I came top in art, sir.'

'Ah, yes indeed, but you also came *thirty-ninth* in geography, out of a class of how many?'

'Thirty-nine, sir.'

'Exactly, boy. *Exactly!'*

At such times Mr Sunderland would shake his head and purse his lips and make little kissing noises with his tongue and stare off into the distance with narrowed eyes and say:

'Ah, your poor, dear mother. Such an intelligent woman. So smart, so beautifully spoken. What a disappointment you must be to her. What a *terrible* disappointment.'

'Yes, sir. Sorry, sir.'

Feeling oppressed by this reminder of his short-comings, Frankie allowed his narrow shoulders to sag as he trudged along while his shadow, as if in sympathy with his shabby grey socks, collapsed in a shapeless heap around his shoes. To his right were the old allotments, mostly overgrown now and ruined by rummaging animals. Against the high perimeter walls lolled the chicken-enclosures with their accompanying crop of ramshackle huts, old tin baths brimming with rancid rain-water, stacks of empty oil cans, old car batteries and coils of wire-netting. As he walked along he passed the weeping willow tree which stood in the very centre of what were originally the formal gardens, where roses and miniature trees had once grown in elegant, carefully pruned order. He was particularly fond of the willow tree. He liked to hide himself beneath it on warm summer days when its leafy branches hung right down to the ground to form a cool, sun-dappled den that nobody else knew about.

The old allotments ended at a thicket of prickly black-berry bushes, and beyond them the land suddenly drop-ped away into a steep, thickly wooded hillside that loomed over Mucky Beck and Dead Man's Alley in a heavy green canopy. All this was Frankie's garden, his private world. While other kids lived in back-to-back houses with out-side lavatories and kitchens crammed into a tiny square at the top of the cellar steps, Frankie lived like a prince in a huge house behind high walls. He knew there was not a kid in Bradford who would not swap places with him in a flash for a chance to live at Old Ashfield. Nobody in the whole country was as lucky as Frankie. He had everything. He was the only kid *anywhere* who had a full cowboy outfit and a pony of his own and a Tarzan swing and a real American dad and a beautiful mam who looked just like a film star from the Hollywood movies.

When he reached the steps and the small iron gate leading to the front terrace, he looked back to see forty or fifty turkeys flinging themselves in frenzied abandon at the unstable fences of the chicken runs. He could see them struggling to reach the lean-to roofs, and from there the freedom of the street beyond. He wanted to observe their escape from that safe distance, but the

23

sound of raised voices drew him to the terrace steps, from where he could see right along the paved walkway at the front of the house. A knot of people were milling about outside the main door. Some women he did not recognize were walking arm-in-arm towards the far gate, all smiling and talking together at the same time, the way women do. A man leaned over to vomit violently into a rhododendron bush, then swilled out his mouth with wine from a bottle, gargled noisily and spat into a nearby patch of dandelions.

'It was a brand new handbag,' a woman by the door complained as she folded her headscarf into a neat triangle, placed it over her hair and knotted its corners under her chin. 'Real zebra-skin it was, too. Real, genuine zebra-skin.'

'You bloody liar!'

So said an older woman who stood with her arms folded across her body and her bosom thrust out like a sturdy soldier on parade.

'It was, too,' the first woman insisted. 'And there was eighteen pounds thirteen and sixpence in it and now it's gone, money and all, stolen by some rotten, light-fingered bugger who . . .'

'Oh! That's a bloody tale, Doris Bickerstaff!'

'Nay, it's as true as I'm standing here.'

'What? *Eighteen pounds thirteen and six?* You never had that kind of money in a month of Sundays. Not in a month of Sundays.'

'Happen she's been upping her prices,' a red-haired woman sniped from a shrewd distance of several feet. A number of people, including the man who had just been sick, guffawed at the suggestion.

'Nay, she'd earn bloody *nowt* if she tried doing that.'

Doris Bickerstaff placed her hands on her hips and shook her shoulders from side to side, spoiling for a fight.

'And what would *you* know about it, you dried up old cow? Ten bob's always been your limit . . . seven and six on a poor night, so I've heard.'

'All right, then, how much? Go on, Miss Fancy Knickers, tell us how much you've been getting and I'll tell you you're a bloody liar.'

By way of reply Doris Bickerstaff made a sudden lunge for her antagonist and both women fell to the ground in a flailing of arms and legs and a spectacular show of undergarments. The two were noisily encouraged by cat-calls and whistles and loud applause from the rest of the group.

'Go on, you give it to her, Mavis,' someone shouted.

'Nay, my money's on Doris,' yelled another. ' Go on, lass, you get stuck in. Show the old cow what you're made of.'

Taking advantage of this unexpected flurry of activity, a tall, skinny, big-breasted black woman slipped from the house and wiggled along the terrace with her coat wrapped tightly around her body and her high heels clacking on the crazy paving. Blossom was on her way back to Howard Street, and as he watched her go, Frankie would have bet his entire secret savings that the missing zebra-skin handbag was clutched beneath the short fur coat she wore.

It was Tom Fish who came with the news that the turkeys were all loose and running amok as far afield as Chesham Grove on one side and Thorpe Street on the other. Tom Fish was the man Frankie hated so much that sometimes just *thinking* about him could bring on a cold sweat and cause the muscles in his face to screw themselves into agitated spasms. Tom Fish smiled all the time, especially when he was tormenting Frankie. Tom Fish was big and arrogant, a good-looking man with sleepy green eyes and a lilting Irish accent that made the women flutter their lashes and turn all coy and silly. Frankie wanted to murder him. He had promised himself

25

that one day he would kill Tom Fish stone dead with the biggest, sharpest axe he could find. Better still, he might knock him down with a wooden club and castrate him the way Buddie castrated the pigs, so that Tom Fish would never again be able to take his pants down and do dirty things with Frankie's mam. Every time he set eyes on the Irishman, Frankie wanted to rush inside and steal Buddie's twelve-bore shot-gun, load a cartridge into each barrel and blow that snide grin right off the man's face.

'I did it for *her*,' he would tell them all when they brought him to trial in a dark and sombre court of law with his head shaved and his hands tightly bound behind his back and heavy iron shackles bolted to his ankles. 'I did it for me mam.'

She would weep, of course, when they hanged him by the neck until dead. She would weep and wring her hands, perhaps even collapse in one of her slow and graceful swoons, but when that trap-door opened to swallow her only son into eternity she would know beyond all doubt that he had done what he did for *her*.

The terrace had been cleared of people for a long time when Frankie began to feel it might be safe to sneak into the house. Everyone who had not gone off home was out chasing turkeys, desperately trying to drive the escapees back into the grounds of Old Ashfield before they were caught by outsiders and killed for the pot, free of charge. Buddie's deep bellow could be heard even from that distance as he chased his property through the streets and scaled mill walls and private gates in pursuit of missing birds. With any luck, Frankie could grab something to eat and be back at school before the round-up was completed. After several deep breaths and a close look in every direction, he gathered up his courage, sprinted along the terrace and ducked into the house by the main door.

'Oh heck! Oh, Jesus, what a mess . . . what a *mess!*'

26

He could not imagine where all the rubbish had come from that was littering the hall and stairs. It looked for all the world as if every room in the house had been ransacked. Clothes and bedding hung over the banister or lay in crumpled heaps on the steps. Newspapers and song-sheets, record sleeves, wire music-stands, shoes, plates and bottles were strewn about the hall. Frankie stooped to pick up a drumstick, looked around until he found its twin and shoved both into the waistband of his trousers for safekeeping. Among the scattered newspapers was one of Buddie's many gramophone records, still inside its cover but broken into three parts. He squinted at the torn centre label and read what was printed there:

'Come Along Down-a My House, Baby.'

It was one of Buddie's favourite Nellie Lutcher records. He would be hopping mad when he saw what had happened to it.

Across the landing at the top of the main stairs the bathroom door stood open, flooding the next flight of stairs and the dark corridor beyond with borrowed light. The bathroom was divided into three sections, each with a window that caught the summer sun at certain times of the day so that the whole place grew warm as a greenhouse and just as bright. Someone had left a tap running, and he knew it was the hot tap because even from down there he could hear the cistern filling up.

'Oh, heck,' he repeated, his face twitching in sudden concern. It had just occurred to him that his own room might have been invaded and his treasures pilfered by dishonest strangers. He thought of the heavy army great-coat that kept him so warm in the night, the forbidden teddy bear concealed under his bed, the little parcels of food and money and photographs, the Oxo tin with its precious contents, the collection of fancy knick-knacks that did not really belong to him. He dreaded the loss of his possessions, but right then their safety had to take second place to more immediate concerns. He must not be discovered. He would be blamed for everything if they found him in the house.

Walking on tip-toe towards the stairs, he passed the playroom on his left, where the window reached almost to the floor and the great fireplace was inlaid with smooth, dark green marble. Children had been allowed to play in that room in the olden days, when posh Quaker people owned the house and all the ladies wore bonnets and long dresses. It was still known as the playroom, but now only the men from the dance band were allowed to play there whenever Buddie could get them away from their wives and girlfriends for a serious session.

The next door was permanently bolted from the inside. Frankie thought it led into the huge curtained alcove in the best room where his parents had their bed, but he could not be sure. Even though he had lived in that big, shadowy house all his life, there were still rooms he had never seen, doors he had never dared open, keys that were never to be turned by prying, inquisitive little fingers.

Just beyond the fancy turn at the bottom of the main stairs, the big hall narrowed into an unlit corridor leading all the way to the kitchens. The first door along this unlit passage was painted a lovely rich green and belonged to the best room, with its fabulous collection of treasures from China and India, Japan, Africa and all those other wonderfully exotic places. This was the room whose shuttered window looked out on to the back yard, and whose secret door, now hung with a display of swords and foils and rapiers, once opened on to a vaulted courtyard big enough to hold a horse and carriage. That cobbled yard was now Buddie's tool-shed, and livestock and dogs and bins of entrails were often kept in there, but that did not make it any less grand in Frankie's estimation. Even if it had originally been built as a humble barn for storing winter fuel or animal fodder, it was still a fascinating place with its arched entrance, vaulted ceiling, ancient stones and mysterious metal wall-fittings.

He held his breath as he approached the best room. She might be in there, resting on her film-star's bed or moving amongst her magnificent bric-à-brac, her footsteps silent on thick, warm carpets woven with such colours as could snatch the breath from a small boy's lungs. He stooped, pressed his ear against the door, heard only the thud of his own heart and the sound of her last warning repeating itself inside his head:

'Listen to me, you little sneak. If I ever catch you creeping about the house, listening at doors and peeping through keyholes, I'll break every bone in your body. Do you hear me? I'll make you wish you'd never been born.'

He sprang nervously back from the keyhole, shuddered and moved on. Now he had to pass the long row of hooks on which were hung layer upon layer of old coats, jackets, rubber aprons, dirty shirts, tool bags, horse leathers, dog chains, blankets, empty sacks and other things that were shapeless and therefore nameless. That weird collection of items, hanging as it did above mounds of old shoes, cardboard boxes and galvanized buckets slotted one inside the other, served to narrow the corridor considerably. Those hooks and their accoutrements were a constant source of anxiety to someone of Frankie's temperament. Their shapes were seldom constant but took on monstrous possibilities in the fickle darkness of the corridor. Sometimes he was convinced that a whole tribe of jet black cannibal savages was lurking there in the gloom, watching and waiting, perhaps for a child to wander by.

To reach the kitchens he had to pass uncomfortably close to that door on the right beneath the stairs, the door with the chocolate brown paint and the stains and splashes that looked like dried blood, the door to the cellars. Here too he held his breath, partly because he was nervous, but mostly because he would never, even if he lived for a hundred years, become accustomed to the smell of slaughtered pigs and gutted turkeys.

He hesitated with his hand on the latch of the kitchen door. He was caught in a dilemma. If he knocked and no-one was in there, the sound might alert someone from another room and he would be discovered. If he did not knock, if he dared to walk right in and found her sitting there before the stove or having a private conversation with a friend, he would be in deep trouble. She would smile and be ever so nice to him until later, when there was nobody else in the house. Then she would punish him really, really hard, perhaps until he disgusted her by wetting his pants or being sick on the floor. And he would deserve it, too, because he knew full well that he must never, ever enter a room where she might be, not unless he knocked first and waited for her to say that it was all right for him to come inside.

He bent to peer through the keyhole and saw what looked like flour or sugar scattered all over the place. Then he dropped down on to his hands and knees and squinted into the gap beneath the door. She was not there. She would never sit in the kitchen unless the curtain was pulled right across the door and the sausage-shaped mat pressed up close to keep out all the draughts. Even in summer she felt the cold. Frankie thought that was because her skin was so white and perfect and must not be dried up or turned a horrible brown by the heat of the sun. And perhaps it was because she wore all those flimsy clothes that let in the cold and sometimes fell down over her arms to leave her shoulders bare. She could not wear things that were thick and warm because they made her feel drab, like a Thorpe Street housewife or a common mill worker. Ladies who could have been famous film stars in Hollywood could not be expected to

30

dress like ordinary people. They were special. They were entitled to the very best.

'I like my home to be warm and comfortable,' his mam always said when Nanny complained about the amount of coal that went into keeping the stove burning night and day. 'Buddie keeps his antiques in good condition by making sure they don't suffer from the cold and damp. Surely I, his wife, the mother of his only son, may expect the same consideration?'

She knew just what to say to shut Nanny up, and Buddie always took her side against his ma and his sisters. That was because Buddie loved her more than he loved anything else in the whole world. He knew, just as Frankie knew, that she was a very, *very* special person.

There was a lot of food in the kitchen but none of it fit to eat. Plates of leftover sandwiches and pastries had been tipped on to the floor with the dirt and the dog hairs. Someone had been using a big bowl of cold rice as an ashtray, and what remained of Buddie's special hot and spicy chicken had been thrown in a bin with the carcasses and all the scrapings from peoples' plates. Frankie went through into the smaller middle kitchen where food was stored on high shelves and cool stone slabs. Here several sacks had been split open and their contents of flour, sugar and tea thrown about or trampled into the floor. Poultry feathers were everywhere. It looked as if someone had thrown the feather-box into the air with not so much as a thought for all the mess it would make.

He was beginning to fear that nothing edible had survived when a glance in the stone crock revealed half a loaf of clean, reasonably fresh bread which had escaped the ravages of the party and its violent aftermath. He selected a large pudding basin, wiped it out with the palm of his hand, then began tearing the bread into small, bite-sized pieces and dropping them inside. This done, he scooped a handful of sugar from one of the split

31

sacks, sprinkled it over the bread, saturated the lot with milk ladled from the big can, then found himself a large, clean spoon with which to eat his makeshift lunch. He did not really mind about the wasted rice and chicken, or the sandwiches that were dirty and unfit to eat. He was well satisfied. He had never before enjoyed such a huge bowl of pobs all to himself.

Sugar crunched under his shoes when he crossed the main kitchen to peer out through the broken window. Nader was lying in the yard exactly where she had fallen when Buddie kicked her into silence. She was still showing the whites of her eyes and panting as if it hurt too much to take a deeper breath. Frankie was sorry for her, even though she always scared him half to death when she was in a fierce mood. He imagined he knew exactly how she was feeling, because once he had suffered a similar injury. Some time ago he had scrambled on to the midden roof of the derelict house next door in pursuit of a wind-blown ten shilling note that had probably fluttered down from Brooke Parker's rear lorry park. The prospect of getting his hands on all that money had made him forget that the stones were crumbling and the cement between them all but flaked away. He had no sooner grasped his prize than the huge roofing slabs shifted under his weight, tipping him over the edge of the midden. Buddie said he was damn lucky not to have fallen in the path of the slabs when they dropped edge-on and shattered against the ground. Instead he had landed flat on his stomach on the pavement, horribly winded but still alive and ten shillings richer for his efforts. His ribs had been sore for weeks, and for the first few days he had breathed the way Nader was breathing now, fearful of the terrible pains that stabbed into his chest whenever he tried to fill his lungs with air.

'Poor old lass,' he muttered, licking milk and grains of sugar from his lips. 'Poor daft bugger. Maybe that'll teach you not to holler at Buddie when he's in a bad mood.'

He ate his pobs quickly, slipping back to the larder only once to steal a little more sugar for the pieces of bread at the bottom of the bowl that had turned soggy in the milk. Although he was still hungry, he did not empty the bowl. Instead, he carried what remained into the back yard and very gingerly approached the Great Dane. He had never trusted dogs. Too many bad experiences in the past had taught him not to get too close or turn his back on them, even when they were chained up or lying quietly, pretending not to have the least interest in him. Nader's eyes rolled and she raised her head a little, making him extra watchful as he tipped the pobs into her metal dish and pushed it towards her. He did not touch her. He knew better than to attempt such a dangerous move, but he spoke to her softly, urging her to taste the sloppy, sweetened mixture.

'Come on, old lass. Good girl, Nader. You'll feel pounds better if you get this down you. There's a good dog. There's a *good* dog.'

She whined, making a small, sad sound in the back of her throat. He watched her closely, wishing he dare pat her head to make her feel better. She was not like Rosie. She did not bite him at every opportunity or leap at her chain, barking and snarling like a wild beast, whenever he came near. Even so, he watched her through suspicious eyes and resisted the temptation to offer his hand in friendship.

The injured Great Dane was attempting to lap up the pobs when Frankie, after first looking in each direction to make sure the coast was clear, slipped from the yard and turned right to hurry along the dirt drive in the direction of the pigsties. He gave the tethered goats as wide a berth as possible, quaking at the way the bearded Billy stared back at him with its pale, oddly shaped eyes. He was making for the tall iron gate at the far end of the

33

drive, where a narrow, neglected pavement would take him up the front of the Brooke Parker building to the top of Thorpe Street. It was here, behind the bins and the big pile of rubbish on the right of the gate, that he concealed his stolen drumsticks with the intention of retrieving them later in the day. Not until he was absolutely certain that he was safe did he break cover and race up the steep slope to the top of Thorpe Street, there to begin the only downward stretch on his long journey back to school.

THREE

He met up with the dinner children as they were making their way back to St Andrew's from Grange Road School canteen, where their midday meal was provided. They marched across Shearbridge Road in a long, double column: the girls leading two-by-two in orderly fashion, holding hands and walking with a quiet sense of purpose; the boys, noisy and prone to spasmodic bouts of scuffling, brought up an untidy rear. The free-dinner kids were not required to make up a separate line on the long trek back to school from Grange Road. Only on the outward journey were they segregated from their fellows, then made to carry their free tickets and their hot humiliation into the dining room after everyone else was seated. Now they were back within the main stream, their shame reconciled beneath full bellies and a lingering taste of shepherd's pie and tapioca pudding laced with warm raspberry jam.

Mr Pocklington was in charge. In order to control both children and traffic, he had placed himself in the very centre of the road with his whistle clenched between his teeth and his arms fanning the air like the sails of an unwieldy windmill. As the last two boys dashed off the pavement and into the road, Mr Pocklington's right arm descended with practised precision and caught one of the stragglers a glancing blow to the back of the head. Tubby Atkinson yelped and staggered drunkenly to one side, where he accidentally stomped upon Herbert Procter's heel and sent the smaller boy sprawling into the road. Mr Pocklington promptly rushed forward to haul young Procter to his feet, smacked him smartly across the ear with the flat of his hand and helped him on his way with a shove that very nearly unbalanced him for a second time. Behind him in the road lay Procter's left shoe, the one with the hole underneath the sole and the heel that was worn right down to its uppers on one side. Procter was snivelling like a girl and being shoved about by several jeering schoolboys by the time the missing shoe was brought to Sir's attention and its owner ordered to retrieve it from the path of a Corporation street-sweeper.

Prior to the arrival of the dinner kids, Frankie had been picking his way very gingerly along the top of a high mill wall with his arms stuck out on either side of his body like a professional tightrope walker. Under cover of the flurry of excited activity generated by Herbert Procter's left shoe, he was able to jump down from the wall and insinuate himself, unnoticed by Sir, into the shuffling crocodile of pupils. By pushing and squirming he soon made himself quite inconspicuous between a spotty kid with glasses and a peevish-looking Roger Smith, who was holding a bloodstained handkerchief to the lower half of his face. Someone jabbed Frankie in the back and hissed:

'Hey, you! You've been home for dinner. You'll get done if Sir sees you walking with us.'

'Oh, shut your mouth, Billy. Old Pocklington will never know I'm here if you keep quiet and I keep my head down. What's wrong with Smithy?'

'Some big kids from Princeville got him when he came out of dinners. Ripped his jacket and bust his nose, they did. He had to sit on a chair with his head right back and a wet cloth over his nose, but Sir couldn't stop it bleeding.'

'They might send him home, then.'

'No they won't,' Billy said, shaking his head. 'They'll put him to bed in Nurse's room with all the lights out and the curtains drawn, and he'll miss history *and* mental arithmetic, the jammy bugger.'

36

'Yeah, I wish it was me,' Frankie sighed, anticipating the afternoon's lessons with the quiet dread of one well-acquainted with personal failure. He glanced around to see if he had been spotted. Sir was now marching on ahead with his whistle in one hand and Procter's shoe in the other, directing his charges round the corner of Shearbridge Road into Longside Lane. This was one occasion when Frankie could be grateful for his lack of height. He was almost certain not to be noticed by Sir amongst all those taller and broader boys.

'What did you have for dinner?' he asked, nudging Billy with his elbow.

Billy poked his thumb nail between the gaps in his teeth until he discovered a morsel of food. He scrutinized it carefully before sucking it back into his mouth.

'Shepherd's pie and carrots and mashed potatoes,' he said.

'And gravy?'

'Course we had gravy, and me and Ronnie McEvoy had seconds of spuds and carrots.'

Frankie nodded, licked his lips, glanced again at the anxious face of Mr Pocklington and demanded in a whisper:

'What was for pudding?'

'Tapioca, and we had seconds of that, too. What did *you* have, Frankie? Did your mam make you something special, like before?'

'Course she did. She always does. Every single day, if I ask her to.'

'What, a proper dinner? *Every* day?'

'Course she does,' Frankie insisted, feeling important. 'Better than rotten old school dinners, any day.'

'Well, what was it, then? What did you have?'

Frankie scowled the way Buddie did whenever he was deep in thought, pulling his brows down over his eyes and pressing his lips together.

'Bacon,' he said at last, pronouncing the fib so clearly and emphatically that it might well have been the real,

37

honest truth. 'A great fat slice of bacon fried in the same pan with two eggs and *loads* of mushy tomatoes, and two thick slices of bread and butter to go with it. Then I had some home-made apple pie with sugar on it and custard with a thick skin on top. *And* I had seconds.'

'Of what? Seconds of what?'

'Of *everything*,' Frankie declared proudly.

Billy stared at him, open-mouthed.

'All that? You had all that for your dinner?'

'Yeah, sure I did.'

'Followed by seconds . . . of *everything?*'

'Sure, and for tea I'll be having stew and dumplings, with as much bread and butter as I can eat and as many seconds as I ask for.'

Billy suddenly scowled and folded his arms across his chest, stretching up tall so that he could look down on Frankie.

'Well, if what you say is true,' he said, narrowing his eyes suspiciously, 'if it's really true, how come you're the smallest kid in the class? How come you never grow any bigger?'

Frankie was instantly on the defensive.

'Are you calling me a liar?' he demanded.

'And what if I am? What are you going to do about it, *Titch?*'

'I'll belt you one, that's what I'll do.'

'Oh yeah? You and whose army, *half-pint?*'

'Just you wait, *four-eyes*, I'll get you when . . .'

'*You, boy!* Yes, *you*, boy! Come here at once!'

Too late Frankie tried to shrink from view. He was caught. Mr Pocklington was glaring at him over the top of his heavy spectacles, one talon-like finger beckoning with silent menace.

'Come here, boy!'

Frankie reluctantly obeyed. Someone sniggered and nipped his upper arm. He reached out and grabbed a twist of flesh from the first available buttock, only to find to his horror that it was firmly attached to big fat Wally Watmough, cock of the whole school. Wally winced and rubbed the offended buttock with both hands. He was quite red in the face when he rounded on Frankie and snarled furiously:

'You just wait, Gyppo. I'll get you back for that.'

The narrow bulk of Mr Pocklington, teacher of art, PT and games, suddenly loomed before him.

'Have you been home for dinner, boy?'

'Yes, sir.'

'And do you have permission to join the school dinner children?'

'Er . . . no, sir.'

The swift, flat-handed blow to the side of his head nearly lifted Frankie off his feet and caused him to see a snow-storm of bright lights dancing before his eyes. It wasn't fair. He didn't think it right that great big teachers should go around smacking small boys across the head whenever they felt like it. It made them daft. He knew it made them daft because his Nanny Fanny had said so lots of times, and if she had *her* way it wouldn't be allowed.

For the offence of being where he had no right to be, Frankie was given fifty lines, to be completed at play-time while the other kids were drinking their milk and playing in the school yard. He copied down the first line from the blackboard where Sir had written in his bold, upright hand:

'I must not walk back to school with the dinner children without the permission of a teacher.'

Unfortunately, he somehow managed to allow a spelling mistake to creep into the word *permission*, a mistake that was subsequently duplicated no less than forty-nine times as he laboured to complete his task within the time allowed and without his usual quota of ink smudges. At the end of it all, Sir was far from satisfied with his efforts and Frankie

39

was required to stay behind after school in order to copy out, one hundred and twenty times:

'I must learn not to make careless mistakes in my school work.'

He was oppressed all afternoon by a dark cloud of depression brought on by the prospect of staying behind to write out Mr Pocklington's lines after all the other kids had been dismissed. Sitting in the empty classroom of a deserted school always gave him the creeps. It made him so nervous and jumpy that he usually messed up what he was doing and had to start all over again on a fresh sheet of paper.

He felt a lot better when he was ordered to stay indoors at playtime in order to make a start. Wally Watmough was not pleased about that. He was waiting in the porch with his fists clenched and his mates gathered round to back him up. Frankie thumbed his nose and stuck out his tongue and the big fat kid turned red in the face with thwarted spite. Everyone knew he would get Frankie, sooner or later. It was only a matter of time. He lived just across the road from the school, so he would find it as easy as eating his dad's apple and blackcurrant pie to get his hands on the last kid out after everyone else had gone off home.

'Bloody, bloody, bloody.' Frankie hissed the word through clenched teeth, wondering why teacher's lines always had to be written out in pen and smudgy ink when all the kids at St Andrew's were still more accustomed to using pencils.

'Bloody!' he repeated, and glanced about him to make sure he would not be overheard when he added, in a clearer, more daring voice:

'Bloody in the Bible,
Bloody in The Book,
If you don't bloody believe me
Have a bloody look!'

Having given vent to his frustrations, he gripped the pen tightly and, biting down on his lower lip as an aid to concentration, hunched himself over his work. After

40

first scraping the nib of his pen around the bottom of the pot ink-well that hung in a neat round hole in the top of the desk, he narrowed his eyes and began to write. Even before the first laboriously executed line was completed, a large, unsightly smudge had appeared on the clean white sheet of foolscap paper.

It was Mr Sunderland, the headmaster, who took Frankie's class for double history immediately after playtime that afternoon. His classroom was brighter and more pleasant than all the others, with each row of desks set higher than the last on wide steps running right across the room. Those on the very back row could look out on the girls' yard or down on the inner corridor leading to the assembly hall. They often saw the girls in their navy blue knickers and little white blouses jumping up and down in PT or playing games with bean bags in the hall. They were luckier than the others because they could see right over those panes of glass opaqued by whitewash or covered by drawings of Jesus healing lepers and Lazarus, the dead man, rising from his hole in the ground. Frankie would be moving into Mr Sunderland's class after the big holidays. He was hoping to get one of the end desks on the very top row, and he was willing to hand over all his best swaps, if necessary, to get one.

Mr Sunderland stood at his upright desk close to the outside window. He was a tall, grey-haired man with scrupulously clean hands and glasses that clung so tightly to the end of his nose that they left deep red marks in the skin. His shoes were highly polished and squeaked when he walked, signalling his approach. His dark suit was worn to a shine in some places and faded in others, and it carried with it the musty smell of mothballs and long-forgotten dinners. Mr Sunderland was an immensely powerful man. He could use the cane harder and better than any other teacher in the school. Mr Sunderland had the power to make or break any pupil in his charge with his scribbled comments on their annual school report. He could even recommend that a child be taken from its family and placed in a Special Home in some foreign town many miles away. He loomed large and formidable in the lives of every boy and girl who attended St Andrew's Primary School, Listerhills. He was lord and master of his domain, and yet his pupils smirked at him in secret because, when deep in thought, Mr Sunderland picked his nose and smeared the results of his explorations along the top left-hand side of his desk.

'And who can tell me what became of them?'

Frankie's arm shot up.

'Please, sir, they were murdered in the tower by Richard's men because he wanted to become King of England.'

'Indeed so. Indeed so. And who can tell me exactly *how* they died?'

Frankie's arm shot up again, but it was Wally Watmough who was selected to answer the question.

'Please, sir, were they stabbed in the back, sir?'

'Don't be a damn fool, Watmough! Where were you last week when we all read aloud from the history book? No, you stupid boy, the young princes were *not* stabbed in the back.'

Class 3 was still tittering over Wally Watmough's blunder when the classroom door opened unexpectedly and a woman stepped inside. A hush immediately descended on the room as all eyes turned in her direction. Then a voice, clear and refined, rang out:

'Oh dear. How terribly clumsy of me. Oh *do* forgive me, Mr Sunderland. I'm here to collect my son, but I've obviously arrived much too early. I think perhaps I should wait outside in the corridor . . . ? '

Mr Sunderland's features softened into a strangely docile expression. He fingered his tie, then his collar, then the buttons on the front of his jacket.

42

'Oh, but I wouldn't hear of it, my dear lady,' he almost crooned, then turned a sudden scowl upon the nearest available pupil. 'Jump to it, Robinson! Where are your manners, boy? Fetch the lady a chair! Quickly, boy! Quickly!'

Ginger Robinson's face and neck turned a hot, flame red as he rushed to obey, and there wasn't a boy in the room who didn't envy him that simple task. In those drab, commonplace surroundings this particular visitor was a visual treasure. She was wearing a blue skirt and tightly-fitting jacket trimmed with huge, mother-of-pearl buttons. Her bright auburn hair was swept up into coils and waves held in place by painted combs. From her ears dangled the biggest, longest, shiniest earrings ever seen before in the classroom of a Bradford school. Like an elegant duchess she lowered herself slowly on to the chair and crossed one lovely leg over the other in such a way that her skirt slithered up to reveal her rounded, silk-clad knees. Her gaze swept the room, came to rest on Frankie, and her smile was as brilliant as sunshine breaking through cloud. Suddenly he was the proudest boy in the whole school, because this beautiful lady was his mam, his own special mam.

'Smallfry!'

He whispered the name under his breath as he felt her eyes and her smile warming his cheeks.

'Smallfry!'

It was not her *real* name. She had heard it in a Bing Crosby song and wanted everyone to believe that Frankie had thought of it all by himself because he loved her and it proved she was different from all the other mothers. At first he had hated using the name, especially when she told Tom Fish and his friends about it and they all roared with laughter because they thought Frankie a puny little runt and by far the smallest fry in *any* pond. Now he was almost used to it, and he tried his best not to enrage her

43

by calling her 'Sweetheart', which used to be her favourite name, or even 'Angel', which she had once preferred above all others. He never dared call her 'Mam'. He wanted to, all the time, but 'Mam' made her feel dowdy and old, so it was no longer allowed. Now he only ever said it inside his head where she could not hear it and get enraged.

He was glad she had worn her American silk stockings with the pattern up the side and the tiny little stones that twinkled like diamonds in the sunlight. And he was glad she had worn her peep-toed shoes, the red and green ones with the high, shiny black heels and slender ankle-straps fastened with silver buckles. He could see the red on her fingernails and the glistening colour on her lips, and he could see how the headmaster was gazing at her from behind his big desk. He sat up straight in his seat, grinning widely, proud in the knowledge that his mam, his Smallfry, was fit to be a famous film star along with Betty Grable, Ava Gardner and Jane Russell.

Smallfry adored the films. Sometimes she would take Frankie to see the same film several times, and afterwards she would pretend to be the heroine, doing the same things and saying the same words that had thrilled him on the big screen. And sometimes she would do her hair differently after visiting the picture house, or sew a glamorous new outfit for herself, or talk in a strange new voice and pout her lips and half-close her eyes the way the beautiful Hollywood actresses always did.

'My mam says your mam's got nowt better to do than traipse around all day done up like a Christmas tree.'

Nelly Belcher was slumped in her seat with her elbows folded on the desk in front of her. Her short fair hair was scraped back from a centre parting and held in place by two long metal grips. She had a big scar on her top lip and most of her teeth were either chipped or missing completely through standing too close to the batter during rounders. Now she lisped out of the corner of her mouth,

44

intending her comments for Frankie's ears alone.

'Shut your mouth,' Frankie hissed in reply. 'Your mam's only jealous because *she's* fat and ugly.'

'Well, my mam says your mam's *bone idle.*'

'That's a lie! My mam's a *lady.*'

'She's got fancy fingernails,' Nelly declared, knowingly. 'My mam says them as have fancy fingernails can't be keeping up with their housework or doing their front doorsteps like they should.'

Frankie glanced at Smallfry's hands. They were small and very white, with shaped nails that glistened and shone like polished pearls. He tried to remember when she had touched him last, and if her hands were really as soft and as smooth as they appeared to be.

' . . . and my mam says your mam never did a day's honest work in her life and wouldn't *dare* set foot in church of a Sunday for fear of being struck down right there and then by the wrath of the Good Lord for being nothing but a stuck-up, painted . . .'

'*Nelly Belcher!*'

Mr Sunderland lifted the lid of his desk and slammed it shut again with a crash that caused forty-three gaping children to gather their senses with a collective start.

'Stand up, Nelly Belcher.'

'Yes, sir.'

'You were talking in class.'

'Please, sir, I'm sorry, sir.'

Mr Sunderland narrowed his eyes menacingly and pursed his lips as he pointed towards the chair that stood with its back to the blackboard as a permanent reminder of his authority. Head bowed, the offending pupil left her desk and descended to the front of the class, where she climbed up on the chair and stood with her face to the blackboard.

Frankie smiled in secret satisfaction. Nelly Belcher thought she was so clever, just because she came third in mental arithmetic and once travelled all the way to Robin Hood's Bay in her Uncle Stanley's motorbike and sidecar. She did not look so clever now, with her hands clasped on the top of her head and her elbows stuck out at such an angle that her frock had grown shorter by several inches. Now everyone could see the places where her navy knickers were darned in green wool, and where the frayed edge of her vest hung down below the elastic of one leg. She did not look so clever now, with her face as red as a brick and her bottom lip trembling because she knew they were all laughing at her behind her back.

'Now, children. I would like you all to close your books and pass them to the end of each row. I want neat stacks ready for collection, and *no* talking amongst yourselves.'

Mr Sunderland's voice had taken on a more refined tone, the way Smallfry's always did when other people were listening. Smallfry had lots of voices. Frankie had learned to recognize them all. He loved her best when she used her nice voice, the one that could always make him smile, especially when she used it to recite the long story-poems that she could say from beginning to end without a single mistake. But she also had a slow, cold, quiet voice that set his face twitching and made him feel frightened and guilty, and a screaming, raging shriek that filled his insides with a different kind of terror. She had a posh voice that she used when she came to school or visited the local shops, and a special-occasion voice that made her sound like a royal princess or a glamorous film star. She rarely spoke like the common people of Bradford, except when she was really angry and the words just came out, or when that evil Tom Fish did something to upset her.

'We will all sit up smartly for the remainder of the lesson. The final bell will ring in exactly two minutes.'

That was the children's cue to stiffen their bodies into military-like positions and remain thus until Mr

Sunderland was satisfied that he could hear a pin drop in the silence.

Smallfry turned her lovely head to look up at Frankie and his cheeks grew warm with pleasure. She always seemed to know when he was thinking about her. She had often warned him that she possessed secret powers nobody else would understand. She knew things. The fact that she had come for him on this very afternoon was *proof* that she knew things. Now he would not have to stay behind all by himself to write a hundred and twenty lines for Mr Pocklington. He would not be forced to sit at a desk all alone, feeling small and nervous because all the other pupils had gone home and every room in the school was deserted. He would not have to listen to the noisy thumping of his heart, the scratching of his pen and all those small, mysterious sounds that were always there in big, empty buildings. Smallfry had saved him from all that, and from the revenge of big fat Wally Watmough, who would surely have waited outside to pay him back for that ill-judged nip in the dinner-lines.

He grinned happily, and suddenly it did not matter at all that he was the smallest boy in the class and had the worst handwriting Mr Sunderland had ever had the misfortune to encounter in a long and varied teaching career. His Smallfry had come to take him home, so today he was not too skinny, too small or too swarthy-skinned for her to be proud of him. Today Smallfry loved him, and that made him feel like the best son any mother ever had.

FOUR

Mr Sunderland held the door open and Smallfry stepped grandly from the classroom, her high heels ringing a brazen tattoo on floorboards accustomed to the more respectful shuffle of Council-approved footwear.

'Good afternoon, dear lady,' he gushed. 'We hope to have the pleasure of your company again soon . . . er . . . very soon . . . er . . . in fact any time . . . any time at all.'

She acknowledged the invitation with a brief turn of her head and a lowering of dark lashes to pale cheek, a practised movement of the type conferred by royals upon inferiors.

'Come, Frankie.'

She swept across the assembly hall with her head thrown back and her hips swaying from side to side in that easy, fluid way peculiar to herself. She looked neither to the left nor to the right, though she must have been aware of the many eyes that followed her as she crossed to the far exit with Frankie, her shabby, devoted young duckling, marching at her heels. They had been allowed to leave a full minute earlier than the rest of the school so that Smallfry might avoid the noisy exodus when swarms of children poured out into the streets. Those pupils already gathered in tidy groups in the main hall nudged and stared and whispered as the *clack*, *clack*, *clack* of specially imported American shoes rang out to announce the rare presence in the building of Frankie's mam.

'Allow me, madam.'

As if by magic, the tweed-suited Mr Horner, recently transferred from Carlton Street Juniors and rumoured to

48

have worked for many years in an iron foundry at Hebden Bridge, appeared in time to swing open the outer doors so that Smallfry might pass through without pause or impediment. Her smile was so brilliant that it made his face redden and caused a cluster of small spots to become more noticeable above his tight white collar. Frankie marched through in her wake, elongating his strides and beaming with newly-acquired self-esteem. She had made a splendid exit, just like in the films. Everyone in the school must have seen her and known she was *his* mam. All the teachers and the other kids would be talking about this moment for weeks to come.

He realized that something was wrong the moment they were outside in the bright afternoon sunshine. Once clear of the school gates, she made an unexpected right turn and began to walk away with such haste that he was forced to make frequent short dashes in order to keep up with her. Disappointment shaped itself into a lump behind his ribs. She had not smiled, spoken a word or even glanced in his direction since the door of Mr Sunderland's classroom closed behind them. A few minutes ago she had made him feel proud and special, but now she was striding on ahead as if he did not exist, or as if his very presence were beneath her contempt. He followed behind in worried silence, fearful of the sudden change of mood that told him he might be in serious trouble. He must have done something very wrong, or not done something he *should* have done, or perhaps said something he should never have said. His mind cast about for clues, and it soon occurred to him that he must have been spotted sneaking about Old Ashfield at dinner time, and now he would be blamed for causing that terrible riot amongst the turkeys.

'It wasn't me,' he mumbled urgently under his breath, a ripple of panic already stirring in his empty stomach. 'I didn't do nothing. It wasn't my fault. It was the Brooke Parker man, not me. Honest to God, it wasn't me.'

Head lowered, lips moving like a penitent in prayer, he trotted behind the beautiful lady in the tight-fitting blue costume and the colourful American shoes, miserable in his assumed guilt.

She neither acknowledged his presence nor slowed her pace until they reached the small picture house opposite the allotment gardens some distance up Listerhills Road. This was one of his favourite picture houses. She had brought him here recently to see a double bill of George Formby films, and he had not really minded too much when she slipped away after the lights went out and didn't come back for him until the last show was over. He could bear being alone in the dark during the cowboy films and the comedies and the musicals, especially when she left him with an ice lolly or a bar of chocolate. It was the murder films that made him nervous, and those grisly horror stories with the scary music and the screams and the monsters that never seemed to go away once they got inside his mind.

While Smallfry paced the edge of the kerb, looking irritably up and down the road, Frankie hung back so that he could see the photographs in the glass display case outside the cinema doors. The film now showing was called *Samson and Delilah*. Frankie's eyes widened as he stood on tip-toe to take a closer look. Here were leather-clad gladiators with swords and nets and shiny metal breastplates, set to do battle to the death with snarling lions and prancing grisly bears. And here was a beautiful young dancing-girl with long dark hair and crimson skirts that swirled in soft waves about her naked legs. Frankie stared so hard at the pictures that he could almost smell the wild animals and feel the crush of spectators and hear the reedy, piping music to which the girl in the red dress was undoubtedly dancing.

'Is my nose clean?'

He started at the sound of Smallfry's voice. She suddenly loomed over him, very tall in her high-heeled shoes. Then she stooped and pulled her upper lip down over her teeth

50

so that her nostrils were stretched open for his careful scrutiny. Frankie stared hard before nodding his head in mute relief. He hoped the day would never come when he was forced to answer differently, when he peered up her nostrils and saw something dark and dirty lurking there.

She was standing so close that he could smell her perfume, the distinctive Californian Poppy she bought from Woolworth's in Darley Street for one and ninepence the smallest size. It came in tiny square bottles with bright red lids and boxes with cut-away fronts and pictures of the famous poppy on every side. He loved her scent. It was the best perfume in all the world, even better than the smell of Nanny's kitchen when she was cooking dinners for the boarders. If ever he went blind in both eyes like Jack Bottomley's gran, he would still be able to recognize Smallfry, just by her Californian Poppy. He did not know a single kid whose mam wore real, genuine scent every day, and even if they could afford to, not one of them would be able to make it smell quite the way Smallfry's did. Californian Poppy was special to her. It was one of the many things that made *his* mam so remarkable.

'For goodness' sake, stop day-dreaming, Frankie,' she snapped, nudging his chest so sharply that he came back to the present with a start. 'Are my seams straight?'

She walked slowly on ahead, looking back at him the way she did in some of her photographs, with one shoulder raised and her face tilted so that her eyes seemed to slant, and a small, secret smile on her lips. Her pose seemed to challenge him to detect even the smallest flaw in her appearance. He found none. The dark seams of her silk stockings emerged from behind the stitching in the heels of her shoes and ran all the way up her legs to the hem of her skirt, straight and neat as if drawn by a steady hand with a pencil and a ruler.

'They're dead straight,' he announced, and was disappointed when she did not return his grin. He watched her rummage for her lipstick and lean forward to study her reflection in the glass front of the display case. She pouted her lips, painted them with rich colour, pressed them firmly together, then touched each corner of her mouth with the tip of her little finger to catch any runs. Finally, she ran a corner of her handkerchief across her front teeth and licked her lips until they glistened before returning her attention to the traffic on Listerhills Road.

Frankie knew, now, that she had come here to meet someone. She had not, after all, come to fetch him from school because she sensed by magic that her little boy was in trouble and needed her. Not for him had she worn her best shoes and stockings and styled her hair like Jane Russell's and put on her brand new dangly earrings. She was waiting for someone, and he felt sick inside because he guessed that someone would be Tom Fish.

He dug his hands so deep into his trouser pockets that his fingers passed right through the holes in the lining and touched the bare skin of his legs. Scowling, he studied the scuffs on the toes of his shoes and almost wished she had *really* come for him because he was in serious trouble with Buddie. It was not fair for him to be blamed for something that was not his fault, yet he would willingly confess to turning all the turkeys loose if it would stop her going off somewhere with the Irishman. He feared his father's anger and he dreaded the sting of the big leather belt on his bare legs and backside, but neither seemed to hurt him quite as much as the pain he felt every time he saw Tom Fish put his big, workman's hands on Smallfry.

'Are we going to the pictures?'

He asked the question half-heartedly, wishing he could just go home for something to eat.

'What?' She frowned but did not look at him.

'The pictures. It's the new one. *Samson and Delilah*. Is that where we're going?'

52

'What, at this time? Don't be so stupid. When did we *ever* go to the pictures at this time?'

'I'm sorry, I just thought . . .'

At that moment there was a long, loud wolf-whistle and the honk of a horn as a big green lorry pulled into the kerb and came to a halt a little further along the road. The driver was no more than an anonymous dark shape behind the cab's small window, but Smallfry recognized him immediately and her face broke into a happy smile. She fished in her purse for a penny, which she pressed into the palm of Frankie's hand.

'Here, get yourself some peanut butter or a lolly or something. Go home the long way and wait for me outside Mrs Midgley's shop. I'll meet you there later.'

'When? What time will you come?'

'I'll come when I'm good and ready,' she snapped. 'You just do as you're told and whatever happens, don't let your father see you. Have you got that?'

'Yes, Smallfry.'

She gripped his shoulders and glared down at him.

'Don't you dare let me down, Frankie.'

'No, Smallfry.'

'And you'll keep out of sight until I come back?'

'Yes, Smallfry.'

The lorry horn sounded impatiently and she turned and hurried away without a backward glance. As she approached, the passenger door swung open and a man's arm appeared to help her inside. Frankie caught a glimpse of her white suspenders and dark stocking tops as she hitched up her tight costume skirt in order to negotiate the high step. Then she was inside and pulling the door closed behind her. He could hear her pretty laughter as the lorry pulled away. On the dark green tail-flap were painted the words: William G Moffat, Coal & Coke Merchant.

Frankie watched the lorry until it reached the main junction and turned right into Cemetery Road before he began walking away in the opposite direction, dragging his feet. Hunger tempted him to go back down the road to Watmough's shop for a penny loaf, but common sense held him back. Wally Watmough would surely spot him there and come after him. Besides, if he saw any of the kids from school they would laugh at him and ask him where his mam had got to so soon after taking him out of class. Still dragging his feet, and with both hands sticking through the holes in his pockets, he cut down the side of Legrams Mill and trudged in the general direction of Great Horton Road. He hated the man, whoever he might be, who had driven away in that big green lorry with his mam.

Mrs Midgley's shop window was set so close to the ground that there had once been a row of thick iron bars set into it to keep the burglars out. Now the bars were gone, taken years ago to help in the war effort, or weighed in at one of the local scrapyards for a few shillings when times were very hard. Someone had cut them out with a special saw, leaving just enough behind to create a row of uneven spikes that prevented small boys from sitting on the windowsill with their backs against the glass. There were heavy wooden shutters behind the window. Mrs Midgley had to unlock them with a key on a string every time she needed to get something out for a customer. The goods on display were all hidden from view, completely covered by sheets of old newspapers to keep off the fading effects of the sun. It was a dark and dingy little shop, but Mrs Midgley sold good comics and best boiled ham cut into wafer-thin slices that melted away in the mouth and left the sweetest, whitest fat behind for sucking on.

'Once nine is nine. Two nines are eighteen. Three nines are twenty-seven. Four nines are ...' He made a rapid calculation on his fingers, '... thirty-six. Five nines are forty-three ... er ... forty-*five*.'

At seven times nine he gave up with a sigh and began again. Most of the other kids in his class knew their times-tables off by heart, but however hard he tried and however often he practised, Frankie could not get the rhymes to stay in his mind for longer than a few minutes at a time. What he needed was one of those shiny red exercise books like the one Ginger Robinson's dad had bought him last Christmas. Pounds and ounces, yards, feet and inches and all the arithmetic times-tables were printed on the back page, but Ginger was too mean to let anyone copy them out unless they gave him something really good in exchange. He wanted Frankie's champion conker, the big one that always smashed everyone else's conker into smithereens, but Frankie had hesitated over the swap until it was too late, and now he would have to wait until the season came around again, and hope the deal was still open to negotiation.

Learning his times-tables was terribly important to Frankie, because what he *really* wanted was to pass his eleven-plus exams next year. His tenth birthday was coming up soon. He would return to school after the big holidays with less than a year in which to prove himself and make the grade. Nobody believed he could do it, but passing those exams was very, very important to him. Michael O'Leary's older brother had passed *his*, and he had gone up to Bradford Boys' Grammar, where they wore special uniforms and learned to speak properly, without swearing. Smallfry would never allow him to go to Grammar School, of course, because that would only make him big-headed and turn him into a stuck-up little snob with no respect for his parents, but if he could only pass his eleven-plus exams, he knew it would make her proud of him. The prospect of success brought a satisfied grin to his face. He could see her now, modestly informing everyone that *her* son was a scholar, that *her* boy could have gone to Grammar School with all the posh kids, only he didn't want to leave his mam

55

and she didn't think it fair to *force* him to go. Frankie knew he would end up going to Princeville Secondary School with all the others, where the lessons were really hard and the big kids would bully him for being skinny, but he wouldn't really mind all that, so long as Smallfry was happy. He *had* to pass. He could make her so proud of him, if only he could learn enough, and remember enough, to get him through those special exams.

'Six sixes are thirty-six. Seven sixes are forty-two. Eight sixes are forty-eight. Nine sixes are fifty-four.'

He had crammed himself into the gap created by the wooden gate in the wall of the Bowling Green Club. It was a narrow gate with a single shallow step, so he sat with his knees bent almost to his chin and one pant leg tucked underneath him to prevent it hanging over the edge of the step. Now he was unlikely to be noticed by any casual passer-by, yet he was close enough to Mrs Midgley's to spot the big green lorry when it eventually brought Smallfry back. From there he could see where Great Horton Road dipped into the hollow that was Shearbridge Corporation Depot before rising again into a steep incline. Up there at the top of the hill were the Sunday Schools and the Grange Cinema, and the ice-cream factory where Mr Bradshaw's crippled sister used to work until she fell out of a delivery window and broke her leg in two places and lost three teeth and the use of all her fingers.

'Ten sixes are sixty,' he chanted softly, picking at a large scab on his right knee, his brows tightly puckered in concentration. 'Eleven sixes are sixty-six. Twelve sixes are seventy- . . . . *two.*'

Unless he craned his neck round at an uncomfortable angle, he could no longer see behind him, where the road curved past Ashfield Place and dipped down by the Technical College and the School of Art on its way to town. When Frankie grew up, he was going to be a model at the School of Art, just like Buddie. He would be drawn and

56

painted in all sorts of poses, as Gypsy horseman or French waiter, as Spanish dancer, Mexican cowboy or turbanned and bejewelled Indian prince. He often practised the poses before the big mirror on the landing, but he was always disappointed with the results. Nobody wanted to paint pictures of a skinny, swarthy-skinned kid with hair like a black thatch and limbs no thicker than bean-sticks. It never failed to amaze him that parents like his should have produced such an unsatisfactory child. Smallfry deserved so much better. He knew she was right to believe that she, with her lovely face, long red hair and perfect figure, could be the best model the School of Art ever had, except that she could never lower her standards so far as to even set foot inside the building while Buddie's sisters were also working there.

It was late when he saw the green lorry come round the corner and pull into the kerb where a wide passage-way separated the Bowling Green Hotel from the row of shops. His legs were cramped. He had walked up and down the road a few times and crouched for a while outside the open door of the barber's shop, listening to the men talking. Then he had sprawled out on the pavement, trying to write out his times-tables on the flags with the sharp edge of a stone. He was so hungry that his stomach ached and so fed up with hanging around that his brain wouldn't work properly. As he shook the stiffness from his legs he saw the green lorry make a wide turn and roar off up the hill, leaving no clues as to the driver's identity. Standing on the pavement with most of her hair now unpinned and hanging loose down her back, Smallfry waved and waved with a big smile on her face until the tailboard saying William G Moffat, Coal & Coke Merchant was no longer in sight. Then she turned and began walking towards Frankie, swinging her hips and her handbag and smiling into the distance somewhere beyond him.

'Have you spoken to anyone?' she asked when he fell into step beside her.

'No, Smallfry.'

'And nobody saw you?'

'No, nobody.'

'Good, good.' She sighed heavily and patted the upswept sides of her hair very gently with her fingertips. 'You can tell your father we've been to visit your other nanny on Park Road. Then we went for a walk in the park and came back over the railway bridge. He isn't really interested, so there's no need for us to tell him anything else, is there, Frankie?'

'No, Smallfry.'

She was no longer smiling. Instead she was looking at him in that way she had of making him believe she could read his mind. Sometimes she did not need to use words like other people. Sometimes she only had to look at him in a certain way and he knew what she was telling him to do or say or think. There were even certain occasions when she instructed him to do something and he just *knew* he was expected to do the opposite, like when she told him in her firm, motherly voice to come out of hiding *this minute* and kiss his aunties or his nanny goodbye. After the first call she would revert to that same coaxing, sugar-sweet voice that could have him standing to attention like a clockwork soldier to impress strangers with his obedience. He knew to remain hidden at those times, even when she looked right into his eyes and *begged* him to come out. He would stay hidden and she would sigh very sadly and say:

'I am so sorry. I can do no more. As you can see for yourselves, the boy simply *refuses* to see you.'

He would never dream of disobeying her under normal circumstances, but he always knew, as if by magic, when she was saying one thing and meaning another. He knew every inflection in her voice, every tone, each subtle alteration. He *had* to know. If he made a mistake he would be in serious trouble, because mistakes meant that he was being deliberately stupid, and she would have to make him suffer for it.

'And we were all alone, of course,' she said, narrowing her eyes a little. 'There were just the two of us. Just you and me, Frankie.'

He nodded his head vigorously.

'Yes, Smallfry.'

'Right, then. Let's go home.'

Her smile was sudden and very bright and just for him and nobody else. He felt its warmth touching him all over, making up for the endless waiting and the sickly emptiness in his stomach. When she reached for his hand he hurriedly wiped it on the leg of his pants to make sure it was clean before slipping it into hers. She was humming softly to herself as they turned into Ashfield Place and headed for home hand-in-hand, swinging their arms and smiling like sweethearts.

FIVE

Two turkeys and a hen were still missing, and Buddie was blazing mad because he knew his profits were going to end up in someone else's larder with their throats cut. There was a family of Ukrainians living in a run-down house in one of the back streets near the corner of Ashfield and Cheshum Grove. The father spoke fractured English and always wore a big overcoat, even in warm weather. He rented just one upstairs room in the house for fifteen shillings a week, and his wife had to do the cooking in a shared cellar kitchen and his five young children all slept with their parents in the same bed. Buddie was convinced the Ukrainian had stolen one of his birds because the family was so poor they never had any decent food to eat. The foreigner was under suspicion, and if Buddie ever found out that he *was* a thief and a liar, there would be a lot more than poultry feathers flying about Cheshum Grove.

Frankie thought about that for a long time. It seemed to him that being really, *really* poor and having to live seven in one room with no decent food must be very hard, even for a Ukrainian. Perhaps the man made a genuine mistake because of his bad English. Perhaps he prayed to God to send him something decent to eat, and one of Buddie's turkeys came fluttering into the back yard so he killed it for his dinner, believing it was manna from heaven, just like in the Old Testament.

'Never look a gift horse in the mouth,' Buddie always said with a knowing wink whenever he came across an opportunity to make a little bit of something on the side. It was clear to Frankie that different rules applied to different people. Gift horses, like stray chickens and unclaimed turkeys, were not meant to be appropriated by neighbouring opportunists or by destitute Ukrainians in need of a decent meal.

'Where the hell have you been until this time?'

Frankie flinched. Buddie was in the back yard, pressing soft putty around a new sheet of glass in the kitchen window. The putty had a nice smell and left pale, oily smears on his dark fingers. He glowered irritably at the boy before looking beyond him to where Smallfry had appeared in the open gateway. Then he smiled. He always smiled when he looked at Smallfry.

She descended the yard steps with all the style and grace of Carmen Miranda making a grand entrance at some glittering function. Her glance took in the pile of old clothes stacked near the dustbins, the tin bucket filled with broken pieces of pottery and glass, the cringing Great Dane, the hose-pipe still leaking a trickle of cold water long after the yard had been swilled down.

'I collected Frankie from school and took him up to his other nanny's,' she explained, smoothing the front of her skirt with both hands and wiggling her hips. 'She gave him a slice of lemon cake and two shillings to spend. My goodness, how that woman can talk. She kept us there for much longer than we intended to stay, didn't she, Frankie?'

'Yes, Smallfry.'

Through the finger-stained glass he could see his fat nanny working in the kitchen. She was Buddie's mam, but everyone else called her Fanny, except when Smallfry was in a bad mood and nobody else was around and she called her lots of other names, some of them so rude that Frankie would never dare repeat them out loud. He guessed that Buddie had sent for Nanny to help clean up the mess in the house. She was wearing her floral wrap-over pinny, the one that had become faded in the wash and had neat white patches stitched over the holes in both pockets. She was standing at the gas-stove in the corner, cooking something in the big iron frying pan. There was no sign of the tiny, purple and black bottle with the ridges on the sides where Smallfry suspected she kept her deadly poison.

'And we called in the park and came back over the railway bridge,' Smallfry was saying. 'Isn't that so, Frankie?'

'Yes, Smallfry.'

'Oh, I almost forgot. Here's your spending money from Nanny, my dear. Put it away safely, and *do* try not to spend it all at once.'

'Yes, Smallfry. Thank you very much.'

He took the two-shilling piece and polished it on his sleeve before slipping it into the tiny breast pocket of his shirt, where it chinked against the penny already there. He was delighted with the gift. There was money hidden away in his secret tin upstairs, but he had to be careful how he spent it in case someone saw what he bought and demanded to know where it came from. He usually squirrelled away every ha'penny that came his way, keeping the coins wrapped up in a big khaki handkerchief so they would not jingle if the tin was disturbed, and keeping the windfall ten-shilling note folded very tightly and concealed in the corner of an old envelope. He was mostly very cautious with his money, but sometimes he just could not resist the temptation to take out a few coins and spend them on himself. This usually happened when he was left all alone in the house and the door to the store-kitchens was locked, or when the bread was a new loaf or the chicken uncut or the cheese unopened, so that even a single slice from either would be missed. Then he would get so hungry that the need to fill his stomach out-weighed his hoarding instincts. He might run down to Bland's at the bottom of Thorpe Street for a teacake and two penn'orth of peanut butter, or to Turner's for a big slice of meat and potato pie. Once he had bought a whole six penn'orth of Mrs Midgley's delicious boiled ham to make a feast with a dollop of sweet pickle and a tuppenny bar of chocolate to finish with. The money hidden away upstairs was a secret and must never be discovered, but now Smallfry's mam had sent a whole two-shilling piece for him to spend openly, whenever he liked, on *anything*. He pressed the flat of his hand against his shirt until he could feel the coin touching his ribs. Now at last he could go out and buy his very own shiny red exercise book with all the times-tables printed on the back.

The kitchen was much tidier now and filled with the most wonderful cooking smells. His fat nanny winked one eye in his direction but did not smile at him. She was cooking spicy egg specials for tea, thick wedges of bread soaked in beaten egg with lots and lots of seasoning and then fried in hot dripping in the big pan. The finished slices, all brown and crisp and crinkly at the edges, were then placed on a meat plate in the oven to keep hot. Each time she opened the oven door Frankie could smell the eggs and see the great mound of specials growing bigger and bigger. His stomach began to grumble so loudly that his nanny, looking stern but not really angry, poured out a full cup of fresh goat's milk and watched him drink it down, right to the last drop.

'Where have you been, Frankie?'

He wiped his sleeve across his mouth and turned to rinse out his cup. The movement caused several large bluebottles to rise from a bucket of poultry giblets left standing in the sink. Outside in the yard, his parents were speaking together in friendly tones while Nader, looking nervous and down-in-the-mouth, half-heartedly wagged her tail.

'We've been to Park Road,' he said quietly. 'My other nanny gave me two shillings to spend and we . . .'

'Is that the truth, Frankie?'

He swallowed hard. In spite of the milk, his throat was beginning to feel very dry.

'Yes, Nanny.'

'The *whole* truth?'

'. . . er . . . yes, Nanny.'

'You know what happens to little boys who tell lies, don't you, Frankie?'

'Yes, Nanny.'

'They get their tongues cut out. Or they get hung up by their thumbs in dark cellars so that big black rats can nibble their toes and vampire bats can suck the blood out of their necks. *That's* what happens to little boys who tell lies.'

He swallowed again.

'Yes, Nanny.'

She opened the oven door and placed two more egg specials on the meat plate before tossing another lump of dripping into the pan. While it melted she crossed to the sink, took up a large scoop of giblets and returned to drop them into the smoking fat, where they sizzled and smoked and gave out a strong, meaty aroma.

Nanny Fanny was a stout, pear-shaped woman with grey-streaked hair that she kept wound up and pinned in a twist at the nape of her neck. She was smaller than Buddie and walked with a waddling gait because her legs had grown very thick and lumpy now that she was getting on a bit. Nanny liked to smoke Woodbine cigarettes and drink milk stout, and she had a terrible temper because she took in boarders who were all theatrical people or circus folk, all black people who were rowdy and needed to be ruled with a firm hand. Nanny had soft white skin like Smallfry's, but she was not a lady, because she had once been married to a big black man from America who sang on stage for his living and had medals with his name on them from the Royal Order of Buffaloes. That black man was to blame for Buddie and his brothers and sisters being so brown, and for people thinking that Frankie was an Italian or a Gypsy kid. He hated to think of his grandfather being jet black with woolly hair and thick lips and a flat nose, even if he *did* come from South Carolina and have a wonderful singing voice. Having a black grandfather would be looked down on by other people. Smallfry had explained to him that being even a little bit Negro was a stigma as far as normal folk were concerned. However friendly they pretended to be, nobody would ever *really* forgive him for it.

Frankie seated himself at the table, head lowered and shoulders hunched, a tendril of thick black hair falling over the bridge of his nose and his gaze fixed on his badly chewed fingernails. He was wondering if Lord Jesus knew about all the little boys who had their tongues cut out and were hung up by their thumbs in dark cellars for telling lies.

When Buddie came in for his tea he had to wash his hands in the sink where the bluebottles were. This reminded him that the sticky brown coils of fly-paper hanging from the centre light fitting were too full of winged bodies to be of further use. He dried his hands on a towel that was scorched at one end from hanging too close to the stove, then he wafted the flies away from the giblets and threw the towel over the bucket to keep it covered. Frankie hoped and prayed there were no hairs on the towel, because of all the things he hated most in the world, finding a hair in his mouth when he was eating came first on the list.

'Here, carry these outside and throw them in the *dustbin*, not the swill-bin.'

Buddie had climbed on a chair to unfasten the used fly-papers from the light fitting. He handed them down to Frankie, who took them carefully by the strings and held them at arm's length because insects, dead or alive, were another thing that turned his stomach and made him want to throw up. When he returned to the kitchen a new fly-paper was in place, its coiled surfaces glistening as if treacle-coated as it turned slow, lazy spirals in the heat of the kitchen.

He managed to eat no less than four egg specials and a generous portion of Buddie's fried giblets before Nanny presented him with a warm fruit scone yellowed almost right the way through with melted best butter. There had always been best butter at Old Ashfield, and plenty of milk and cheese and other things that some people didn't have because of Government rationing. Frankie was luckier than all those other kids who had to go without such things as sugar and meat and butter for their bread. It had something to do with Buddie being a small-holder and having his own stock, and with all those secret ration books and petrol coupons that Frankie must never, ever talk about to *anyone*. The Government did not allow people to kill their own animals or do private deals for things that were still difficult to get, even so long after the war. They called it 'black market trading' and sent people to prison for doing it, so Frankie was very, very careful never to talk to outsiders about the things that went on at Old Ashfield. He did not want his dad to be sent to prison so that there was nobody left to take proper care of Smallfry and to keep Tom Fish from moving in and taking over the place.

'Careless talk costs lives.'

That was what Buddie always said when he had to warn Frankie to keep his mouth shut about something he had seen or overheard. It was a warning the boy always brought to mind whenever outsiders became curious about his life behind the high walls and locked gates of Old Ashfield.

Frankie worried about Buddie. Sometimes he worried about him so much that he had horrible nightmares, or bit his fingernails so far down that they bled and were very painful. And sometimes he became so anxious that he wet his bed in the night and had to find another spot to sleep in that was dry but not so warm as the deep hollow in the centre of the mattress where he usually slept.

Some weeks ago Smallfry had told him a secret, and now there were times when her words preyed on his mind until

66

he felt sick from hearing them over and over. She said Buddie might be going away. Such small words, spoken on a warm, sunny day when Smallfry was wearing her bright yellow dress and peep-toed sandals; yet they were big words too, frightening and threatening words. She had hinted that his father might be planning to go back to sea, but she had said it in such a way that he knew he was not supposed to believe it *exactly*. Then she had whispered to Park Road Nanny that Buddie was *out on bail*, and Frankie knew that *out on bail* was a special order to attend Leeds Assize Courts on very serious police business. Perhaps Buddie had been caught doing something wrong, and when the magistrates saw him they would send him away to prison, and people would pretend he had joined the Merchant Navy, except that everyone would guess the truth when the family started queuing up for Prisoners' Aid. Perhaps he had decided to go back into the Army, where he had once been a truck driver, or to rejoin the trawling ships, where the big blue skull and cross-bones had been tattooed on his arm and would never come off as long as he lived. What tormented Frankie was the suspicion that Tom Fish wanted Smallfry and Old Ashfield and all the farm-stock and dance-band kit for himself, and that the big, grinning Irishman would slaughter Buddie and hang his body in the cellar with the bleeding pig carcasses, just to be rid of him.

'And when does *Madam* intend to eat?'

Nanny's sharp voice brought Frankie back to the present with a start.

'Too hoity-toity to sit down with the rest of us common lot, is she?'

'You know she'll eat when she's good and ready, Ma,' Buddie growled. He ripped a chunk of bread from what remained of the loaf, dipped it into the fat from his giblets and pointed with his fork at the oven door. 'Any more eggs in there?'

Nanny shook her head and pushed a warm scone in his direction. Her lips had tightened into a thin line. The thoughts in her head were making her cross. Frankie could see the bad temper growing on her face.

'You should put your foot down, Buddie,' she said. 'She's your wife, isn't she? You shouldn't let her get so finicky over everything. Why can't she clean up after her own bloody parties? Why can't she learn to cook a decent meal and sit down with her family instead of picking at her food in secret, as if eating was something to be ashamed of?'

'Now, Ma, you know she won't eat in front of other people.'

Frankie frowned at his tea-cup and pretended not to be listening. He had never seen his mam eat. He wasn't even sure if *anyone* had ever seen her eat. She took weak, milky tea from an elegant china tea-cup and saucer with real painted rose-buds and shiny gold trims, but he had never seen her eat.

'Bone idle, that's what she is. Bone idle,' Nanny said, chewing tea leaves.

'Leave it, Ma,' Buddie growled. 'I'm not complaining. She's a good lass. She does all right.'

'What? *What?*' Nanny retorted. 'She does *bugger-all!* She never lifts a damn finger unless it's to tart herself up to go prancing around the streets making sheep's-eyes at everything in pants.'

'I said *leave it*, Ma,' Buddie warned.

'Neither use nor ornament, that's her. Neither use nor bloody ornament.'

'That's *enough!*'

Frankie sat up with a start. He could feel the muscles in his face begin to twitch of their own accord, and he knew that Buddie would slap him hard if he noticed. In the tense silence that followed he managed to stammer out the words Smallfry insisted upon hearing after every meal:

68

'Thank you for what I have eaten, now please may I leave the table?'

Buddie nodded sharply and the boy slid from his chair and made a dash for the door leading to the hall. He pulled back the curtain and slipped out like a nervous shadow. As he closed the door behind him, he heard Buddie bang his big fist down on the table and growl:

'Now look here, Ma. I won't have it, do you hear? I won't have you running my wife down every time you open your damn mouth.'

Frankie tiptoed away, groping his way along the unlit hall where coats and jackets brushed his cheek and unidentified objects nudged him in the darkness. He jumped sideways in sudden alarm as the door of the best room swung open and a figure loomed at him from the brightness within. It was Smallfry, still wearing her high-heeled shoes but with her costume jacket removed and a thin white blouse clinging to the thicker fabric of her brassiere. He could see the firelight twinkling on all the brasses, copper, silver and pewter ornaments in the room at her back. She made him imagine that she was a fairy-tale Queen with magic powers, guarding the gates of Aladdin's cave.

'What have you told them?'

His face twitched.

'Nothing, Smallfry.'

'Liar!'

She was using her quiet voice, the scary one that came out like a hiss between her teeth.

'I d-didn't tell,' he protested in a whisper. 'Honest, I d-didn't tell. I only said like you t-told me. Nanny wanted to know where we were and I said at P-Park Road, just like you t-told me.'

'Is that all?'

'Y-Yes, Smallfry.'

'If you're lying to me . . .'

'No, honest. Honest to G-God,' he swore. 'I didn't ... I didn't say *anything*.'

She looked down at him for a long time while he tried desperately to control the nervous spasms in his face and shoulders.

'All right,' she said at last. 'Now get outside and don't come back until you're called. Go on, you fool. *Out!*'

He scuttled off in the direction of the front door, only to skid to a halt halfway across the main hall when her voice, sharp as the crack of a whip, rang out behind him.

'*Frankie!*'

He hurried back, cautious and watchful. She was still standing in the brightly illuminated doorway with lights dancing in her long auburn hair and her face set like a mask. Without speaking, she extended her right hand, palm uppermost, and snapped her fingers several times. He knew exactly what she wanted. His heart sank as he fished the two-shilling piece from the breast pocket of his shirt and returned it, still warm, to its rightful owner.

SIX

Beyond the big front door the terrace was a patchwork of unevenly cut stones separated by tufts of grass and yellow-headed dandelions. Sunlight still filtered through the trees to lay itself in bright stains across the stones. Out there was warm and friendly, but the house itself was a scary place. It was big and dark, with lots of doors that were never unlocked and many places that always felt cold, even in summer. In winter the wind howled down unused chimneys, windows rattled in their frames and tall trees tapped and scratched at the house with bare branches that were mysteriously transformed into ghostly fingers in the dead of night. Sometimes the hall became inky black, so that Frankie had to feel his way through it without breathing, lest the darkness invade his lungs and suffocate him, or cause his heart to beat so fast that it burst inside him. Upstairs on the first landing, a pale grey light from the lamp in the back yard, filtering through frosted windows, pushed the darker shadows back against the walls, but from there a lesser flight of steps led into the total blackness of the first-floor corridor. Frankie's bedroom was at the far end of that corridor, beyond the final turn of the banister, beyond all those other doors leading to attics, store-cupboards, box-rooms and bedrooms, and to reach it he had to pass the most frightening thing in the whole house; the Bogeyman's door. Frankie's home was not like the cramped and ordinary homes of other boys. Even now, on a day that glittered and shone with summer sunshine, it was a gloomy, scary place.

Frankie was sitting on the front step with his face close to the door so that he would know if anything happened. He was skinny enough to have squeezed through the gap without disturbing the big security chain that allowed the door to open only a few inches. He knew he could not be seen from the kitchen, and if anyone came after him, he would be long gone and hidden before they even got the chain off the door.

He could still hear voices coming from inside the house. Nanny always made trouble when she came to Old Ashfield. She complained about the house and the way Frankie was dressed, about Smallfry's clothes, or mice in the pantry, or wet spoons in the cocoa tin, or Nader's fleas. And she often complained about the stove being lit day and night because that, in her opinion, was a wicked waste of fuel. Smallfry did not like Buddie's ma. She said she was jealous because her own house was over-run with lodgers and her daughters were all ugly bitches, even if two of them *were* artists' models and one a professional dancer who had travelled the world many times over in spectacular musical shows. Smallfry told Frankie that Nanny's house in Lansdowne Place was a gin-shop for black men, lunatics and whores, but he must never repeat that to anyone, and especially not to Buddie, because it had to be kept secret, even though it was the truth.

'Red, purple, green and orange.'

He had spit on his fingers and rubbed at a patch of floor tiles in the corner just inside the door. Sunlight warmed the pattern beneath the dust, lifting the bright ceramic rectangles back into life. He counted the colours aloud:

'Red, purple, green and orange,
Blue, gold, brown, turquoise.'

The tiles were beautiful. They had been imported from Italy a long time ago and laid by an artist in a very complex design that covered the entire hall. Even the narrowest part on the left of the stairs, that dark passageway leading to the cellars and kitchens, was set with the same wonderful patterns beneath its strip of chocolate brown linoleum. It had only recently been revealed to him that a wealth of jewel-like colours was lying right there beneath everyone's feet. The discovery had taken place just before Rosie killed herself by chewing through the gas pipe in the tool-shed, in the very recent past when the big brindle Great Dane and her bulldog companion had terrorized Frankie even while they were chained up. Rosie had eaten a pile of raw turkey entrails and then been sick and done her diarrhoea all over the hall. Both dogs had then slithered about in it and trodden it everywhere in their panic to get away from the awful, stinking mess. An infuriated Buddie had taken them, a collar in each fist so that even the huge Rosie had to walk on her hind legs, and dumped them in the pigs' water trough to cool off and clean off. Both were given a scrub and a beating and locked in the coal-hole for a whole week, and at times their howls had sounded so pitiful that even Frankie, fearing them as he did, had felt sorry for them.

On that occasion Buddie had brought a bucket of hot water and some soap flakes and scrubbed up the mess with the long-handled broom from the yard. Then he had swept the filthy water straight out the front door to the terrace before rinsing off the tiles with a strong solution of disinfectant and ammonia. With the door standing back on its hinges so that sunlight flooded in, the floor had soon dried to reveal the colours previously dulled by years of dust and grime. The moment the coast was clear, Frankie had crept downstairs and crouched on the bottom step to gaze in wonder at this newly-discovered delight. It had filled him with amazement that something so colourful and beautiful could, even on warm summer days, strike at the under-sides of bare feet with a chill that seemed to reach right to the bone.

'Frankie!'

He leaped to his feet as the kitchen door flew open and

Buddie's big, deep voice boomed along the corridor and across the hall.

'*Frankie!* Damn it, where *is* that boy?'

Frankie made as if to flee, but his body checked itself in mid-stride, plucked to a halt by the twin barbs of cowardice and obedience. Even now he could run down the garden steps or jump the steep rockery and be hidden among the weeds and thick bushes before his father came in search of him. Even now he could probably make it to the pigsties at the far end of the terrace and hide there until the row in the kitchen blew over. He might have escaped, had not his father's voice, like the roar of a dangerous beast, struck fear into his heart and pulled the anxious, almost automatic response from his lips:

'I'm c-coming, B-Buddie. I'm c-coming.'

He squeezed through the gap below the safety chain and raced for the kitchen door. On tile and linoleum his footsteps rang out to alert his parents to the presence of school shoes in the house, and although he yanked up his socks as he ran, by the time he reached the kitchen they were bunched in untidy heaps around his skinny ankles.

Nanny was now wearing her overcoat as she stood before the mirror, pinning on her headscarf with her mouth pinched into a thin, angry line. Buddie was frowning as he neatened the toes of his thick white socks before stepping into his boots. As if totally oblivious to their presence in the room, Smallfry sat near the pantry door in her favourite chair, the one with the pretty fringed shawl thrown over its back and the silky cushions padding out the seat. Her legs were crossed one over the other and she was polishing her fingernails with a wad of soft silk cleverly rolled into a neat sausage-shape. She seemed happy. She was smiling gently to herself and was too preoccupied with her own private thoughts to notice the arrival of Frankie.

Buddie looked pointedly at Frankie's shoes, then deepened his frown and said:

74

'I'm going back to Lansdowne Place with Nanny to pick up a few bits of scrap iron. How'd you like to come along for the ride?'

Frankie beamed and nodded his head vigorously. Nanny's house was always warm and crowded and very noisy. It was cram-packed full of strange sights and interesting smells and weird and wonderful people with funny accents.

'Yeah, please, Buddie . . .'

Too late his senses registered a minute tightening of Smallfry's features, a pause, an almost imperceptible stiffening of her body as she continued to smile down at her long red fingernails. What passed between the boy and his mother was a private thing as brief as the tiny space between one heartbeat and the next, and yet her wordless anger reached him like a well-aimed blow.

'No . . . no . . . I can't . . .' he immediately blurted. 'I'm sorry, Buddie . . . I can't come . . . I have to stay here . . .'

'What? What's that you say?' Buddie tapped one foot on the flagged stone floor and gave the leather top-stitching of his boot a final tug for good measure. Then he stood to his full height with his fists on his hips and his legs wide apart, glowering beneath his black brows.

'Quit that stammering, boy. Pull your socks up and speak properly. And stand up straight when you're talking to me.'

'Yes, Buddie.'

Frankie snatched at each sock in turn before jerking himself to attention with his hands clasped behind his back. As if to declare an act of mute defiance on his part, both socks slowly collapsed into ragged concertinas around the tops of his shoes.

'Well, boy? What have you to say for yourself?'

'I'm sorry . . . er . . . I can't c-come to Nanny's . . . er . . . I forgot . . .'

'Forgot what? Stop twitching your face, damn it.'

'Yes, Buddie. I'm s-sorry, Buddie. I forgot . . . I forgot . . .'

75

He fell silent, his mind casting itself frantically this way and that in search of a believable explanation. The saving fib steadfastly eluded him.

'*Well*, boy?'

He could tell by the set of those dark features that Buddie was rapidly running out of patience.

'. . . er . . . er . . . I have to stay with S-Smallfry,' he blurted.

'What? Are you saying you'd rather stay home with your mam than help your father with a spot of man's work?'

'No . . . er, yes . . . er, I think . . . I mean . . . I promised . . .'

'Make your mind up, boy! Stop pissing me about! Do you want to come with me or stay home?'

Frankie lowered his eyes and said miserably:

'I-I think I should s-stay here with S-Smallfry.'

At that Buddie curled his lip in disgust and spat:

'*Mammy's boy!*'

The way his father sneered at him made Frankie feel ashamed. From the corner of his eye he could see Smallfry still smiling down at her nails, seemingly unaware of his predicament. Knowing he was doing exactly as she wished did not make the confrontation any easier. He feared his father's contempt. It was somehow more painful, more deeply wounding, than his anger.

'*Bloody Mammy's boy!*'

Buddie spat the words again and shoved the boy roughly to one side as he yanked open the back door. 'As soft as shit and just as useful, that's what you are! Come on, Ma, let's be off. This little sissy's no son of mine. He's nothing but a bloody *Mammy's boy!*'

Nanny did not kiss him goodbye. Instead, she picked up her woven string shopping bag and waddled through the open door smelling of fried eggs and chicken giblets and face powder. He watched her pass the kitchen window in Buddie's wake and guessed that she, too, was cross with him for being a Mammy's Boy. And Nanny would not forget. She would poke fun at him and talk about him to other people, and then they in their turn would laugh at him for being a big sissy and a dreadful disappointment to his father.

'Come here, Frankie.'

Smallfry's voice was as smooth as a caress. It made him nervous. It reminded him of the last film they had seen together at the Empire, when Mata Hari spoke so softly to the German double-agent and then shot him right through the head with the miniature pearl-handled revolver concealed in her fur wrap. He snatched at his socks and shuffled forward, halting a measured distance from her chair. Smallfry was very particular. She did not like him to stand too close.

'Would you mind very much if your father went away?'

'Pardon?'

The words had made a sudden cold patch inside him.

'Tell me, how would you feel?' she cooed. 'Would it make you happy? Sad? Indifferent? *Miserable?*'

Frankie swallowed hard. The cold patch was spreading outwards and upwards. He wasn't sure what she wanted him to say.

'I . . . I d-don't know, Smallfry,' he stammered. 'I d-don't want B-Buddie to go away.'

'Oh?' She stopped buffing her nails, all movement so abruptly arrested that her fingers remained frozen in mid-air. Her eyes widened in surprise, then became all sad and glittery, as if she were about to weep.

'Oh,' she said again. 'Oh, I *see*. You don't want him to go away because he's your *favourite*. *He's* the one you love the best.'

'No, no, Smallfry . . . I didn't m-mean . . .'

'Oh, Frankie, Frankie,' she sighed. 'How cruel one's own precious children can be. And I was foolish enough to believe that I, who willingly made so many sacrifices on your behalf, must be the one you care for best of all. Oh, what a wicked waste of my affection, and I could have enjoyed such a wonderful, glamorous life had it not been for you and my beholden duty as a mother.'

'N-No, please, S-Smallfry . . . I d-didn't m-mean to s-say . . .'

She dismissed his feeble protests with a small, elegant fluttering of her fingers.

'Your father doesn't care a damn for you, Frankie,' she informed him. 'He might leave here tomorrow, or even tonight while you're asleep. Who knows the way that man's mind works?' She shuddered, sighed heavily and fixed her troubled gaze on the flames licking around the front grids of the stove. 'He might simply pack his bags and vanish back to sea one day while you are at school or out playing somewhere. Are you aware of that, Frankie?'

'Yes, Smallfry.'

'He might just decide to leave here without so much as a *word* to you. He could go at any time. You'll never know when, or why, or how long he intends being away. One day he'll be here and everything will be as normal, and the next day he'll be gone. Just like that. Do you understand, Frankie?'

'Y-Yes, Smallfry.'

The prospect filled him with a familiar, aching distress. He could not bear to think of Buddie leaving forever.

'While I, on the other hand, am obliged to stay,' Smallfry continued in her soft, Mata Hari voice. 'I have already made my sacrifices and swallowed the bitter pill of self-denial. I have already given up everything, *everything*, for the simple reason that my son, my only son, means more to me than anything else in the world.'

Frankie tried to swallow the lump that had begun to fill his throat with a bile made up of guilt and fear and uncertainty. He sniffed and wiped the back of his hand across his nose, willing himself not to cry.

'And where on earth do you think you'd be without your

78

mother to take care of you?' she suddenly demanded in a harsher voice.

'I-I d-don't know, S-Smallfry.'

'Buddie would beat you and neglect you. He'd make your life a misery and eventually the authorities would have to put you away in a Children's Home for your own safety.' She sighed again and shivered a little. Her voice had altered to a softer tone when she added:

'Oh, such hateful, uncaring places. How could it be that *my* child, my own darling son . . . ?'

Frankie swallowed again. A tear squeezed itself from one eye and ran down his cheek to hang in a salty droplet from his upper lip. She had often told him about the Homes, where children were forced to scrub floors all day long and were then beaten with sticks every night, where unwanted boys and girls were starved until their ribs stuck out and tortured by evil keepers just for sport. He knew he would die if they put him in a Home. It would be the end of him if Smallfry went away and left him and he was locked up in one of those terrible places.

'Oh, but how could I leave?' she suddenly asked. 'How could I possibly desert you now, after all I've done for you these nine long years? Unless, of course, I suspected that deep down you really *wanted* me to go . . . '

'No,' he sniffed noisily. 'Oh, n-no . . . n-no . . . '

' . . . because you prefer to live with your *father*.'

'Oh, no, Smallfry,' he protested. 'I n-never said that. I love you b-best of all. I d-do. Honest to G-God, I do, I love you b-best of all.'

'But you love your father, too, of course?'

'Well, yes,' he sniffed, then added hastily: 'but not a lot . . . only a little bit . . . '

'Ah, so I was right! You *do* want me to go!'

'No . . . no . . . '

'But you openly admitted just now that you love your father!'

'Yes, but not . . . well, I d-didn't mean, that is . . . I . . .
I . . . '

Confused and frightened, Frankie blinked his eyes furiously and felt his entire face begin to jerk itself into unsightly twitches.

'P-Please S-Smallfry,' he stammered. 'I love you *best*.'

'Oh? Then you *don't* love your father?'

He shook his head, spraying tears, and said in a small voice:

'No, Smallfry.'

'And if you don't love him, you must *dislike* him.'

'Y-Yes, Smallfry.'

'And if *that's* the case, you wouldn't care a damn if he *did* go away, would you?'

'N-No, Smallfry.'

'Or if he never came back?'

Although the word *never* made him wince, he answered without hesitation.

'No, S-Smallfry.'

'And why is that, Frankie?'

'Because I l-love you b-best.'

She suddenly dropped her hands into her lap and smiled brilliantly, showing the wide gap in the centre of her beautiful white teeth, and all those pretty little laugh-lines at the outer edges of her eyes.

'And that, my dear child, is exactly how it *should* be. No woman likes to work her fingers to the bone for nine long years and then find out that her son is an ungrateful little bastard who doesn't appreciate the debt he owes her. But I'll be watching you, Frankie. I'll be keeping my eye on you, and heaven help you if I find out you've been lying to me.'

'I haven't . . . I d-didn't . . . '

He wiped his nose on his forearm and tried desperately to halt the flow of tears that were now coursing down his face. He saw Smallfry's smile fade away as she began to polish her nails in that same easy, refined manner, resuming her

80

original task as if their conversation, and his distress, had never taken place.

'You may go, Frankie.'

Aching with the fear that he might have condemned Buddie with his disloyalty, Frankie made his way to the kitchen door.

'Haven't you forgotten something?'

'Oh, y-yes . . . I'm s-sorry, S-Smallfry.'

He hurried back to her chair, wiped the back of his hand across his mouth to clean the germs away, then leaned his upper body towards her. Still polishing her nails, she turned her face away but lifted one cheek sufficiently to receive his kiss. Against his pursed lips her skin was soft and smooth and very cool, despite the heat from the fire. Her aloofness reminded him that this ritual was solely for his benefit. Smallfry did not enjoy being touched. She was not like all those coarse, inferior women who could afford to let themselves be mauled about and slobbered over by grubby children with sticky hands and runny noses.

Frankie tiptoed out to the front steps and sat there for a long time, watching busy insects in the rhododendron bushes and listening to the rustling sounds of a breeze among the leaves. He liked the trees of Old Ashfield. They were big and old, and they seemed to be everywhere, lurking like a band of patient bailiffs determined to take over the place the moment its owner's back was turned. Sometimes they frightened him with their gnarled shapes and eerie shadows, but mostly they were harmless things to climb into and swing from and hide in.

He was still sitting on the front step when Smallfry left the kitchen and went into the best room, where she could be surrounded by all those beautiful things she prized so dearly. He heard the key turn in the lock, and then the sound of music coming from the wind-up gramophone in the carved mahogany cabinet.

You must remember this . . .

81

A kiss is still a kiss . . .
A sigh is still a sigh . . .
The fundamental things apply, as time goes by.

It was growing late and the light was rapidly changing. It left trails of dark shadow like deep stains along the terrace, and it robbed every living thing of its colour so that all the vibrant greens and reds and yellows turned to black.

Frankie was worried. He did not know how to undo all the unkind things he had said about his father, and long ago he had learned to fear the power of the spoken word. He knew there were times when just *saying* something made it so, like that day when Georgie Hemmingway climbed up to walk along the guttering of the main porch roof for a dare. He was doing all right until Miss Jeffries with the fat legs came along and cried out at the top of her voice:

'Oh my good Lord, he's going to fall. That child is going to fall.'

And sure enough, Georgie Hemmingway was so startled by the words and so upset by the sudden arrival of Miss Jeffries that he put his foot down in the wrong place, skidded on a wet leaf, wobbled like a panic-stricken jelly and fell to the ground with a scream and broke his arm in two places. The words had made it happen. There was also that time when Buddie was away and Smallfry became uneasy because she suspected the Bogeyman was about to come looking for Frankie in the middle of the night. She had warned him in a frightened whisper that had made the blood run cold in his veins. He had begged to be allowed to sleep in her bed until Buddie came home, but she had told him to run along like a big, brave boy because perhaps she was wrong and nothing was going to happen, after all. But sure enough he had been awakened that night by scratching noises at his door and horrible groaning sounds coming from the corridor outside. Frankie had curled up under his army greatcoat, stiff with fear lest the broken chair leg rammed into the space at the bottom of the door proved ineffectual in keeping the Bogeyman at bay. It was all to do with words. Just saying them out loud, a person could sometimes *make* things happen. That was why he so often chanted certain phrases, or prayers, over and over in a quiet voice:

'Please God, don't let Buddie or Smallfry go away so that I have to be put in a Children's Home.'

He would count the repetitions on his fingers, saying them twenty-five, thirty, forty, sometimes even *fifty* times to be on the safe side.

'Please God, help me to learn all my times-tables so I can pass my eleven plus and make them both proud of me.' This he always repeated on his way to school, especially on those days when it was mental arithmetic or double maths. And every night, or whenever it was very dark, and always when he was in the house all by himself, he would chant:

'Please God, please Jesus, please Holy Ghost, please don't let the Bogeyman get me.'

Frankie was not really convinced that boys like himself stood much chance of being listened to by someone as important as God, but there was just a possibility that he might catch Him on a good day, when He was feeling particularly generous, or simply stumble across that magic formula that would make the words come true, if he repeated them often enough.

With this in mind he waited on the front steps and counted out the prayers on his fingers, always coming back to the most important prayer of the moment:

'Please God, send Buddie home.'

The sky was as dark as pitch and a solitary owl was hooting mournfully on the hillside when Frankie heard the back door open and Buddie's big, Fats Waller voice fill the kitchen with song. Like a swift shadow the boy squeezed through the gap in the door, scuttled across the hall and crept silently up the big staircase with his school shoes clutched in his hands and a broad smile on his face.

His father had come home. He had not become sick and tired of Frankie being a Mammy's Boy and decided to go away again, after all. The long vigil on the front step and all the chanted prayers had been worthwhile. Frankie had made it happen. He had said the right words and Buddie had come home.

Frankie waited in the darkness at the top of the stairs to watch Buddie carry the big white mug and the delicate china cup and saucer to the door of the best room. For a moment the two people he loved most of all in the whole world were silhouetted like strange, picture-book figures in the twinkling firelight. Then the door of the best room closed and the big key turned in the lock, leaving the rest of the house blacker than blackest midnight. Now he, too, could go to bed.

With his out-stretched arms wafting the air ahead of him for unseen dangers, Frankie picked his way gingerly across the small landing and up the seven wooden steps leading to the first-floor corridor. A slender sliver of pale grey light seeped from beneath the Bogeyman's door. Its presence quickened his heart and pulled his scalp so tightly across his skull that he was forced to hold his breath for fear of breathing something dangerously evil into his lungs. Then he screwed his eyes tightly closed and raced as fast as he dare along the inky corridor to his own room.

SEVEN

Frankie's bedtime ritual seldom varied. Once inside the room, he closed the door quickly to shut out the creaks and shadows of the corridor, only to find himself standing in a thick darkness that seemed to close in around him like a sprung trap. He dare not open his eyes and he could not pray out loud for fear that something nasty would fly into his open mouth. Instead, a frantic little voice cried out somewhere deep inside his head:

'Oh, God, please keep me alive. Oh, God, don't let me die in the dark. Please don't let me die in the dark.'

He dropped to his hands and knees and groped blindly in the pile of litter stacked in the corner behind the bedroom door. His heart was pounding. His fingers had become fat and clumsy, but at last they closed around the stolen box of matches and the precious stub of a candle hidden away amongst the junk. In the sudden flare of light his face was pale and ghostly, with twin reflections of the candle's flame shimmering in his eyes. This was the worst time, the moment he dreaded most of all, when he might have made it safely to his room only to find that the Bogeyman was already there, lying in wait for him.

By the meagre light from the candle he examined the room with meticulous care, squinting into every recess and corner, searching for the smallest hint of change, the tell-tale extra shadow. He even sniffed the air, convinced the Bogeyman would have its own distinctive smell to give warning of its presence. It would be a smell like that which sometimes seeped from beneath the dark brown door at the other end of the corridor, a peculiar concoction of moth balls and camphorated oil, stale food, mouldy newspapers, snuff and damp carpets, and perhaps something really bad, like dog dirt. And there would be the scent of blood, of course, thick and cloying and sickly, like the awful stink that rose from the cellars and drains whenever Buddie and his helpers slaughtered the pigs for the secret black markets.

Shielding the candle flame with a cupped hand, he checked the space beneath the big iron bed, where mounds of worn-out rugs and old clothes and discarded strips of linoleum made familiar humps and mounds that could not be disturbed without his knowledge. The gap at the bottom of the chest of drawers was still stuffed with screwed-up newspapers, as was the wider, deeper cavity at the foot of the wardrobe. He was always worried about the wardrobe. It was huge, easily large enough to hold a fully-grown man, with no handles on the outside and a rusty lock holding the narrow doors together. Sometimes he imagined that horrible things had been hidden away in there in the days when the room was used for storing old furniture and dusty, moth-stained curtains. One of his worst nightmares was the one where he was fast asleep in bed in the middle of the night and the wardrobe doors began to open very slowly from the *inside* and the beast living in there reached for him in the darkness.

Only when fully satisfied that he was alone in his room did Frankie dare to ram his wooden wedge, broken from the leg of a discarded dining chair, under the door so that it could not be opened from the corridor outside. His parents would shout from downstairs if they wanted him. They never came up to his room, except at those frightening times when Smallfry crept upstairs and suddenly pounded on his door with something hard and he knew he would have to follow her downstairs to be punished, even though she did not speak a single word to him.

'That bedroom is your responsibility,' Buddie had told him a long time ago. 'Keep it clean and tidy and don't go making extra work for your mam by leaving your toys all over the place.'

'No, Buddie.'

'You're a lucky young fellow, Frankie. I betcha there's not another kid in the whole of Yorkshire who has his own private room with a big double bed all to himself.'

'No, Buddie.'

'Me, I had to sleep in a long, draughty dormitory and share everything I had with thirty other kids. Never had a thing to call my own. Little chance of that in a damn lousy orphanage. You're a lucky young fellow, Frankie, and don't you ever forget it.'

'No, Buddie.'

Frankie had stared hard at his father's face, seeing the grim tightness that always came into his features when he mentioned the orphanage in Harrogate where he was put when his father dropped dead on stage during a charity concert at the Star Hotel in Eccleshill. The black American bass singer had left his family to fend for themselves, and so poor little Buddie, only eight years old and the youngest boy, had been locked up with strangers in a prison-like house in a strange town. The loss of a father was a terrible thing. The very idea of it struck cold terror into Frankie's heart.

He always tried to do what was expected of him so that he would not get into trouble or force his parents to think about leaving him, but looking after his bedroom was not easy. The place was full of old junk. There were piles of newspapers and old tarpaulins crammed into corners, stacks of broken furniture and unwanted mattresses shoved against walls, bits of damaged garden tools stored in old tea-chests. And there was no light. He could not remember there ever being a bulb in the socket. Once he had managed to steal one from the cupboard in the pantry, only to find that no amount of climbing or stretching would make him tall enough to reach up and fix it in place. There was no light on the front terrace to filter through into his room and even if there *had* been a lamp out there, he was not allowed to remove the dark army blanket that had been nailed across the window since the days of the blackouts when he was just a baby. Frankie could not really complain. He had his store of candle stubs and stolen matches, and sometimes, on winter nights when it was very cold and very dark, he made a fire of old rags and papers and bits of rubbish in the little iron fireplace set into the wall at the foot of his bed.

Now he stood beside the bed with his candle balanced on the lid of his Oxo tin and two spare matches at the ready. He had pulled back a corner of the blackout blanket and hooked it around the stuff on the windowsill so that light would flood into his room as soon as the sun was up. It was so dark outside that the glass panels in the window looked as if someone had daubed them with a thick layer of black paint. He stared all around him, eyeing the many shadows that flickered and jerked just beyond the limits of his small candle. They might have been tethered creatures straining to break free of the walls and fly screeching across the room to cling to his face until he suffocated to death or choked when they got into his throat. He shuddered at the thought. He had forgotten to go to the bathroom. The level in his pot had reached the curve just below the lip of the rim, which meant that it was already too full for him to carry all the way to the lavatory without mishap. He needed to go. He had gone twice in the bushes on the front terrace, leaning back and sticking his hips forward so that the flow of pale liquid arced with a tiny hiss of steam into the garden below. Now he needed to go again, because coming up to bed in the dark by himself had made him nervous, and being nervous always made him want to wee.

After stripping off his shirt and pants he folded them neatly and hung them over the rail at the bottom of the

bed so that Sir would not scowl at him and tell the whole
class his clothes looked as if they had been slept in.
Then he squatted over the pot and managed to empty
his bladder with just a fraction to spare before the contents spilled over on to the already stained floorboards.
Tomorrow, when it was not so dark in the corridor, he
would bring an empty tin can and ladle out some of the
wee before attempting to carry the pot to the lavatory.

He made a swift but careful check under that side of
the bed to make sure all his secret treasures remained
intact, then pulled a small parcel from the folds of a
piece of carpet and hugged it to him as he scrambled
into bed. He was glad Smallfry would not see his room.
She was a lady. She liked pretty things and nice smells,
and Frankie's room was not the kind of place where such
a lady would feel comfortable. It made him feel ashamed.
Although he was almost ten years old he still wet the bed
regularly, so he could not be allowed clean sheets and a
fresh mattress and new blankets just so that he could mess
them up all over again. His bed stank, but if he wanted a
clean, nice bed like Smallfry's, all he had to do was stop
wetting in the night. It was entirely up to him, yet no
matter how he tried, or how often he weed before he went
to sleep, there were still times when he woke up lying in a
wet, smelly patch that never seemed to dry out properly.

Frankie snuggled down beneath his blanket and adjusted
the big army greatcoat so that it hugged his body in a warm,
protective embrace. Then he undid his parcel and let the
paper fall to the floor. By the light of the candle, Mr Ted
stared back at him with beady black eyes and a lop-sided
smile. Mr Ted was Frankie's teddy bear. He was a small,
hard-packed, balding individual with dingy fur that had
once been a bright golden brown, black ears and black soles
to his clumsy round feet. He had hinged limbs that allowed
him to sit or lie and move his arms in any direction, and
the permanent tilt of his head gave a friendly, inquisitive

89

expression to his worn features. Mr Ted was Frankie's best friend. If the house caught fire and Smallfry and Buddie were saved, Mr Ted would be the one Frankie rushed back into the flames to rescue. He was supposed to have been thrown on the bonfire years ago, when Smallfry called him dirty and flea-ridden and not a fit toy for a big boy to play with, but Frankie had cheated his mam when she was not paying attention. He had thrown an old shoe on to the bonfire in Mr Ted's place, and had kept the bear carefully hidden ever since then. He could not imagine ever being grown-up enough to part with his shabby little friend. He loved his teddy more than all his other hidden treasures put together.

When he blew out the candle the room closed in as if some heavy invisible cover had suddenly been thrown over his head. He forced himself to breathe steadily and evenly as he hugged Mr Ted with one hand and fingered the spare matches with the other. The Oxo tin was right there on the mattress close to his head. If the darkness became unbearable he would simply relight his candle and wait until it was safe to try again. He screwed his eyes tightly closed and told himself that everything would be all right. However wickedly he had betrayed his father for Smallfry's sake, Buddie was still here, and as long as he was here in the house, everything would be all right.

'God forgive me for all my sins,' he declared out loud, and then repeated the same words many times to ensure extra strength and potency by the repetition. 'And God bless Smallfry and keep Buddie from going to prison, and please God make me grow taller, and please make my skin turn white like Smallfry's, and please make me stop wetting the bed.'

After several minutes of intense chanting he opened his eyes in the darkness and added passionately:

'*And I hope Tom Fish gets eaten by the Devil.*'

The sound of his own voice was a source of comfort to him. It made him feel that he was not really alone in the big room where shadows lay one upon another like crowds of living things.

'Someone might buy me a proper torch for my birthday,' he told Mr Ted in a whisper. 'A silver and blue torch with two spare batteries so that I can always see my way around in the night. And Smallfry might ask Buddie to climb up and put a light bulb in the socket for me, just as she promised to do, ages and ages ago, only I think she forgot.'

Mr Ted lay small and hard against the boy's chest, a silent and trusted confidante.

'Maybe I'll find a key to my room so I can lock the door behind me and then nobody will ever be able to get inside when I'm not here. Better still, my birthday present might be a move to the big back bedroom where light comes in from the lamp in the yard, so it never, ever gets *really* dark. And there's no blackout blanket on the window and hardly any furniture at all, and there's a long string hanging down with a knob on the end that you pull to switch out the light *after* you've got into bed.'

The owl on the hillside called its melancholy cry and the ancient house creaked and sighed as it settled down for the night. The hint of a breeze invaded the chimney, where it was checked by heaps of yellowed newspapers scrunched up and stuffed into the sooty aperture to keep the night-things out. Curled up in the big bed with his eyes tightly closed, Frankie hugged his teddy and desperately tried not to think about the creepy-crawlies that might be lurking among the lumps of musty flock inside his mattress.

Bright sunshine and the sound of bird-song woke him in the early morning. His bladder was full again, but in spite of his anxieties of the night before, he had managed to sleep through without wetting his bed. In daylight there was nothing sinister or particularly scary about his room. The piles of old furniture and bits of carpet, the stacks of newspapers and magazines, even the battered chest whose drawers were all jammed shut with wads of trapped paper were innocent enough when there was light to see them for what they really were. He knew there were mice. They came sometimes in the night to rummage about and scare him with their scratchings, and they left little piles of torn-up paper and droppings that hardened into dull black beads. The funny smell of their bodies never went away, but he did not really mind them being there. It was the rats he feared, the big, black, poisonous rats that lived in the tunnels of Mucky Beck and were so cunning that Smallfry believed they might one day find a way up to the house through the main outlet pipe and the well in the cellar where the pigs were killed. He sometimes dreamed they were swarming up the stairs and along the corridor to his room in a glistening black wave, drawn by the one scent rats found totally irresistible, that of a human child.

Frankie dressed himself, restored the bottom corner of the blackout curtain to its original position, picked up his school shoes and stepped outside his room. The rest of the house was still in darkness, with only the faintest glimmer of light touching the glazed panel in the bathroom door, shining from the inside to give the opaque glass a pale, ghostly glow. His bare feet made no sound on the narrow strip of carpet that had worn so thread-bare in places that it looked as if someone had stuck it down in fragments, like the pieces of a jig-saw puzzle that was no longer complete. With a shoe clutched in each hand he tiptoed along the corridor to his special watching-point just beyond the attic door. Here the heavy wooden banister, supported by ranks of slender, carved pillars, ended its long journey from the main hall. The wood was reddish brown in colour and as smooth as satin, with joints here and there that could be seen only when the light was good and could never be detected by touch alone. He had often trailed his hand from the snail's-shell twist at the very bottom of the main staircase to the graceful curve on the landing outside the bathroom door, then up the steeper flight of seven wooden steps and along the corridor to the final bend where the banister vanished into the wall. Here he could squat in the shallow recess created by the banister and the high stone step that jutted out beyond the bottom edge of the attic stairs. On his right the wall was always cold to the touch because of the draught from the attic door. On his left the Bogeyman's door was only the width of the corridor away. It was a scary place to wait, but from there he could see right down into the lower corridor, to the best room, the cellars, the kitchens, and the long row of coat-hooks where all those unwanted garments clung like dark vampire bats to the wall. He could also see the whole of the main staircase, the landing and the bathroom door. It was by far the best look-and-listen-place in the whole house, and safe enough so long as he never, for so much as a tiny split-second of time, allowed himself to forget the proximity of the Bogeyman's door.

After many long minutes spent squatting with his head thrust between two banister-rails, he concluded that it was safe for him to go downstairs. He stepped very close to the banisters where the floorboards and stair-treads were at their most firm, because nobody knew better than him just how penetrating the sound of a creaking board could be when the rest of the house was quiet and still. At the bottom of the main stairs he felt the chill from the hall tiles and the familiar draught blowing under the front door. The last stair curved to the right into the pitch blackness of the lower corridor. He took a deep breath and held it until the blood pounded in his ears. He wanted to hug the panelled wall below the staircase to avoid passing too close to the humps of old coats on his left, but that would only bring him into contact with that other horror, the cellar door. Instead, he stretched his arms out in front of him, closed his eyes and hurried in a straight line down the very centre of the corridor, ignoring anything that touched him in the darkness. Moments later he was inside the big, warm room where a welcoming light flooded through the uncurtained window from the lamp outside the back yard gate. He let the air from his lungs in a long sigh of relief.

'Easy, Nader. Don't start your barking, old girl. Easy, now. Keep quiet, there's a good girl. Good dog. *Good* dog.'

He spoke softly to the tall, toffee-coloured Great Dane, fearful that at any moment she would leap to her feet, barking and snarling and straining at her chain the way Rosie had done whenever he entered the room. Nader was tied up next to the stove, in the deep alcove Rosie had once occupied. She growled softly, showing the whites of her eyes as she strained to watch Frankie without bothering to lift her chin from where it rested comfortably on her front paws.

'There's a good dog,' he told her, smiling nervously and trying his best to conceal his fear. 'There's a good, nice, clever dog.'

Unlike her predecessor, Nader was not in the habit of lulling him into a sense of false security before exploding in a savage frenzy just when he least expected it. Even so, he gave her a very wide berth as he crossed the kitchen. Buddie liked his dogs to earn their keep. They were not pets to be played with or trusted like other dogs, and when they were set to guard the house at night, he did not defeat his own intentions by chaining them up beyond reach of any would-be intruder. Nader's chain looked adequate enough for its purpose, but Frankie knew from past experience that it was fastened to the wall with only a few twists of light-weight string.

Someone had left a dinner plate under an up-turned basin in the centre of the kitchen table. On the plate were two thick wedges of bread, a lump of smooth white lard wrapped up in grease-proof paper and a portion of cheese that had started to go dry and hard around the edges. Some salt, a butter knife and a penny had been placed beside the plate, and nearby stood his own chipped cup with a measure of cocoa powder and sugar already inside. Someone had gone to a lot of trouble to prepare his breakfast, and the unexpected kindness of it filled him with guilt. Last night he had upset his mam by saying the wrong thing, then betrayed his father by speaking words that were meant and yet not meant, both at the same time. Once again he had fallen short of their expectations and let his parents down, yet here was a good breakfast and a penny piece to spend, all neatly laid out for him on the kitchen table as if he had done something to deserve a special treat. It made him feel deeply ashamed of his own short-comings.

He unwrapped the lard and spread it carefully across the bread in layers thick enough to satisfy his appetite and leave the marks of his teeth behind with every bite. When he lit the gas under the kettle to heat water for his cocoa, he removed four matches from the half-empty box, rolled them in a scrap of newspaper and stuffed them inside his sock. He was always on the look-out for matches and spare bits of candle for his Oxo tin. It was a terrible thing to be caught in the dark and to know there was nothing, not even the flame from a single match, to help him through the night.

Although Frankie did not want to share his breakfast with the dog, he broke off little bits of crust from time to time and tossed them into the corner, where they were snapped up greedily. He desperately wanted to stay on the right side of Nader. She was a big, muscular animal with sharp teeth and an uncertain temper and, just like Rosie before her, she would learn to make his life a misery unless he gave her some reason to like him. With this in mind, he poured milk into a saucer, laced it with warm, sweet cocoa and placed it gingerly on the stone floor as a peace offering.

'Friends,' he told her firmly. 'You and me's *friends* now, Nader, so no biting and no snarling and no pinning me against the walls like Rosie used to do. All right?'

Nader tilted her head on one side and puckered the flesh above her eyes as if to mimic a real human frown. He wanted to reach out his hand and pat her head or tickle her ears to reinforce the pact, but however much he tried to summon up the courage, he just could not bring himself to place that much trust in one of Buddie's animals.

The clock on the shelf above the dresser said twenty minutes past seven when Frankie climbed up on a chair to unfasten the top bolt on the back door. He sat down on the low threshold to pull on his shoes, wrestling with the broken laces and trying to get a hole in the heel of one of his socks to lie flat under his foot so it would not show. It was too early in the morning for any of his school friends to be around, so he would have to go up to Thorpe Street and sit on Valance Fraser's doorstep until it was time to set off for school. He glanced up at the enormous window on his left, with its concertina shutters and its rich velvet curtains that could not be seen from the outside. His parents would still be asleep in the big bed in the alcove, with fluffy pillows under their heads and a fringed cover thrown over them that had a brightly coloured Indian pattern sewn here and there with gold and silver thread.

'I love you both the same,' he suddenly protested in a whisper. 'Honest to God, cross my heart and hope to die, I love you both the same.'

The impassioned words seemed to burst from his mouth of their own accord. He hoped that God was awake and listening, so that He and all His Angels would know the honest truth, because now Frankie was dreading the day when Buddie, too, might take him aside and ask that terrible question:

'Which one of us do you love the best, Frankie?'

EIGHT

On Friday morning, just as the bell was being rung to signal the end of playtime, Frankie presented himself at the door of the staff room to hand in his final sheet of lines. Mr Pocklington scanned the page of foolscap paper with a minimum of interest, grunted twice and let it fall into the wastepaper basket standing beside his chair.

'Let this be a lesson to you, boy,' he said, speaking around the stem of his pipe.

'Yes, sir.'

'I will not tolerate careless work.'

'No, sir.'

Frankie stood with his hands behind his back, pressing his knees together in the hope that by doing so he would prevent his socks from falling down. He had spat on his fingers and rubbed the toes of his shoes so that the scuffs from climbing up trees and mill walls would be less noticeable. The same amount of spit had slicked the front of his hair and that awkward bit at the crown that grew in untidy tufts and stuck itself out in all directions while he slept. He stared at the sheet of foolscap paper with its double side of laboriously executed lines. He had the distinct impression that Sir had forgotten why he had given him all those lines to do in the first place.

'And don't let me see you here again, boy.'

'No, sir. Can I go now, sir?'

'Yes, off you go.'

Frankie left the room and closed the door quietly behind him. He lifted his shoulders and let them fall again with a deep, exasperated sigh. There were ink stains on his fingers and little grooves in the flesh where he had gripped the narrow wooden shaft of the pen too tightly. It did not seem right, somehow, that he should miss all those playtimes and worry about neat writing and ink smudges and careful spelling, just so Sir could grunt at his work and throw it straight into the wastepaper basket as if it were of no importance to anyone. It seemed to him that going to school and writing lines was no different from anything else in the world. The *Bigs* made the noise and the *Littles* did the work. He promised himself that he would double his efforts in future so as not to be thin and weedy forever. Big people always ruled over little people. It was what Buddie called a *fact of life*, and Frankie had always feared that Bigs and Littles were *also* a fact of life, like Great Danes and Jack Russells, and they could not be altered no matter how hard a person prayed or did his body-stretching exercises.

His fears seemed to be justified that very day, not ten minutes before the bell for afternoon lessons, when he found himself shunted into the farthest corner of the boys' playground by the self-styled 'Cock of all Listerhills' and his gang. He had managed to avoid Wally Watmough on the long march back to St Andrew's from Grange Road dinners, but once inside the school grounds he became fair game for a big kid with lots of mates and a week-long grudge. No longer protected by the lengthy periods of detention during which he focused his attention solely on the task of producing one hundred and twenty neatly-written lines, Frankie was at last brought face to face with the consequences of his own folly.

'You nipped me, Gyppo.'

'I didn't mean to,' Frankie protested. 'It was an accident.'

'Oh yeah?'

Wally Watmough was tall and fat, with big hands and a body that lumbered around on such massive thighs and calves that his feet seemed almost dainty by comparison.

He was two months older than Frankie, which meant that he was already past his tenth birthday. He was also the undisputed cock of the school, even bigger and tougher than any of the boys in the top class who would be moving up to Princeville after the big holidays. It was much better to be Wally's friend than his enemy, but Frankie had too many faults to qualify, and Wally Watmough would lose face if ever he allowed any skinny kids to join his gang.

'You nipped my arse, Gyppo.'

'I'm *not* a Gyppo, and I didn't mean to nip you. I thought I was nipping Freddie Binns.'

'Yeah, pull the other one,' Wally scoffed.

'I did. Honest.'

'He's yellow,' a voice announced from the small knot of onlookers.

'Yeah, he's a rotten little yella-belly,' scoffed another.

'Bash him, Wally. Bust his nose,' demanded another.

'No, that's not fair,' someone else shouted. 'It's a punch for a punch and a nip for a nip. Give him a nip, Wally. You're good at nipping.'

Everyone laughed and the group moved in a little closer. Frankie's heart sank. Wally Watmough could pinch a lump of flesh until it burned like Hell's fire and turned every colour of the rainbow.

'You nipped my arse, Gyppo.'

Fat fingers suddenly closed around the meagre flesh of Frankie's upper arm and squeezed with all the ferocity of a crab's pincers. Not since Trigger had bitten his thigh or Rosie had tried to eat his hand had he felt such agony. He yelped and danced from one foot to the other, twisting his body into the pain in the vain hope of lessening the damage. Wally Watmough held on, his eyes beady-bright and his features screwed into a gleeful grimace. He bit his bottom lip and narrowed his eyes as, with no more than two fingers and a thumb maintaining the grip-and-twist hold, he forced the smaller boy to his knees.

100

'Say you're sorry,' he growled.

'I'm sorry. I'm sorry.'

'And you won't do it again.'

'I won't do it again. Honest, I won't do it again.'

'And you're really, *really* sorry?'

'Yes, yes. I'm really sorry.'

The bell sounded for afternoon lessons.

'You watch it, Gyppo. Just watch it, that's all.'

Wally Watmough waddled off to be first in the queue outside the boys' entrance, leaving Frankie to pick himself up off the floor, hugging his injured arm and trying his very best not to burst into tears. The razor-like pain was quickly replaced by that awful burning sensation that hurt all the way down to his finger-ends. With his free hand he dashed tears of pain and humiliation from his eyes. At that moment he would gladly have given everything he possessed to get his own back on that sniggering, wet-lipped bully who was as bloated as a porky pig because his dad let him eat anything he wanted from the bakery and his mam gave him sweets and puddings every single day. Wally Watmough was big enough to torment any other kid in the school and mean-minded enough to make a career out of doing just that. If there was any justice at all in the world, he would move up to Princeville Secondary School next year and be just a rolly-polly new kid for all the older lads to pick on.

'Bloody bugger,' Frankie muttered, limping across the school playground with his arm on fire and his face contorted in agony. 'Bloody fat bugger.'

He ran all the way home after school in the hope of catching Buddie before he set out on his swill-collecting rounds. He ran and ran until he had a stitch in his side that caused the breath to catch in his throat and a stabbing pain to shoot right down into his groin, but he was too late. Nader was rummaging in the dustbins near the tall iron gate down the side of Brooke Parker's and the big

101

American Jeep, nick-named 'The Duke', was nowhere in sight. Frankie was disappointed. He always enjoyed those times when Buddie invited him along for the ride. The smell of the swill-bins sometimes made his stomach retch, but there were plenty of stops on the way and Buddie always drove with the windows wide open, even when it was cold and raining, so the feelings of travel sickness came and went and were never severe enough to cause any real problems. Frankie liked to fold up the old blanket from the tool box and pack it on the passenger seat as a cushion to make him sit up taller. He would ride with one elbow stuck out of the window and his cowboy hat pulled low over his eyes and pretend that he and Buddie were both grown-ups and living in America and the very, very best of friends forever.

Nader lifted her head and wagged her tail in greeting as he entered the gate. Then she stepped back, looking sheepish and nervous. Lying between her front paws were the chewed remains of his drumsticks. She had found them hidden among the rubbish around the bins. She must have spent the better part of the day reducing each one to a wet and ragged stump.

'Oh, you bugger,' he said, seeing his best swap ruined. 'You bugger.'

Nader's tail slid between her legs. She hung her head and whined. That kick to the ribs had made her nervous. Enjoying the sense of power this gave him, Frankie stamped his foot and yelled:

'*Gercha!*'

The animal leaped away from him with her tail hooked between her legs and the whites of her eyes showing. She was afraid of him. She stood as high as his chest and weighed a lot more than he did, and yet she, the guardian of Old Ashfield, was scared of *him*. That would make her a useless animal as far as Buddie was concerned, and for that reason Frankie felt sorry for her.

102

'Easy, Nader,' he offered in a more friendly tone. 'Take it easy. I'm not going to hurt you. You and me's friends, remember?'

She cocked her head on one side and moved her tail as if reassured by the sound of his voice, but she kept her distance. Frankie picked up a stick and offered it at arm's length, then tossed it into the weed patch beyond the dustbins. Nader made as if to race after it, hesitated, wagged her tail a few times, then backed away and growled softly, eyeing him with obvious suspicion. She did not trust him. She wanted to play just like any other dog, but she did not trust him. He shrugged his shoulders and walked along the littered drive, past the tethered goats and the first of the turkey houses and on towards the back-yard gate. He was on his guard, even though he made a point of pretending not to notice that the big Great Dane was padding along some distance behind him. He had learned the hard way that it was dangerous to turn his back on one of Buddie's dogs, no matter how docile and nervous it pretended to be.

The back door was locked from the inside. He peered through the kitchen window and saw that the front of the stove was wide open and the kettle was simmering over a low light on the gas-oven in the corner. Smallfry would never go out and leave things like that, and if she had gone out somewhere with Buddie, he would have made doubly sure that nothing could catch fire while they were away. Safety in the house was very, very important. That was why Frankie hid his matches and candles so well. If he was ever caught lighting fires in his room, his father would take a belt to him and his mam would make him wish he had never been born.

'Hey, Frankie, lost your mam, have you?'

'What's the matter, Frankie? Got yourself locked out?'

The Brooke Parker men were up there again on the high wall. They guffawed and shoved each other around in playful scuffles. Frankie set his features, determined not to

103

respond in any way to their taunts. He marched up the yard and through the gate, turned sharp left as the gate closed on its sprung hinges behind him, and strode purposefully toward the less exposed area at the side of the house. Nader unfolded her elongated legs from a tumble of old potato sacks and slunk after him with her head lowered and her tail still hanging between her legs.

'Where is she then?' one of the men called out to him. 'Where's your mam, Frankie?'

The boy quickened his pace. He would not give them the satisfaction of seeing him break into a run, no matter how much he hated their teasing. All he could do was lengthen his stride until the heels of his shoes struck the ground ahead of him with twice their natural force.

'Hey, what's up with you, kid? Got the sulks, have you, just 'cause your old lady's locked the door on you?'

Frankie rounded the corner to the sound of fresh laughter, collided with someone standing in the shadows of the empty house and came to an abrupt halt with a small cry of alarm.

'*Buddie!*'

A huge brown hand grabbed him by the collar, its fingers trapping a cluster of small hairs in the nape of his neck so that he winced in unexpected pain.

'What was that all about?' Buddie demanded, jerking his head in the direction of Brooke Parker's wall and somehow managing to pull his scowl right down over the flattened bridge of his nose.

Frankie hunched his shoulders, grinning despite the sudden spasm of twitching that attacked his muscles. Frankie grinned a lot. Sometimes he smiled even when he did not want to, when he was scared, or in big trouble, or really sorry about something. He could not help it. The stupid smile and the twitching were something that just happened, like biting his nails or wetting his bed in the night.

'Well?' Buddie hissed. 'Answer me, boy. What was all that about?'

'Nothing, Buddie. Just some Brooke Parker men shouting and laughing.'

'Friends of yours?'

'No, not mine, honest.'

'So what're they doing up there?'

'Just looking . . . I don't know . . . It wasn't my fault . . . honest . . . I didn't ask them to come.'

Buddie grunted and measured with his dark-lashed eyes the distance between the top of the wall and the turkey-pens. His fingers were still gripping the fine hairs at the nape of Frankie's neck.

'What were they saying about your mam?'

'Just asking,' Frankie said, wincing.

'They been up there before?'

'Yes, sometimes . . . '

'Asking for your mam?'

Frankie stiffened, his sense of danger alerted. He would have to be very careful what he said. He could not allow those leering Brooke Parker men to get Smallfry into trouble, just because she was lovely and smiled a lot.

'Sometimes they do,' he admitted. 'They like to whistle at her and make kissing noises when she passes, but it isn't *her* fault, Buddie. She never answers them. Honest, Buddie, she never pays them *any* attention at *all*. She never even *looks* at them.'

Buddie nodded, his mouth pinched into a tight line.

'What were they saying about her?'

'Nothing. Just asking. Just asking where she is.'

'Nothing else?'

'No, Buddie, except . . . '

He had not intended that word to slip out. Now it hung in the air like a shout and Buddie's grip tightened on his collar until the buttons on the front of his shirt dug into his windpipe.

'Except what?'

Frankie wished he could bite off the end of his tongue.

' . . . except I saw them . . . ' he blurted, ' . . . one time . . . throwing their tab-ends down into the turkey-pens.'

'What?'

'I did, honest. It made the birds jump about and get all scared and noisy.'

'By bloody hell! So *that's* what happened! It was *them*. Those bastards panicked my birds and cost me a bloody tenner in lost profits.'

Buddie fell silent, lost in his own thoughts while Frankie dangled helplessly by the scruff of his neck from a big brown fist. It was a long time before the grip began to ease and he could lower his heels to the floor and breathe more easily and turn his head without pain.

'Where's your mam?' Buddie asked, after a long silence.

'I don't know. I just got back from school.'

'Well, she didn't go out, that's for sure, because the back door's bolted from the inside and the front door's fastened on the safety chain.'

'I can get in,' Frankie said, eager to please his father and deflect his attention from the men still gathered up there on the wall, out of sight but clearly audible from that side of the house. 'I can do it, Buddie, I can easily squeeze through, even when the chain's on, so I can go in first and open up the back door for you.'

Buddie nodded grimly.

'And after tea I want you to gather up all the empty bottles from the bottom of the hill and stack them over there, in the corner by the terrace gate. Milk bottles, beer bottles, wine bottles . . . bring the lot. Makes no difference if they're broken, just bring 'em all, as many as you can find.'

'Right, Buddie.'

'And watch you don't cut yourself.'

'Right, Buddie.'

106

'And don't say anything to your mam. This is something for you and me to sort out by ourselves.'

Sudden pride made Frankie stand up with his back so straight and his head so high that he felt he had grown a whole inch in just ten short seconds.

'Right, Buddie,' he beamed.

'Now git. Let me in by the back door. Git!'

'Right, Buddie.'

Frankie raced down the side of the house and round the corner to the steps and the narrow iron gate that led to the front terrace. He was laughing as he ran along the crazy paving, avoiding the holes and the bigger tufts of weeds and counting out the forty-seven strides from the gate to the front door. He squatted down, threaded one leg and one arm through the gap below the safety chain, turned his head to one side and squeezed his body through into the hall. Once there he closed the door to release the safety chain, then pulled it open as far as it would go, flooding the hall and stairs beyond with light. Moments later he was standing quite still at the foot of the stairs, staring up, wide-eyed, at the figure just emerging from the bathroom.

To his left the door of the best room stood open. He could see the edge of the bed, with its clean white sheets and colourful cover, and Smallfry's pale, bare feet groping for the pretty slippers lying discarded on the rug. She leaned forward, stretching her arms out on either side of her body and letting her long hair fall over her face like a veil.

Tom Fish finished buttoning up his flies as he crossed the landing and started down the stairs. He grinned that charming, easy, lop-sided grin that only Frankie seemed to find in any way sinister or unpleasant. He was wearing a white shirt with its top buttons undone, and a wide-bottomed, fancy tie that hung from each side of his collar without the benefit of a knot. In the light from the bathroom his hair looked almost blond as he raked it into place by using his fingers as a comb. He was a big man who walked with a lazy swagger and always managed to give the impression that he was laughing at everyone else behind their backs.

'Frankie? *Frankie!* What the hell are you pissing about at in there? Open this bloody door, will you?'

Buddie's voice bellowed from the back yard as he banged his fist on the door. Frankie hesitated. In the best room, Smallfry was pulling on her dressing-gown and tossing her hair back from her face, as lovely as a princess rousing herself from a long sleep. Still grinning, Tom Fish walked down the wide staircase, hooked his jacket from the curve at the bottom of the banister, then strolled across the hall and out into the bright afternoon sunshine.

'Frankie! Frankie! Open this bloody door, for Christ's sake!'

It was Smallfry who opened the back door. She unfastened the bolts and stood back, gripping Frankie by the shoulders and pulling him backwards against her soft, warm body. He could not be sure if she was hiding herself behind him or trying to shield him from his father's temper. The scowling Buddie seemed to fill the entire doorway, not with his physical size but with the terrible force of his anger.

'What the hell's going on here?' he roared. 'Why was this door locked?'

Smallfry touched her forehead with the back of one hand and held on to Frankie with the other as if she might swoon and fall down without his support.

'Please lower your voice, Buddie,' she said softly. 'Can't you see I'm unwell? Have you no consideration?'

'What's that? What's wrong with you? Why are you undressed at four o'clock in the afternoon?'

'I was feeling ill, dear. I developed the most appalling headache and simply *had* to lie down for a while. I must have fallen right off to sleep because of the pills I took for the pain. I was absolutely dead to the world until Frankie shook me awake just now. Isn't that so, Frankie?'

'Y-Yes, Smallfry.'

He could feel her long fingernails pressing against his shoulder and smell the strong tobacco scent of Buddie's breath. Held fast between the two, he felt the way a cornered pig must feel on slaughtering day.

'And why on earth is everyone home so early?' She glanced sleepily at the kitchen clock, then brought one hand to her throat as her eyes widened in surprise. 'Oh, my goodness, is that *really* the time? I must have slept for at least *two hours*. Oh, Buddie, thank heaven I remembered to lock all the doors. Why, I might have been murdered in my bed . . . '

Frankie heard the loud click as the yard gate opened and swung closed again on its sprung hinges. Tom Fish had walked all the way round the house to amble down the back yard with his jacket flung casually over one shoulder and that same easy smile on his face.

'Hello there,' he drawled in his soft Irish brogue. 'Just got myself a lift from Clayton and wondered if you might be needing a hand to shift that old pig-swill boiler.'

Buddie nodded and began to prise off his boots.

'I'll need a hand, right enough,' he confirmed. 'It'll be a job and a half, shifting that lot.'

He seemed suddenly short, standing beside the Irishman in just his socks, a man of five feet two inches looking up at a broad-shouldered giant of over six feet. But Frankie knew that in every other way that mattered, his dad was much, much bigger than Tom Fish. He would *always* be bigger than Tom Fish.

Smallfry gathered her hair into a neat bunch and pulled it over one shoulder. She was smiling and her cheeks were flushed. She reached up to get cups and saucers and the dark blue teapot from the top shelf, and when she lowered her arms the neck of her robe gaped open to reveal the froth of peach-coloured lace decorating the front of her nightdress.

Frankie swallowed hard and wondered why there was a hollow feeling behind his ribs that made him want to cry. Without asking permission to leave the room, he slipped away quietly and seated himself outside on the front steps. He needed to be alone to think about all the ways in which he could kill the hated Tom Fish stone cold dead.

NINE

He ate his tea outside on the step. He was called in to eat at the table with the others, but after a short while he noticed that they were talking over his head in half-sentences and mouthing certain words so he would not understand what they were talking about. They were all having stew, except for Smallfry, who didn't like to eat in company. The vegetables and dumplings had thickened up and sunk to the bottom of the pan in a solid mass that left a rich and greasy gravy floating on the top. Frankie got the gravy. It was hot and tasty and there was plenty of it served up for him in a pudding basin with a wide blue stripe around the outside. He was not ungrateful or greedy. He just wished he had been given a big chunk of neck of mutton, like the ones on Buddie's plate, and he was stung with jealousy when he saw how many dumplings and potatoes and lumps of meat were ladled on to a dinner plate for Tom Fish.

Buddie cut up a whole loaf, measuring it off so that each piece was a fist-sized cube of fresh white bread with a golden brown crust that crunched when it was bitten into. He cut it with the big knife he always carried, the one he used for gutting animals or digging out nails from planks of wood, for slashing open pig-feed sacks or spearing decent apples from the swill-bins. He was proud of his big knife. He said it was the perfect tool for every job around the place, and when he used it at the dinner table he first polished the blade clean by rubbing it up and down the leg of his pants. The loaf was a large crusty white from Mrs Midgley's, delivered that very day in the dark blue van marked: Watmough &

Son, Bakers. How Frankie envied Fatty Wally Watmough. It made his mouth water just to imagine how good it would be to live every single day of his life among loaves of freshly baked bread and scones and bannocks, golden-crusted fruit tarts, sugary cream cakes, chocolate eclairs and spicy, juicy apple turnovers.

'Little pigs have big ears.'

Frankie dunked his bread in his gravy and pretended not to notice the remark. He knew what they were all talking about so secretly, anyway. A load of corned beef had gone missing from a meat storage depot in Dewsbury Bottom two nights ago, and a chap called Norman Slater from Thorpe Edge was getting pretty jumpy because the police had already been round to his place asking questions and if they came back again with a search warrant he would really be up Shit Street. Frankie liked corned beef, especially when it was sliced up and dipped in batter and fried in the pan with onion rings. If Buddie decided to help get rid of the load before the police went sniffing around there again, there would probably be a few tins going buckshee for his trouble. Buckshee was just one of the many foreign words Buddie had picked up in the Army. It meant that something was free and for nothing, or found on a tip, or fell off the back of a lorry, or simply didn't belong to anyone. Old Mr Ramlaj Dilip Shah, who lived in Morley Street and had once sailed all the way from Bombay harbour on a cargo ship, said it was a real Indian word and ought to be pronounced *baksheesh*, only Frankie didn't dare tell Buddie he was saying it all wrong. He could not really see that it mattered to anyone except Mr Ramlaj Dilip Shah how one little word was said, so long as the buckshee corned beef was good enough to make a tasty hash or a decent pile of fritters.

'Little pigs have big ears,' Tom Fish said again.

Smallfry agreed with him.

'Tom is absolutely right, my dear,' she said, lifting her cup to her lips so delicately that her little finger stuck itself

112

straight up in the air, just the way a lady's finger should. 'Certain matters of business should not be discussed in the presence of the boy.'

Buddie tipped his chair forward and leaned over the table to scowl into Frankie's pudding basin. His scowl deepened. He stirred the soup around with the blade of his knife while Frankie sucked the gravy from his bread with an audible slurp.

'Here, kid, let me stick a few guts in there. You're a growing boy. You need guts, real meat and spuds and a dumpling or two to fill you out a bit, and maybe a scraping of the burnt bits off the bottom of the pan to make your hair curl.'

Frankie grinned and happily surrendered his basin. He could not always tell if Buddie was teasing or serious when he talked about his hair being as straight and coarse as a Chinaman's instead of growing in tight, shiny, corkscrew curls the way his own did. Frankie did his best to encourage it to curl. He ate all the sooty burned bits from his toast instead of scraping them away as most folk did, and all the crusts on his bread, no matter how hard and stale they had become. He did his best and it wasn't really his fault that his hair refused to curl the way it was meant to. He just hoped his father would pay no attention when certain people told him that the only solution was to shave it all off, smooth as an egg, and start again from nothing. He did not want that. He would rather eat blackened toast for the rest of his life than be forced to go to school with his head shaved.

He watched Buddie carry the blue and white basin to the stove and ladle in a great pile of thickening from the bottom of the stew pan. It forced the level of gravy right up the sides of the bowl until it covered Buddie's thumb all the way to the first knuckle and very nearly spilled over the sides. Smallfry made little tut-tutting noises of disapproval and moved her dressing gown so it wouldn't get stained by gravy spills.

113

Instead of returning the basin to the table, Buddie reached over to grab a fistful of bread from the bread-board, then jerked his head for Frankie to follow and moved off towards the door, walking with extra care. As he drew level with the stove, Nader raised herself from the corner, cautiously eyeing the basin with her ears pricked up and her jaws glistening with saliva. A soft whine caught in her throat when she realized the deliciously scented food was not for her, but instead of making her usual fuss she simply hung her head and, whining quietly, recurled herself on the sacking in the alcove.

'Get the door, will you?'

Frankie slid from his seat after first looking to Smallfry for permission. She merely closed her eyes, pursed her full lips and arched her brows the way Bette Davis always did to convey a meaningful message without words or actions. It reminded him that his friendship with Buddie must never be allowed to upset his mam and drive her away from home. Now he ducked under Buddie's out-stretched arm, pulled back the curtain and opened the inner door leading to the hall. He closed it again as soon as Buddie had passed through, but not before he had taken a last envious glance at the couple still seated at the kitchen table. Smallfry was laughing in that special way she had that made her face light up and her eyes sparkle. Tom Fish was leaning close to her, and the grease on his lips from the dumpling stew seemed to turn his lop-sided smile into a leer.

Outside the front door, Buddie waited until Frankie was seated in his usual corner below the safety chain housing, then set the basin down on the step and dropped the bread into the boy's lap.

'And don't forget there's a job needs doing, straight after tea,' he said, winking one eye and touching the side of his nose with his forefinger as a reminder that the job was a secret to be kept strictly between the two of them.

'I won't forget, Buddie.'

'Take anything you need from outside the main pigsty, and watch out for that glass.'

'Right, Buddie.' He saluted smartly with his spoon, but Buddie had already turned away and the big front door was swinging closed behind him.

So it was that Frankie finished his evening meal whilst sitting outside on the front doorstep with the terraced gardens dropping away into a jungle of wild greenery and the trees wafting their leafy branches high above him. He saved his piece of mutton until last, then picked it up in both hands and sucked every last bit of meat and fat and marrow from the bone. Only then did he wipe the basin clean with the last of his bread and lean back against the wall with a sigh of contentment, his stomach bloated and a meaty, fatty after-taste lingering on his tongue.

The others had not yet started on their tea and wafer biscuits when Frankie roused himself and went in search of the tools he would need for the job he was to do for Buddie. He found a coil of light-weight rope, frayed in places but strong enough to support his weight, on the scrap-pile round the back of the main pigsties. Nearby was a large enamel bucket, discarded when a cracked and rusting base made it unsuitable for boiling large quantities of water on the gas-ring. Frankie hung the coil of rope around his body and found a small piece of cloth to protect his hands from the sharp handle of the bucket where the wooden bit for holding and lifting had been burned away on the stove. Then he hunted around until he found part of an old garden rake before marching off with his selection of tools, back along the crazy paving of the front terrace, through the narrow iron gate at the far end, down the steps and on towards the hillside above the beck. The coil of rope was heavy. It chafed the tender skin at the back of his neck and bumped awkwardly against his shins with every stride, but he was able to ignore the discomfort. He was being trusted to do a very important job for his father, and for that he would

115

happily tolerate the chafing of a dozen ropes across his shin-bones. With the rusty rake slung over his shoulder and the battered bucket swinging at his side, he took great big strides and whistled as he walked, striding out like a real-life Huckleberry Finn with a brand new adventure in the making.

During the days following a party, Buddie always took the beer and wine bottles back to the pub and claimed a refund from the man who collected them all up for the brewery to wash and re-use. Any broken bottles, and all those that were not sporting the familiar brewery label, were disposed of down the hillside. Frankie usually helped gather them all up and sort out the brewery bottles from those that were to be thrown into the big wheelbarrow. Then he would stand with Buddie at the top of the hill and watch them cascade down the steep slope to join all the other rubbish at the bottom. It was his job to scramble down with the long-bristled yard-brush to dislodge anything that got stuck amongst the tree roots or in the mud if the weather had been bad. It had taken a great many parties and band practices, and hundreds of breakages and missing brewery labels to amass the great mound of glass that leaned like a dark, surrealistic hedgerow against the lower boundary wall.

Frankie set down his special implements and stood for a long moment with his hands on his hips, surveying the thick knot of woodland that was part of his home. On the far side of the beck rose the sheer backs of woollen mills and blind foundry walls, and beyond them the black slate roofs of back-to-back houses stretching all the way up to Listerhills Road. There was little to see while the trees were in leaf, but if he bobbed down in a crouch and squinted between the branches, he could just make out the spire of St Andrew's Church and a small corner of the nearby school. Standing there was like standing at the top of the world, and it was all a part of his back yard, his own personal back yard.

116

'You're a damn lucky kid to have so much,' Buddie was constantly reminding him. 'Damn lucky. You can bet your sweet life *I* never had anything like this when I was your age.'

With a grin Frankie unfastened the length of string that held his Tarzan swing against the trunk of the oak, the biggest of all the trees. He grabbed the thick, heavily knotted rope in both hands and positioned his feet with careful precision on the top edge of the hill where the nettles grew sideways in search of sunlight. He knew just the right launching spot and the exact angle at which to jump in order to make the highest, widest swing and return without mishap to where he started from. The slightest miscalculation and he might smash into one of the trees and kill himself stone dead, or end up tangled and badly injured amongst the uppermost branches. He might even find himself swinging short and unable to get back to firm ground, left to hang helplessly in mid-air until his grip weakened and he plummeted to his death at the foot of the hill. Buddie had taught him exactly how to do it. Buddie was the best. Frankie knew he was good, but Buddie was undoubtedly the Champion. With a whoop and a holler, that tough little man could soar out into the space between the trees and hang there, some sixty feet above the walls and paving stones of Mucky Beck, for one breathless, timeless moment before turning in the air with the backward swing of the rope and sweeping back to home base.

Now it was Frankie's turn to soar. With barely more than a moment's hesitation he pulled the rope as far back as it would come and then leaped into the air. For an instant he released his grip in order to grab the rope at a higher point, then his fingers locked together and his feet found the knots and wedged tight and he was away. The earth seemed to open up and swallow the entire hillside, so swiftly did it drop away beneath him. The great bough on which the rope was hung creaked as the noose turned and twisted across

117

the bark. He reached the highest point with cold, sweaty fear shrinking the skin on his face and forcing the air from his lungs so that the emptiness left behind rang in his ears. For a sickening moment he hung in the sky, staring down at the rusting carcass of a car far below, at the twinkling mounds of broken glass, the wheelbarrow-loads of rubbish and the ancient stone wall that snaked along Dead Man's Alley like a meandering reptile. Then he was yanked into the reverse swing as his own momentum catapulted him towards the sloping hillside. It was a dangerous game to play, but Frankie was second only to the Champion, so he always made it back to within inches of the original launching spot. He landed nimbly on his feet, then tied the trailing string to the tree with as many loops and knots as its length would allow, because he knew that if the rope ever got free it would seek its own level and then hang, inaccessible and useless, over the steepest drop, and that would be the end of his Tarzan swing forever.

'*Wowee! Woweeeeeee!*'

He was breathless and his knees were trembling. Fear always made him believe he was dying, yet there were occasions when the very thing that filled him with terror also made him feel good. Sometimes he did things that frightened him half to death and yet made him feel bigger afterwards, and capable of doing something really brave. That's why he liked the Tarzan swing best of all, not just because it made him look good in Buddie's eyes, but because it made him feel scared and brave, sick and clever and excited, all at the same time.

Now it was time for him to begin work. He uncoiled the rope and secured one end to a stout root that stuck out of the ground like a bent elbow. The other end he tossed down the hillside along with the bucket and the rake. He scrambled after them, using the rope to check his speed. It fell short of the bottom by a long way, but he knew it would help him a lot on the uphill hauls when the bucket was full and

118

the ground slippery beneath his feet. Once at the bottom he used the rake to sort out the glass from all the other rubbish and pull the best pieces to the front so that he could get at them without risk of injury. These he piled into the bucket until it was full and ready to be carried back to level ground.

He made eleven trips altogether, and with each load of glass he managed to retrieve, the pile at the top of the hill grew larger and more impressive. It was no easy task. By the seventh trip his palms were sore and he was bringing the bucket up only half full because any more than that was too heavy for him. He felt as if his arms were slowly being prised from their sockets. He had to pull on the rope with one hand and haul the bucket after him with the other, and whichever way round he chose to do it, his shoulders ached and the bruise raised on his upper arm by Wally Watmough's fat fingers gave him hell. On the last trip he slipped and lost his grip on the bucket before he had climbed high enough to grab the rope for support. The bucket rolled over and over all the way back to the bottom of the hill, and when he slithered after it he skinned the big scab right off his left knee so that it bled even more than when he had first injured it on the metal spikes on the gates of Shearbridge Mills. Now his knee was in an awful mess and he was not sure what to do about it, because Buddie had told him to be sure and not cut himself on the glass, and if he saw all that blood he would think Frankie had not followed his orders properly. In the end he decided to plaster the wound with a handful of the good earth, just as Tonto had done when the Lone Ranger's old friend, Prospecting Pete McGinty, had been shot in the belly by bandits who were out to steal his mine and all his newly discovered silver nuggets. If the remedy was good enough for the old prospector, it was certainly good enough for Frankie, even if it did smart like blazes and make his leg throb.

'Heap big medicine, Kemo Sabe,' he said through his teeth. Then he screwed up his face and moaned out loud because it really did sting like blazes.

He did not see Buddie again until a few minutes after his mam had ordered him off to bed. It was still daylight, and he had been hoping to stay up late because there was no school in the morning, but Smallfry just sent him to bed without even looking at the clock to see if it was the right time for him to go. He was sure it was all the Irishman's fault. All Frankie did was knock at the kitchen door and wait for her to call him inside in case there were any jobs for him to do. It was Tom Fish who moaned out loud and muttered something about kids who listened at keyholes, and the next moment Smallfry was speaking in a sharp voice and telling Frankie to say goodnight to his father and then get the hell upstairs, out of her sight.

He was taking his tools back to the pigsty when he spotted Buddie mucking out at the top end of the pens. Cold water poured from a hose pipe attached to the tap inside the sty, and the heavy yard-brush made loud scraping noises as it brushed all the filth into great glistening piles of sludge. As usual, the big saddle-back boar, Pee-Wee, was sniffing about and grunting peevishly. He was looking for a chance to make mischief, even though he should have known that Buddie was too quick ever to let a pig, even a big one like himself, get the better of him. Each time the boar came too close, Buddie simply turned up the head of the broom and jabbed at the softest part of its snout with the bristles. The pigs went crazy when he did that because the yard brush had bristles as sharp and as stiff as wire prongs that must have hurt a lot on their tender snouts. Outsiders might think it was a cruel sort of treatment, but Frankie knew it was both sensible and necessary. A fully grown pig could weigh anything up to thirty stones and turn pretty nasty if it was pregnant, or feeding a new litter, or out of sorts, or just plain mean-minded

120

like Pee-Wee. A person could very easily get knocked over and trampled to death around pigs. It was best to be always on guard and extra careful when mucking out or feeding, and even more so on slaughtering days when the animals saw the rubber aprons and the big knife coming.

'Hi there! How ya doing, Frankie?'

Buddie called out to him in his best American drawl as Frankie tossed the bucket and rake back on to the pile of scrap beside the main pigsty. He tipped the brim of his Stetson, cowboy fashion, and beckoned the boy over.

'Come on up here, Frankie. I could use the company.'

The boy hurried up the side of the house, giving the gates of the pens a wide berth and being very careful where he placed his feet. When he drew level with the top pen he climbed up to hang his body over the wall, wrinkling his nose at the foul smell.

'Hi, Buddie.'

'Hiya, kid. Why don't you hang around here for a while, then help me finish that little job you started? I'll be needing a hand in a couple of hours' time, when I'm through with this lot.'

'Can't,' Frankie said, shaking his head. 'Smallfry says I have to go to bed.'

'What, right now?'

'Yeah, after I've put my things away and said goodnight to you.'

'Why? You been doing things to make her mad?'

'No, I don't think so.'

'Then why the hell is she sending you to bed at this time when there's work needs doing and no school in the morning?'

Frankie shrugged again and stuck out his lower lip.

'I don't know, Buddie. I just went in and she sent me to bed. I didn't do nothing wrong, *honest*.'

He watched his father set down the big brush and clasp his fingers over its handle, then rest his chin on his hands,

121

scowling. Pee-Wee edged closer, sniffing the air. He looked
as if he was wearing four dark boots right up to his thighs
where the mud had dried to a cake that was almost black
against his pink skin. Like all the pigs Frankie had ever
seen, the big boar appeared to be smiling when viewed in
profile, but he knew from past experience that Pee-Wee's
benign expression was just a trick. There was nothing
even remotely friendly about that particular animal. Only
a month ago he had pushed a way through the wire fencing,
sneaked up behind Frankie, stuck his snout right between
his legs and tipped him over into some stinging nettles. If
Pee-Wee could *really* smile, he would only do it to show how
good he felt after doing something mean and spiteful.

'Sent you off to bed, eh?'

Buddie was still standing with his chin resting on the
upright handle of the broom. He was looking into the
distance, right down to where the outhouses finished and
the weeds grew thickest as if trying to help the old wall
hold back the cinder-tip left behind by the mills. His eyes
were narrow black slits below his scowl and his jewellery
seemed to shine with an extra brightness to compensate
for the shapeless, filthy clothes he wore for the mucking
out. His thoughts were obviously on things other than
his son. Frankie waited and hoped for a reprieve, but
only if one could be had without making Smallfry want
to get her own back on him later, when his father was
not around.

'Well then,' Buddie said at last. 'I reckon it's only fair to
do like your mam says.'

'Yes, Buddie.' He was disappointed.

' . . . but I hear she's planning on going out later, so maybe
I'll come up and give you a shout around half eight or nine
o'clock, so we can have that little job finished before she
gets home. Well, what do you say, kid?'

'Oh, yes, Buddie, I'd like that,' Frankie beamed. 'Did you
see all the bottles I brought up? Did I get enough?'

122

'I sure as hell did see them, and I reckon there's plenty for what I need to do. You did a great job, Frankie. Reckon there might even be a shilling or two to be earned here, provided you keep up the good work and no slacking.'

'Oh, thanks Buddie. There's something really special I need to buy, and I have to get it soon. It's a red exercise book with all the times-tables printed on the back, and weights and measures tables and . . .'

'*Gercha!* Git the hell out of it, you mean old bastard!'

A jab from the big brush sent the boar scuttling away with a squeal and Buddie, muttering a string of obscenities under his breath, returned his attention to the job in hand.

'Be seeing ya, Buddie,' the boy offered, but his father was already hard at work again, hosing the pig-yard down and brushing the smelly mess into the channels at the bottom near the gate.

TEN

'Yes? Come in.'

Her voice sounded sharp and impatient. Frankie entered by the back door to find his mam still sitting in her favourite chair by the stove. It had grown very warm in the kitchen, even for her, so warm that she had opened her dressing gown at the neck to leave her throat and shoulders bare. Because her legs were crossed one over the other at the knee, the dressing gown had gaped open from the waist to reveal the sheer, almost transparent nightdress beneath. She was jogging one foot rapidly up and down the way she often did when she was in a bad mood. One of her pretty pink slippers was clinging by its fur to the tips of her toes, wiggling with every movement of her foot and ready to fall off at any moment.

'I've come to say goodnight,' he offered, self-consciously lifting each leg in turn so that he could pull up his socks. He became acutely aware of his dirty hands and untidy hair. The clothes he was wearing fitted his skinny frame so badly that a mere glance from her was enough to tell him he resembled a shabby rag-bag.

Tom Fish was lounging against the sink with his jacket off and his sleeves rolled up to show muscular forearms. There was a pale strip around his wrist where his watch had kept the sun from browning the skin. He was just leaning there against the edge of the sink with his long legs stuck out in front of him and his wide shoulders blocking some of the light from the window. He made Frankie feel very small.

124

Smallfry glanced in the boy's direction, then turned her head in such a way that he knew what to do without being told. He wiped the back of his hand over his mouth and walked over to kiss her cheek as he always did before going upstairs to bed. Her skin was as soft and as cool as silk, and she smelled so wonderful that he was tempted to fling his arms around her and bury himself in all her fragrant softness. He stood back quickly, startled by the strength of the urge. The clock on the wall told him it was only a few minutes past seven. He could not understand why he was being sent to bed so early when he had done nothing wrong that he was aware of.

'Goodnight, Smallfry,' he said, but it wasn't him she was looking at when she gave a little smile and lowered her eyes as if something had suddenly made her feel shy.

'*Oh, goodnight, Smallfry!*'

The Irishman's voice was filled with sarcasm as he mimicked Frankie's words in a girlish, high-pitched voice.

'Listen to that, now. Just hear the way this half-grown little whelp dares to call his mam *Smallfry*, of all names.'

'Don't be a tease, Tom,' Smallfry smiled very sweetly. 'You know he absolutely *refuses* to call me anything so commonplace as Mam or Mother. I suppose he's paying me a compliment, in his own childish way. He thinks I'm special, so he calls me by his special name. You mustn't tease him for it.'

Tom Fish snorted. The sound was full of ridicule.

'And a while ago it was Sweetheart, of all things, as if you were his girl-friend instead of his mam. And before that it was *Angel*. Now I ask you, what kind of a name is that for a kid to call his mam? And now it's *Smallfry*, as if short-arse himself was big enough to call *anyone Smallfry*. He's got no respect, that's his trouble. No bloody respect.'

125

'Now, Tom. Leave the boy alone.'

Her glance at Frankie was frosty above her bright smile. He could tell she was cross with him for upsetting Tom Fish. She never seemed to understand that it wasn't his fault, that he only had to walk into a room for Tom Fish to start picking on him and making fun of him, and if that made him mad it was surely his own doing, not Frankie's? Now Smallfry was cross and that would be another mark against him, and it wasn't fair, because all he had ever wanted to call her in his whole life was *Mam*. With his face burning all the way round to the back of his neck, he left the room and hurried upstairs to bed.

In a way he was glad to be going up so early, especially now that Buddie was planning to call him down at nine o'clock. It was still light. If he opened all the doors in the bathroom and then pulled his blackout curtain back as far as it would go, there would be enough light to illuminate the long first-floor corridor and much of his bedroom. If he was careful and very quiet, he should be able to tip-toe backwards and forwards as many times as it took for him to empty out his brimming chamber-pot without being caught in the act. He had found a tin that very morning in the ash bucket outside the back door. It was not very big, but it would do the job well enough until the pot was only half full and he could carry it along to the bathroom for emptying.

By climbing up on the chest of drawers and then on to the piles of newspapers and bits of wood that were stacked on the windowsill, he was able to pull one corner of the blanket right up and hook it over the thick metal rod that had been a rail for proper hanging curtains in the days before he was born. As he lifted and fixed the blanket, more light flooded into the room than he could ever recall seeing in there before. It showed up the brass-ended bed with its bare and lumpy mattress, the acres of chocolate brown paint, the frieze of faded toy soldiers still visible in those places where mould had not stripped them away. He could see the deep corners of the room where the shadows were always thickest, and the piles of broken furniture, bits of carpets and old junk that looked so scary in the night but were really nothing at all with the sun shining on them.

He prised off his school shoes and stood them by the door so he would remember to wipe them over with a wet cloth or some screwed-up newspaper to clean off all the mud from the hillside. Then he crouched over his chamber-pot and very carefully dipped the rim of his can into the liquid so that only a thin, slow trickle went inside and none of it spilled over on to the floor. With the door of his room standing wide open, the corridor outside was illuminated by a pale glow that seemed to struggle against the gloom. It was reinforced by the light coming from the bathroom, but their combined forces were not enough to push back the shadows clinging to the high ceilings, or to convince Frankie that the swaying humps in lofty corners were not blood-sucking bats but harmless, lifeless, cobwebs.

He hurried along the thread-bare carpet, down the seven steps and across the landing, up three more steps to the bathroom door and into the small cubicle on the far left where the lavatory-pot stood. As he emptied his tin very slowly, letting the liquid run down the inner side of the pot so that it made no noise at all, he was reminded of his own good fortune in living where he did. Not once in his life had he ever met another kid with an indoor lavatory and a wash-basin and a real fixed bath with hot water in the tap. All the kids he knew had to go outside, some all the way down a dark passage to the middens in the yards out back, in all weathers, day or night, summer and winter alike. And they only knew the galvanized baths that hung from nails in tiny cellar heads and were dragged out every now and then for the whole family to take turns in having a proper scrub-down in front of a blazing fire. Frankie was luckier than all the other kids in Bradford put together, because sometimes his mam left her hot, foamy, perfumed water in the bath after she had finished washing herself, so that he could soak himself in the luxury of it until the water cooled and the skin on his hands and feet turned pale and crinkly. Then Buddie would pace all around him with a serious face, sniff the air and say:

'By Jove, young fella, you smell like the inside of Marilyn Monroe's liberty bodice.'

When his makeshift ladle was empty, he hurried back to his room and repeated the process several times until at last he was able to carry the pot to the bathroom and dispose of its unsavoury contents in one go. His pot had become badly stained, with a wide ring of brown scum sticking to the hollowed-out shape just below the rim. It smelled, too, just like the men's urinal that was set into the wall of the Corporation Depot at the corner of Great Horton Road and Shearbridge Road. He did not like that smell. It made him think of filthy old tramps and dark places where rats were breeding. He was pondering what to do about it when the idea occurred to him that he could sneak downstairs when Smallfry went out and steal some soda crystals from the little top kitchen where the chicken carcasses were cleaned out. The stains might fade away if he stood the pot in the bath, filled it up with hot water, threw in a handful of soda crystals and left it to steep until Buddie sent him back to bed after his work was finished. By then the pot should have cleaned itself. It would no longer smell nasty, and nobody would be any the wiser so long as he remembered to take it with him when he went to bed.

Feeling very pleased with himself, he went back to his room and began to tidy up. He made the bed, pulling his blanket straight and adjusting his army greatcoat so that it looked neater and less crumpled. He even punched the pillow a few times to get rid of the dip in the middle where his head had pressed it flat, but he didn't disturb the flock in his mattress, even though it was lumpy and unevenly distributed. Once he had tried to turn his mattress right over, the way he had seen his nanny and his auntie doing when they made the beds for the boarders, but the attempt was a failure. He had wet the bed so often that the striped ticking had turned rusty in places where it touched the metal mesh of the bed's base. The fabric had rotted away and the flock filling was poking out through the holes. If he tried to turn it over, the ticking would simply fall to bits and leave him with nothing to sleep on but the rusty mesh base. So now he treated his mattress with extra care and hardly ever tried to scrunch up the flock filling so that it felt more comfortable beneath his body.

He tidied his room by making sure that all the bits and pieces of things that had fallen down were thrown back on the piles where they had come from. Then he gathered up some of the balls of dark fluff that grew under the bed and wafted about in the slightest draught. He straightened up the piles of newspaper and kicked at the things under his bed until they sat more neatly out of sight. And all the while he told himself that one day, when he was properly grown up and could be trusted not to wet the bed any more, he would persuade his parents to move him into the front bedroom where it was never really dark and no old furniture was stored. Then he would take every penny of his savings down to the open market and buy himself a brand new mattress with clean white sheets and two soft blankets and a pillow that didn't have stains on it.

When the work was done, Frankie climbed up to sit on his windowsill with his back against the wooden frames where shutters had once been folded away on tiny brass hinges. From there he could see the cinder-pile bending its dark hump beyond the trees, and way below the terraced gardens that patch of grassy field where Trigger was tethered. Trigger was Frankie's very own pony, bought from a circus for next to nothing because he was too small for adults to ride and too bad-tempered to be trusted around children. Trigger had a will of his own. He was stubborn and uncooperative. He liked to bite people, and he would always rear up, kicking and complaining, when it was time for him to be saddled. He also had a habit of standing in one spot and refusing to move so much as an inch in any direction, no matter how much he was pulled or pushed or yelled at.

'Stubborn as a goddamn mule and twice as stupid,' Buddie would bellow in fury. He would use his whip until he eventually mastered the situation, but he kept his distance to avoid a nasty nip on the thigh or a sudden sly kick to the shins.

Frankie did not see a great deal of his pony. A horse was neither a toy to be played with nor a pet to be fondled until it was soft in the head. He was allowed to ride Trigger only when Buddie could spare the time to act as trainer and supervisor. Then Frankie was expected to get all dressed up in his cowboy suit and his Stetson hat and his wellington boots, ready for a serious riding lesson. They would always go out on the streets where people could stare at them in admiration and all the kids in the neighbourhood would run after them, wide-eyed and green with envy, wishing that they could be as privileged as Frankie, with their very own pony to ride. Buddie would trot alongside with his coiled leather whip in his hand, keeping pace and shouting out orders:

'Rein him in! Hard, boy, *hard*. Don't let him get the better of you! Head up, boy! Square those shoulders! Give him more rein! Woah! *Woah!* What the hell are you playing at, boy? Goddamn it, won't you *ever* learn?'

130

They would come back to Old Ashfield with Buddie in a foul mood and Frankie bruised across his thighs where he had been punched for not getting it right. And then he would wish to God that Trigger didn't belong to him, and feel useless and ungrateful because after all his parents had done for him he was too damn stupid to master an under-sized circus pony that any idiot with half a brain should have been able to ride.

Frankie sighed heavily as he watched the short, stocky, piebald pony moving behind the trees in the bottom field. He *could* ride his pony, he *could*, but he would never dare admit as much to his father. It was the saddle Trigger objected to. One day Frankie had plucked up the courage to try riding him bareback, without even a bridle for guidance, and sure enough, Trigger had performed like the neatest, most obedient mount anyone could wish for. But that was a long time ago and Frankie was scared of getting caught, and the longer he stayed away the more reluctant Trigger was to let him make friends again. It was a rotten shame, because Buddie would never know how obedient he could be without the saddle, and he would never see how well his son controlled that cantankerous little circus pony.

He was still perched on the littered windowsill when he heard a door slam downstairs and the ring of Smallfry's high heels on the tiles in the hall. He strained to watch her as she left the house and walked, swaying her hips exactly like Jane Russell, along the crazy paving to the side of the house. She was wearing her shiny red skirt, the swirly one with the ribbon of white lace stitched just under the hem so that it looked as if her pretty petticoat was peeping out by accident. Over this she had pulled her mustard-coloured swing-back jacket with the big padded shoulders and the lapel brooch designed like a bunch of fruit. Her hair was swept up on top of her head and held with decorated combs and pins so fine they were barely

131

visible. Her earrings were long and sparkly, and her shoes were the black patent leather ones that she cleaned with Vaseline and trimmed at the front with mother-of-pearl buttons. She looked so beautiful that he felt his heart turn over as he watched her. He even crouched on his sore knee in order to press his face against the glass to keep her in sight until she was through the iron gate and down the steps and gone.

'That's me mam,' he said aloud. Pride brought a smile to his lips and a happy twinkle to his eyes. 'That's me mam. Me *mam*. Me *mam*.'

After first making sure that Tom Fish was no longer in the house, he crept out to stand his chamber-pot in the bath. He turned on the hot tap and let it run until the steam came, then pushed the pot beneath the flow so that the scalding water could run inside. While it was filling up, he hurried downstairs to scoop soda crystals into his tin from the bag under the sink in the little kitchen. This done, he ran back upstairs to the bathroom, checked that the tap was properly turned off, swished the soda crystals into the pot and quickly returned to his own room. In all this time there had been no sound from any of the other rooms, and no sign of life from the gap beneath that one door he dreaded above all others. The Bogeyman hated light. It was almost a certainty that one single light-bulb, placed in the socket at the top of the short stairs and kept burning day and night, would keep the Bogeyman trapped in his room forever.

Frankie's knee was beginning to throb again. The skin felt tight when he bent his leg, and instead of forming a protective crust over the wound, the soil from the hillside had simply made the exposed flesh dry and dirty. He jumped down from the windowsill and practised walking around the room without limping. Then he shook out his best bomber jacket, pulled it on and fastened the front right up to his neck. There was nothing else he

132

could do to pass the time, so he pulled Mr Ted from his hiding place, climbed on to his bed and prepared himself for the long wait until Buddie came to fetch him at nine o'clock. The very last thing he had intended to do was fall asleep with the door wide open and the blackout curtain hooked back and the forbidden teddy bear clutched in his arms.

The flashlight stabbed into his dreams like a sword. One moment he was drifting through waves of sweetly scented water in some safe and quiet place, the next he was yanked from sleep to face a beam of brightness that stung his eyes.

'You deaf or something, boy? I've been calling you for ten minutes.'

'What? Oh! Oh, heck! I'm sorry, Buddie. I'm ready, er . . . I just fell asleep for a few minutes . . . I . . . '

In his panic the words came out on a stammer. He was trying to stuff Mr Ted out of sight and still hold Buddie's attention so that he would not have the time to take a close look around the room. It was growing dark. The curtain had slipped from the metal rod and fallen against the pile of newspapers on the windowsill, blocking out most of the window, and there was no longer any light filtering from the bathroom at the other end of the corridor.

'I'm coming, Buddie. I'm coming.'

He scrambled from the bed and groped for his shoes, praying that his father had spotted neither the battered old teddy bear nor the army greatcoat Frankie had stolen one winter night when a sick man was brought to the house and hidden upstairs in the attic. If Buddie saw any of these things he made no comment as he marched from the room, swinging the flashlight at his side while Frankie followed at a rapid trot with one shoe unfastened and the other still clutched in his hand.

'We've got work to do, kid.'

133

'I know, Buddie.'

'You don't have to help if you'd rather be in bed. I can just as easy finish it myself.'

'No, it's all right. I *want* to help. Honest, I do. I didn't mean to fall asleep. Bringing the bottles up must have made me a bit tired.'

It was a lame excuse and he hated himself for being too much of a sissy to stay awake just a couple of hours. He hurried after his father, trying to stay within the flashlight's brilliant beam. The corridor shrank back into its customary darkness in their wake, except for one pale band of light that showed, grey as cemetery dust, beneath the Bogeyman's door.

They went out through the yard and turned left, their footsteps crunching along the drive until they reached the wide wooden gate near the chicken-pens. This was the main gate, badly in need of a lick of paint and so rusted around its hinges that it had to be hand-lifted clear of all the ruts and pot-holes making up the steep, uneven drive known as Ashfield. Unlike the tall iron gate at the other end of the drive, the one leading up the side of Brooke Parker's to Thorpe Street, this one was wide enough to allow a vehicle to pass through, though the neglected condition of the approach made it a bone-jolting ride. Now Frankie strode on ahead, leading the way and keeping the beam of the torch aimed low on the ground so that Buddie had light enough to manoeuvre the wheelbarrow safely around the rocks and holes and toughened clumps of weed.

Much further up, the drive began to level out until it met a flat, wide section divided into two parts by a neat stone wall, each part having a row of big houses with long front gardens set side by side amongst the trees all the way along to Great Horton Road. Just before the boundary wall of the first house, the drive opened to the right into Brooke Parker's lorry yard, with a cobbled pathway leading past the top side of the building and almost into Thorpe Street. It was a long way up the drive to where the first of the houses was set, and until then the whole of the drive belonged to Old Ashfield, and nobody was entitled to use that part of it unless they had business with Buddie.

Buddie huffed and puffed under the weight of the heavy wheelbarrow as they crossed the lorry park and came to a halt in the very farthest corner, close to the high brick wall. The glass from the bottom of the hill was already there, carried up from Old Ashfield in the barrow and dumped against the wall. Nearby was a small wooden step-ladder, its two parts held together by several twists of stout wire and a length of electricity cable. Buddie hoisted Frankie up the ladder to the top of the wall so that he could play the full beam of the torch down over the other side to the turkey-pens way below. Everything looked very different from that unfamiliar height and angle. There were even windows in the roofs of the three houses that he had never seen before. He squinted into the shadows beyond the front bedrooms, to the slant of the roof where it dipped between two chimney stacks, and he wondered if the small rectangle of dark glass he saw there was the skylight window of the Bogey-man's room.

Father and son worked silently by the light of a torch encased in metal so that its beam was restricted and less likely to be seen from a distance. It grew very dark and chilly, and so quiet in the lorry park that every movement of the spade or trowel made sounds that seemed to carry for miles. Perched on the highest rung of the step-ladder, Buddie piled the wet cement in a rough layer along the top of the wall. With his hands protected by clumsy canvas gloves, he embedded sharp pieces of broken glass, points uppermost, in the mixture. It was Frankie's job to sort out the chunks of glass, stack them in the bucket and hold them up within Buddie's reach. The task made his arms and shoulders ache, but he was glad to be of use and proud of the way the glistening glass barricade grew and grew until eventually it covered the entire length of the wall, even at the far end where no man could possibly climb. To do that part, Buddie had walked along the very top of the wall with spade-fulls of cement and bucket-loads of glass and a small, bent trowel shoved down his belt. He worked his way backwards, one section at a time, moving like an agile shadow in the dim light. Not once did it occur to Frankie that his father might miss his footing and fall upon a bed of glass of his own making, or worse, that he might over-balance and fall the forty feet to certain death on the rear drive of Old Ashfield. Buddie was a champion. He might go away to sea, or abandon his family to travel around the world, but he could no more die of a common fall than the King of England could choke on a lump of poor man's tripe.

Before the job was finished they ran out of cement and had to return to Old Ashfield for a second mix. Buddie rested for a while on the yard steps and rolled himself a long, thin cigarette that flared when he put a match to it and was burned right away after only a few puffs. Minutes later he grasped the handles of the barrow and hoisted them upwards.

'Right, then, Frankie,' he growled. 'Let's be going. Another twenty minutes or so and we'll be through.'

It took them half an hour to finish the job. When Buddie stood back and shone the torch on his handiwork, the top of the wall glowed and glittered under its lethal load. Some shards of glass protruded at least eight inches into the air. No two were set more than a couple of inches apart. It was a job well done. There would be no more grinning Brooke Parker men hanging over the wall to make fun of Frankie, or to whistle and blow kisses at Smallfry, or to send the turkeys into a blind panic with lighted cigarette ends.

Weary but satisfied, Buddie and Frankie gathered up their tools and made the tricky journey back down the rocky route to Old Ashfield. On the rear drive they stood to relieve themselves against the wall of one of the empty houses, each aiming his jet so that it ran down the stones to the grassy patches growing along the narrow pavement.

Once inside the house, Buddie flung open the door of the stove so that the dying fire was shocked back to life by the sudden draught. Then he boiled up the kettle and made two cups of sugary cocoa while Frankie spread slices of crusty bread with dripping from the frying pan and sprinkled the dark grease with a good helping of salt and pepper. Father and son then seated themselves on either side of the fire, both drinking noisily to take in enough air with every gulp to cool the steaming liquid before it reached their throats. They chewed their food thoughtfully whilst staring into the fire in silent camaraderie. From time to time Buddie glanced up at the clock on the shelf. It was after eleven. She was very late home. Buddie's perpetual scowl began to deepen. At last he fished in his back pocket, pulled out a coin and handed it to the boy.

'This is for you, kid,' he drawled. 'You worked damn well tonight. I appreciate it.'

Frankie stared at the big silver coin that was pressed into his palm. It was a half-crown, two shillings and sixpence that he did not have to hide away and could spend just as he wished.

'Heck, thanks Buddie,' he beamed. 'Oh, thanks a lot.'

'Now it's time for you to hit the sack, kid, before your mam gets back and wonders what the hell we've been up to all this time. Go on, *git*.'

'Yes, Buddie.' Frankie gulped the last of his cocoa. It had thickened with the sugar in the bottom of his cup. It scorched the back of his tongue but slid down his throat like a thick syrup, sweet and chocolatey.

'G'night, Buddie.'

'G'night, kid. Will you be OK?'

'Course I will.'

'Want me to come up with you?'

'No, 'course not.'

'You sure? I don't mind taking you up . . . it's pretty late, you know, and it must be dark as the jaws of hell up there.'

Frankie shrugged and shook his head. Something chilly stroked along his spine, making him shudder.

'No, that'd be sissy,' he said, hating every word. 'I don't need taking up. I *always* go to bed by myself.'

'You don't get nervous in the dark, then?'

'Who? Me?' Frankie forced himself to laugh out loud as he opened the inner door on to the pitch darkness of the corridor beyond. 'Me? Scared of the dark? 'Course I'm not, Buddie. I'm no sissy.'

'G'night, then, soldier.'

'G'night, Buddie.'

Frankie grinned again and returned his father's two-fingered salute before closing the door behind him and stepping into the waiting void. Only now did the grin vanish from his face. Now he had to pass between the cellar door and the ominous row of garments crowding against the wall. Now he had to grope his way along the corridor to the dark well of the hall, climb blindly up the main stairs to the eerie half-landing, retrieve his chamber-pot and brave the inky blackness of the next floor. It was a fearful journey that dried his mouth and stopped his breath and made his heart pound like a snare drum in his ears, but he could bear the terrors snapping at his heels, knowing that he had not shamed himself. He had done everything his father wanted him to do and he had done it well, even when it was very late and he was dog-tired and his muscles ached from holding the bucket above his head. No, he had not shamed himself. He had not made any silly mistakes and most of all he had not let Buddie know that he was frightened of the dark.

ELEVEN

The night seemed to pass in the winking of an eye and the sun was up long before his body was fully rested. Its brightness tugged him from his bed with the promise of a good day for those sharp enough to take advantage of its opportunities. It was Saturday, the best day of the whole week.

Frankie stretched his arms above his head and yawned until his jaw bone wanted to spring from its hinges. By nine o'clock he had been hanging around the pigsties for the better part of an hour. He was hoping Buddie would put him to work on a few odd jobs that would not involve passing too close to the pigs or putting his hands in their feed. If he worked hard and made no mistakes, he might be lucky enough to be invited along on the swill-round. The Saturday swill-round was the best one of them all. First they would go to the butchers' shops and workmen's cafés, then the hotel kitchens at the back of the Empire Theatre, and late in the afternoon they would collect all the bins from the meat and fish markets, and all the boxes of bruised fruit from John Street open market in Westgate. Along the way Buddie would pick up a few bottles of *buckshee* brown ale or milk stout and several parcels containing left-over fish, suspect meat or dry, discoloured cheese, all too good for the pigs, yet too far gone to sell over the counter now that the war was over and people were getting more and more choosy. Frankie did not think too deeply about the parcels, especially the fishy ones that sometimes stank so badly he could pick out their distinctive smell above that of all the swill-bins on the truck. After the fish was sorted into which bits were fit to eat and which should be thrown down for the dog, the washing and cooking of it would make everything all right. Buddie never complained about what he ate, so all Frankie could do was surreptitiously examine the food on his own plate every swill day to make sure no maggots or bluebottle eggs had slipped unnoticed into the frying pan. His parents hated him to fuss over his meals. They did not seem to understand that the sight of even a small human hair floating in his food could cause his stomach to heave and churn until he wanted to throw up.

'Is your mam up and about yet?'

Frankie shook his head. 'I don't think so.'

'Anyone in the kitchen when you came through?'

'Nope,' Frankie said, shaking his head again. He was hovering on the safe side of the pigsty wall, making himself conspicuous and hoping to do a bit more fetching and carrying to earn his place in the passenger seat of the big swill truck. He had already fed Trigger and topped up his trough with fresh water carried all the way down to the bottom field from the stand-pipe outside the pigsty. Then he had polished all the chromium-plated fittings on Buddie's big American truck, the headlamp casings and the fancy badges and the trims that shone like pure silver when the dirt was rubbed away. For his final job he had been forced to climb on to the front bonnet where the spare wheel was stored with coils of rope on its inside. From there he had washed the windscreen and polished the painted sign that said 'The Duke' in neat white letters.

'I cleaned the truck,' he announced, proudly.

'Did you now? Good kid. Old Duke was due for a bit of spit and polish about now. Hand me that bucket, will you?'

Eager as he was to prove himself a willing helper, Frankie reached for the handle gingerly. The heavy metal bucket

141

was coated inside and out with layer upon layer of dried swill that never got washed away between feeds. There was no point in Buddie making extra work for himself when the swill buckets were only ever used for doing the same job over and over again. Gritting his teeth and holding his breath against the smell, Frankie dragged the bucket to the pigsty gate and hoisted it over the low, uneven step. Then he dipped his hands in one of the rain-water troughs and dried them on his pants before sniffing carefully at each finger in turn to make sure no trace of the swill remained on his skin.

His socks had gone to sleep again. They were bunched up uncomfortably around his toes so that his wellington boots, bought on the large side so they would not be wasted if his feet suddenly started to grow, were rubbing a big, round, tender spot on each unprotected heel. Buddie did not have that trouble because his feet had stopped growing and his wellingtons could be bought in the correct size. Whenever he wore the khaki army shorts that left his legs exposed, he also wore thick socks knitted in soft white wool that folded over the turned-down tops of his boots. And when he wore his cowboy denims he tucked them inside his boots so that his socks never became twisted up or out of place and uncomfortable for his feet. Grown-ups were lucky. They were never troubled by blistered heels or sore toes, and even in wet weather their legs did not become chafed to rawness by the tops of their boots rubbing against the skin with every stride. This was one of Buddie's *facts of life*: that adults were lucky and youngsters had a whole lot of growing to do before they were big enough to claim similar privileges.

Buddie tipped the last bucket of swill into the bottom trough and stepped back to allow several snorting, jostling pigs to ram their snouts into the sloppy mixture. He gave one hairy pink rump an affectionate blow with the flat of his hand, then turned to observe Frankie, his dark brows lowered in a thoughtful scowl.

142

'How're you feeling, kid?'

'I'm OK,' Frankie shrugged.

'You sure? No aches and pains? No stiff muscles?'

Frankie shook his head vigorously. He would not be allowed on the swill-round if Buddie suspected that he was not really up to it.

'I'm fine,' he insisted, crossing his fingers behind his back to neutralize the fib. 'Not a single pain anywhere, not even a *little* one.'

Buddie nodded and pursed his lips. 'Tough little critter. Did you get a good look at the factory wall this morning?'

'Oh, yes, and it's beautiful,' Frankie said with genuine enthusiasm. 'Just beautiful.'

And it *was* beautiful. In the vivid morning sunlight the broken bottles glittered and gleamed against the sky. Some were as clear as sparkling ice, some warm brown or amber, others glowing with their own particular shade of summer-rich green. They were set like hundreds of jagged jewels in a bed of concrete that seemed to wink an eye whenever its trapped particles of sand caught the light. The whole wall now resembled the battlements of some ancient castle, its sheer expanse of red brick topped by a crown of shining, multi-coloured glass. Buddie had shown a lot of cunning when he did the work under cover of darkness without making any complaint to the management about his violated privacy or missing livestock. Now the workmen and the overlookers would all think the Big Bosses had ordered the work done during the weekend. On Monday morning nobody would suspect that the faceless Top Brass, who were not expected to concern themselves with small matters, had been blown a vulgar raspberry by the little guy who lived over the wall in Old Ashfield. Perhaps the truth of it would never be known, but heaven help the next Brooke Parker man who tried to climb to the top of that wall again.

'I'll be doing my rounds after I grab a sandwich and a cup of tea. You coming?'

'Oh, yes,' Frankie beamed. 'Yes please, Buddie.'

'You'd better go inside and smarten yourself up. And put the gear you're wearing on the laundry pile before it crawls in of its own accord. Jesus, Frankie, you're a bloody ragamuffin. You're old enough to be taking a pride in your appearance, boy. You shouldn't need me to remind you when to wear a clean shirt.'

'No, Buddie. I'm sorry. I'll go inside and change . . . er . . . ' He hesitated, daunted by the sheer enormity of the task now facing him. He would have to wake his mam from her beauty sleep just to ask for a clean shirt and pants, or else confess to his father that he had no idea how or where to find a change of clothes. ' . . . er . . . er . . . '

'You're stammering again, Frankie.' Buddie's voice had a warning edge. Stammering made him mad as hell. Only sissies and babies and half-wits stammered.

Frankie felt his eyes screw themselves shut and then spring open, stretching the muscles around his mouth. If his twitch started up he would be smacked over the head and sent back to his room until his father was in a better mood. He was losing ground. The helper's place on the swill-round was suddenly hanging in the balance.

' . . . er . . . *my cowboy outfit!*' he blurted in an unexpected flash of inspiration. 'Please can I wear my cowboy outfit?'

'Well, I suppose you could . . . '

Buddie rubbed his chin thoughtfully with one hand. He had not yet shaved his face, so the dry skin on his palm scraped over the stubble with a harsh rasping sound.

'And my Stetson?'

'Well, now, I don't see why not . . . '

'And my gun belt and holster?'

Buddie grinned, and his chuckle was like a deep growl rumbling in the back of his throat.

'Sure, kid, why not? You'll find the whole kit and kaboodle in the wooden chest in the playroom, and watch out for those records of mine. I don't want any more breakages.'

144

'Yes, sir, I'll be careful,' Frankie called over his shoulder as he ran off towards the front terrace, his face bright with excitement.

'And for Christ's sake, Frankie, do something with your bloody hair, will you?'

'Yes, *sir!*'

The playroom was at the front of the house on the left of the main door. It was a very large room, with a window so long and wide that when it was opened a person could step right through to the crazy paving on the front terrace. There was a big fireplace made of green and black marble on the wall opposite the door, with deep alcoves on both sides and a high mantel thick enough and strong enough to hold stacks and stacks of gramophone records. This was the room where Buddie's dance band practised, and where crowds of visitors gathered to listen to the records on party nights, when the house was filled to bursting with fascinating people and lots of noise. Frankie liked it best when the servicemen came, those handsome, good-natured Americans with their smart uniforms and loud voices, those heroes from the good old '*US of A*' who were always taller and broader and richer and had more teeth than ordinary folk. Smallfry liked the Americans because they brought her nice things like decorated silk stockings and special underwear, Yankee comics and exclusive movie magazines that nobody else had ever seen, and sometimes bits of beaded jewellery made by genuine Red Indian tribes-people just like the ones Frankie had seen on the films.

Much of the playroom was littered now with the debris of a recent band practice. A dozen or more upright chairs and high stools were set at higgledy-piggledy angles, each one accompanied by a metal music-stand perched on three spindly legs. Against a wall leaned Buddie's guitar case, specially made in shiny imitation crocodile skin with gleaming silver catches and a lining of orange plush to hold the instrument in a tender, protective embrace. There

145

were dinner plates here and there containing stubbed-out cigarettes and cigars, used matches and twists of discarded chewing gum left to harden in the ash alongside bits of stale sandwiches. Empty beer bottles and loose sheets of music lay on every surface, and there was a smell in the air that was sharply masculine, like stale sweat and musty old leather.

The wooden chest stood in one of the alcoves, its lid pinned shut by a collection of gramophone records and two pint mugs in which an inch or so of tea had grown a covering of mould. Frankie cleared the surface very carefully, sliding the records into their strong paper cases and stacking them one atop the other in a neat and tidy pile. Inside the chest, the cowboy outfit nestled on a bed of folded garments Frankie was not allowed to touch. He lifted it free one piece at a time, shaking out the creases, touching the shiny bits, plumping out the Stetson. His cattle-man's shirt was made of crimson and black Scotch plaid with lots of little white buttons and a fancy boot-lace tie fixed under the collar. His mam had made that shirt for him with her own hands. She had taken one of Buddie's thick cotton working shirts and cut it down to Frankie's size, trimming and stitching and reshaping until it became a perfect fit. It did not matter that the points of the collar were too long or the cuffs too deep, or that the button holes down the front were too widely spaced for his small chest. What mattered was that he owned a real cowboy shirt that was not for sale in any shop in the whole of England, and his mam had really and truly made it especially for *him*.

He stripped off his clothes and pulled on the long denim pants that were brought from America by a friend of Buddie's and had to be turned over several times to prevent the bottoms trailing on the floor. Next came the shirt, the leather spats cut from a cobbler's apron, the belt with its big buckle and rows of pointed brass studs, the sleeveless leather waistcoat and, finally, the wide-brimmed Stetson with its exclusive badges and long, knotted thongs. The hat was still too large for him, so to keep it from falling down over his eyes he tried to keep his head slightly raised. He had also developed the standard tough-guy habit of nudging up the brim with his stiffened fingers the way the men did in all the best westerns. Once fully attired, he hurried upstairs to the half-landing and opened the bathroom door to its widest so that the small area was flooded with daylight. He stood with his legs apart and his shoulders squared, studying his reflection in the dusty old mirror that leaned, chipped and frameless and mottled with mildew stains, in one of the corners.

'Reach for the sky, Kid McCormick!' he told the skinny cowboy in the over-sized Stetson hat who stood in the dark mirror with his eyes narrowed into dangerous slits and his gun-hand poised over his holster. 'Reach or die!'

Making fullest use of the element of surprise, he suddenly drew on his old enemy Kid McCormick. He crouched and fired, voicing every shot until his bullets were all used up. Then he blew imagined smoke from the ends of his fingers and stuck them back into their empty holster as yet another lawless gun-slinger bit the dust. He nodded solemnly into the mirror, confident that he would make a damn good cowboy if ever he was called upon to show the world his mettle.

Before going downstairs he thrust his head under running water and fingered his unruly black hair until it was thoroughly doused and stuck out from his scalp in thick tufts. It took a lot of tugging and wincing to ease the tangles out with his special nit comb. It was difficult to use because it had been made with slender, close-set teeth that could scrape out creepy-crawly eggs before they had a chance to hatch. The fine-toothed comb had been given to him by his nanny when he caught nits from some kid at school and had to be de-loused with a thick, foul-smelling concoction made up by the herbalist who had his shop in the alley near the bottom of Manchester Road. The nits had frightened him. He did not like insects, especially tiny ones that might crawl into his eyes or down his ears, up his nose or into his mouth while he slept, and lay thousands of eggs in his brain that would one day hatch out and begin to eat him alive from the inside.

His nostrils were filled with the smell of frying bacon when at last he flung open the kitchen door and swaggered through with his dirty clothes balled under one arm and his wet hair neatly flattened by his cowboy hat.

'Howdy, pardner,' he declared, imitating Buddie's best American drawl. 'Whatcha got cooking there? Say, fella, that chow sure smells good enough to . . . Oh! Oh, heck! . . . er . . .'

He stopped, his face crestfallen, his voice trailing off to a more timid greeting:

' . . . er . . . hello, Smallfry.'

He found himself standing motionless in the centre of the room as if caught beneath a bright spotlight, pinned helplessly in the glare of his own boldness. He had not expected to find Smallfry up and about so early in the morning, especially when she had been out until quite late the night before. Yet there she was, standing by the sink with a tea-cup in her hand, watching him. The front of her hair was set in two deep waves, with the sides swept up and pinned in coils and the back brushed into a neat bun that sat on the crown of her head without a hairpin to be seen. She was wearing her maroon costume skirt and a shiny white blouse with a lace collar and sparkly glass buttons. She was staring at him with her eyebrows arched and her lips slightly parted, as if this grubby, lilliputian cowboy was the very last thing she had expected to see come swaggering into *her* kitchen *without knocking at the door.*

Frankie sucked in his lower lip and fixed his gaze on the floor where Nader had left a half-chewed piece of black rubber inner-tubing. He was not sure what to do. He could

148

go back into the corridor and knock politely at the door before coming in again, but that would only draw more attention to the fact that he had broken the rule in the first place. He could apologize and make up some excuse for the lapse, but that might cause him to stammer and twitch, and then Buddie would get mad and his day would be entirely ruined. In the event he did absolutely nothing. He simply stood with his head bowed for what seemed an eternity before Buddie lifted the cast iron frying pan away from the flames and said:

'Howdy yourself, pardner. Time to eat.'

For a moment his shoulders sagged with relief, then he set down his ball of dirty clothes near the hearth and scuttled to his usual place at the table. When he removed his Stetson and hooked it carefully over the back of his chair, he could not help noticing that Buddie's gaze flickered to his slicked-down hair before he and Smallfry exchanged one of those glances that seemed to say private things without any words needing to be spoken. They both smiled. Frankie smiled too, because now he could see by their faces that he was not in any trouble. He was not yet in the passenger seat of the big American truck, but he was *almost* there.

His bread was saturated in bacon-flavoured dripping and fried to a crisp on one side while still quite soft on the other, exactly the way he liked it. Bits of bacon rind were floating in a pool of hot grease on his plate, which meant he would be allowed at least one more slice of bread for the purpose of mopping up the goodness and wiping his plate clean the way he was supposed to do.

Buddie's pint mug already contained two heaped spoons of dry tea-leaves when Smallfry filled it three-quarters full from the little silver teapot kept warming on the stove. He topped up the mug with milk and spooned in plenty of sugar from the blue paper sugar bag, then proceeded to stir and stir as if the mixture had to be perfectly blended before the taste could be properly savoured. Buddie liked his tea sweet and strong, with a bed of tea-leaves at the bottom and a few stray ones floating on top for good measure. It coloured the inside of his cup with dark brown stains and made Smallfry curl her lip in distaste, but Buddie enjoyed his cups of tea the way he enjoyed a glass of rum or a bottle of ale.

'Give me a drink I can really *taste*,' he always insisted. 'Give me something with a wallop, something that grabs me by the throat before it kicks me in the head like a bad-tempered old mule. Now that's the way I *really* like it.'

Smallfry's mam usually brought him a few bottles of really strong dark beer when she came to visit from her little house in Park Road. It was special stuff that came from the brewery where she worked in Manchester Road, and Buddie said it was the best darn beer he ever tasted. Frankie loved his Park Road Nanny, even though she *did* make lemon sponge cakes as dry as feathers and dotted with caraway seeds that looked like dead insects and tasted foul. Nanny never frightened him or lost her temper for no reason at all, and she never, ever blamed him for things that were not his fault. She had gentle hands and a quiet voice and she smiled a lot, and that was why he did not have the heart to tell her that her cake was awful and the seeds made him feel sick. He just hoped that when she shook her old tab rug against the back wall to clean it, she would not notice the hundreds of little black specks he had picked out of her cake and hidden there rather than risk hurting her feelings.

Now Frankie watched and listened as he hastily devoured his own meal, mopping every last drop of grease from his plate with little wads of bread, then sucking the tasty smears away one by one from the ends of his fingers.

With a sound like water rushing down a narrow plug-hole, Buddie tipped back his head and siphoned the last dregs of tea through the thick bed of leaves in the bottom of his mug. He seemed to trap the mess against the outside of his teeth and suck until the leaves were dry. He was the only person Frankie had ever seen who could drink a cup of tea and then spend ten minutes chewing the bits that had trapped themselves between his teeth.

'Thank you for what I have eaten, now please may I leave the table?' Frankie chanted politely.

Buddie scowled and nodded sharply as if he did not really appreciate such rituals. That was probably because his mother was a Jewess who was supposed to go to church on Saturday, instead of Sunday, and was only allowed to read the front part of the Holy Bible. Smallfry, on the other hand, showed her approval in a warm smile because she was an Irish Catholic who was allowed to read *both* ends of the Bible and could even recite the titles of all the books of the Bible in perfect order from start to finish, including the Apocryphal section. The differences were a constant source of puzzlement to Frankie, especially since his school was Church of England and some of the kids there went to a Methodist Sunday School where the hymns and prayers were not quite the same. He would never understand why God Almighty, who was supposed to be the smartest person in the entire universe, did not send down a list of clear instructions like the ones stuck on the insides of wireless sets. Then everyone would know exactly what He wanted and they could stop bickering amongst themselves about rules and regulations and which day it was when God rested from His labours.

He blushed hotly when Smallfry ran her fingers through his hair before handing him his Stetson.

'Oh, Frankie, whatever are we going to do about your hair?'

'I could go to the barber's and have it cut short, Yankee-style,' he offered. All the American servicemen had crew cuts. It would make him feel pretty good to be the first kid at St Andrew's to turn up at school sporting a real American hair-cut.

'Oh, I don't know,' Smallfry sighed heavily in her disappointment. 'If only it could have been curly, like your father's, or dark auburn, like my own.'

Frankie pulled his Stetson hat down over the offending thatch of hair and stood on tip-toe to kiss Smallfry's cheek. She was wearing White Fire today instead of Californian Poppy. Its scent reminded him of those tiny, red, perfumed sweets called cherry lips that herbalists sold by the half ounce in pointed paper bags with tucked-in tops. One cherry lip could leave its taste behind to sweeten the breath for a long time after it was sucked away. Smallfry kept hers in a miniature tin in her handbag, or sometimes she bought the coloured, violet-scented sweets that came in their own little box with a see-through lid that clicked when it was opened and closed.

Smallfry's words caused him to frown as he hooked his thumbs into his gun-belt and tried to imitate Buddie's easy swagger while following him along the dirt drive. He was sorry his hair stuck out in all directions instead of curling neatly the way it should, but he was not at all sure he wanted to be auburn. Smallfry's hair was such a beautiful, glossy shade of red because he helped her plaster it in graduated-henna once a month and then she had to sit for an hour with the sticky mess covered in strips of newspaper and a warm towel until it dried to a cake that he scraped off and rinsed away down the kitchen sink. This was one of the special secrets Frankie shared with his mam and never spoke of to anyone, not even his father.

The henna came in a greenish powder that had to be mixed to a paste with hot water in a big bowl. It looked and smelled like steaming cow dung, but it preserved the rare shade of her hair so well that some people even maintained that she was not a natural red-head at all and had to have the colour dyed in. It was not true, of course. The people who said those things were just jealous that so many men turned to stare at her in the street and whistle after her because she was so lovely. She was not *really* cheating when she used the henna and told everyone her hair was natural. This was just her clever way of making the most of her beauty, and it was only a closely guarded secret because outsiders would deliberately misunderstand and call her a liar if they knew about it. In Frankie's measured opinion, being a natural red-head amounted to a great deal of trouble that he was glad not to have for himself. Besides, Buddie's hair was as black as coal, and if that colour was good enough for his dad then it was certainly good enough for him.

Loaded with empty swill-bins, The Duke pulled out of the rear gates with its temperamental first gear groaning under the strain and its big tyres throwing up dirt as they dipped in and out of pot-holes in order to negotiate the steep, unmade drive. This was the way they had come last night with wheelbarrow-loads of broken bottles and freshly-mixed cement and an important, clandestine task to perform. Now they were heading for the very top of Ashfield, where the narrow track joined up with Great Horton Road and the Saturday swill-round really began. Buddie was singing as he drove, his big, Fats Waller voice filling the cab while his hands drummed out the rhythm on the rim of the steering wheel.

'*I don't want ya 'cause your feet's too big.*'

He bellowed the words at the top of his voice, at times sounding just a little bit like the famous Louis Armstrong.

'*I don't like ya 'cause your feet's too big.*

I can't stand ya 'cause your feet's too big.'

Frankie sat up tall in his seat, nudged back his Stetson and grinned as The Duke lurched drunkenly up the rocky incline. Then driver and passenger leaned towards each other and rolled their eyes upward, each mimicking the same Fats Waller expression as they sang in unison:

'*I really* hates *ya 'cause your feet's too big.*'

TWELVE

At the back door of Hahn's the butcher's they picked up the first of the day's bins. It contained a full week's collection of unwanted meat scraps, the fat and gristle that could not be sold and the bones nobody wanted for their dogs. It had been filled to over-flowing, and now a small cloud of bluebottles had attached itself to the gap where the lid no longer fit snugly enough to keep them out. Frankie wondered if that was because the butcher and his family came from Germany and were too penny-pinching to spend money on a second bin so that the first one did not have to be crammed so full that the stuff at the bottom turned putrid before the week was out. It seemed a likely explanation. He knew from all the war films he had seen at the pictures that Germans, just like most other foreigners, were very peculiar people. The war had ended in 1945 when he was only four years old, but he knew all about the Germans. He did not really think it was right that a man who was once a soldier in the British army could not tell those who had been on the losing side in the famous Battle of Britain to get themselves an extra swill-bin. And it should not matter that they had since become good friends of the family. The thin Mr Hahn had once given Frankie a meat and potato pie that was fresh out of the oven, and the other Mr Hahn was always slipping him boiled sweets from the pocket of his big white apron, but that did not make it right that they only had the one bin. If Frankie ever became a multi-millionaire, or the King of England, or even the next Prime Minister, he would see to it that a law was passed making it illegal for anyone, especially German butchers, to over-fill a swill-bin so that the lid did not fit properly.

'Here iss sweets only for my gutten friend Frankie ze cowboy.'

The oldest of the Mr Hahns thrust his grinning face and one long, white-clad arm through the open window to drop a handful of mixed humbugs into Frankie's hurriedly cupped hands. Mr Hahn was one of the cleanest men Frankie had ever seen. His skin was a translucent pink that always gave the appearance of being newly washed. Whatever the time of day, his hands and fingernails were spotlessly clean. Even his white overalls and starched white apron, presumably worn to protect his everyday clothes from contact with animal carcasses, were without blemish or blood-stain. He even *smelled* clean. Frankie had never found anything in the war films to explain this phenomenon, but he had noticed the same traits in all the other German people known to his parents. He had long ago arrived at the conclusion that these strange people were so unwilling to get themselves dirty that they had abandoned the war rather than fight in the muddy trenches where Winston Churchill kept all his best soldiers. That was obviously what the Americans meant when they boasted about rubbing Hitler's face in the dirt and grinding the evil Nazi Party into the dust. The Germans did not like to get themselves dirty, so they gave up and surrendered and lost the war instead.

'Thanks, Mr Hahn,' he smiled.

'Ant here iss un pound off my werry best beef dripping for your dear *Mutter*.'

The German's eyes were so watery and pale they gave the impression that all the colour had been rinsed away, leaving behind only a hint of faded blue. He was a very pleasant man, though Frankie would never dream of admitting as much to the kids at school. It was enough for them to know that he was actually on speaking terms with a family

155

of real, born-abroad, foreign-speaking Germans.

'Thanks a lot, Mr Hahn,' he said again, returning the man's cheerful wink.

'See you maybe next veek, my friend, huh?'

'Maybe,' he nodded. 'Maybe.'

As the butcher hurried back to his shop, Frankie turned in his seat in time to see his father grasp a metal handle and, with what appeared to be no more than a mere flick of his wrist, swing the heavy swill-bin on to his back. This was the way the coal men always carried their sacks, with the open end close to their heads so that fine coal dust often trickled down the inside of their collars. It was lucky for Buddie that his own collar was stiff and high and could be yanked up around his ears, because the stuff that oozed from the bins was much less savoury than coal dust. When he swung the bin into the truck and climbed up to manoeuvre it into place, the swarm of bluebottles followed, unwilling to relinquish their claim on these rich, meaty pickings.

They did the Alexandra Hotel next, picking up two bins, a parcel of *buckshee* offal and a bag of fresh prawns soaked in vinegar to eat along the way. Frankie sometimes worried about Buddie's habit of licking his fingers and rubbing them across his palms to ease the constant dryness there. He had the most incredibly dry palms. They made a funny rasping noise like sandpaper when he rubbed them together, and the dryness made his fingers clumsy when he needed to do finicky jobs. Fat Nanny was forever slapping his hands away from his mouth and telling him that one of these days he would kill himself with germs from the animals and the swill-bins. Buddie washed his hands and smeared them with Vaseline whenever he visited her house, but during the day when he was working hard and not wearing gloves, his mind got full of other things and he forgot her warnings. Then his fingers would creep back to his tongue for damping every few minutes with never a second thought for what poisons he might be licking off. Buddie liked to tell people he had never had a day's illness in his life, or at least not since he was let out of the orphanage to go back home to his mam. Not like Malcolm Turner's dad, who eventually lost his job in the mill through taking time off with a bad cough, and now had to sleep downstairs because the bedroom was damp and he was coughing up blood. Then there was Sammy Peacock's brother, the thinnest man Frankie had ever seen and the best jazz drummer in all Yorkshire. He had died of consumption when his lungs got sick and no amount of sunshine would make them better. It was frightening to think how people he knew could die like that. It was a comfort to him that his own dad was fit and strong and had never had a day's real illness since he left the orphanage all those years ago.

Frankie did not mind too much when Buddie parked up in a side street at the back of Aldermanbury and told him he would have to eat his dinner all by himself. He could pretend to be a hired hand riding shotgun, guarding Buddie's valuable property the way Rosie had done before she gassed herself outside the tool-shed. Buddie went off for a few minutes and came back with a rolled-up comic, a big portion of thick tripe wrapped up in newspaper and sprinkled with pepper, half a buttered flat-cake and a small bottle of orange juice.

'Will that do you for a while?' he asked.

'It sure will. And Mr Hahn gave me some humbugs. Want one?'

'You betcha!'

Buddie suddenly reached through the open window and made a grab for Frankie's sweets, his big brown hand seizing the lot. After a good-natured scuffle he settled for a single humbug, which he flicked high in the air and caught in his mouth the way he always did with salted peanuts. Then he pulled off his smelly working coat, tossed it across the bonnet of the truck and swaggered away

157

with a nonchalant wave of his hand. Frankie watched him go. Under the big working coat he always wore American blue denims or strong army pants and a decent shirt. At his waist was the broad, big-buckled belt with the studded sheath that hung at a slant on one hip. He was also wearing his fancy gold chain hung with scary-looking animal and human teeth, his gold wrist watch and his impressive collection of chunky, gold and silver rings. Buddie always knew how to impress people, even when he was out on his swill-rounds. Today he had also tied a leather boot-lace around the long corkscrew curls that hung down over his collar, pulling them all together in a crinkly black pony-tail. He looked like something out of a travel book or a movie magazine. It was no wonder the ordinary folk turned to stare after him wherever he went. Buddie was unique. There was no man to match him for sheer style in the whole of Yorkshire.

Frankie watched until his father was out of sight before turning his attention to his midday meal. This was better than school dinners, any day. He shook his orange juice vigorously to make sure the sediment from the bottom became evenly distributed. It was a short fat bottle exactly like the morning and afternoon milk bottles at school, holding just one third of a pint. He rummaged in the dashboard compartment for a pencil, punctured the flat foil lid and pushed his straw through the hole. He drank half the contents, then balanced the bottle on the dashboard and spread his legs wide to clear a flat space on the seat for his food. The tripe was in a single piece and wrapped in grease-proof paper so that its wetness would not soak right through the newspaper in which it was carried. Frankie tore a corner from the grease-proof paper and used it to wipe some of the pepper away. Buddie always put too much salt and pepper on his food. It had something to do with all the travelling he had done around the world and the funny foreign food leaving him with a taste for strong spices and

158

hot, peppery things. Sometimes he would spoon raw salt into the palm of his hand and lick it away as if it were sweet-tasting, like sugar. Frankie wondered if that had made his skin so crinkly, but Smallfry knew differently. She said such over-dry palms came from having a heavy gin drinker in the family, and far be it from her to make accusations, but it was common knowledge that Nanny enjoyed the occasional swig of *mother's ruin* as a change from milk stout.

The tripe was delicious. This was exactly the way he enjoyed it the most, thick, cold, uncooked and as firm as Nanny's jelly in his mouth. He nibbled all around the edge of the portion until its size was reduced by half, then pressed the remainder into his flat-cake to make a tasty and more manageable sandwich.

His comic was the latest edition of the *Eagle*, so he was able to catch up on the Dan Dare space adventure he had been following right up until the time the dreaded Mekon managed to get his evil hands on the secret formula that would wipe out the whole Earth and its inhabitants in a matter of seconds. That was when Valance Fraser's dad had a short week and his mam could not afford to pay the paper bill, so nobody knew what happened next because no-one else's parents could afford to buy the *Eagle* every week. Frankie was going to feel really smug on Monday morning when they all clamoured round to discover just how Dan Dare had out-smarted the evil Mekon right in the nick of time and saved the Earth from certain destruction.

Buddie had gone to visit the New Inn on the corner of Tyrell Street and Thornton Road. It was a dirty-looking place that was supposed to be the oldest pub in Bradford and to stand in the very centre of the city. Smallfry did not like the New Inn any more. She reckoned all the men who went there were scruffy no-goods and all the women had bad names. Mucky Ethel Warden did most of her drinking in there, and everyone knew that she and her friend Mavis

159

were recently arrested and brought before the magistrates for picking up men for money in Swan Arcade. And it was not the first time either, which *proved* what a den of iniquity the New Inn really was. Buddie did not seem to care about anything like that. He just smiled and shook his head and said it was all just a *fact of life* and did not matter one bit. Buddie liked the New Inn, even if Smallfry did not approve of him going there. He often went there at night with a couple of men from the band and his second-best guitar to play for beer-money and a sandwich for his supper, and sometimes he would arrive home roaring drunk and shouting about what a bloody good night it had been.

Frankie wafted a hand in front of his face as a large fly buzzed between his bowed head and the comic lying open across his knees. There were two wide flaps of leather hanging down behind the front seats of the truck to separate the driver and his passenger from the rear area. While they lessened the smell of the bins and kept some of the draughts out in winter, they were no real barrier against hungry flies. The appetizing aroma of tripe sandwich and orange juice had alerted the bluebottles to an alternative food supply. One by one they buzzed between the leather curtains to settle on the soggy tripe wrapping or hover around Frankie's face in search of somewhere to lay their eggs. Waving them aside with one hand, he popped the last bit of sandwich into his mouth and drained his orange juice with that noisy guzzling sound adults hated and schoolboys found so satisfactory. Then he twisted round in his seat and slid the tripe-paper into the back of the truck, pushing it as far between the bins as his reach would allow. The bluebottles followed, just as he had hoped they would. With that small problem solved, Frankie flopped down in his seat, propped his feet on the dashboard and returned to the pages of his *Eagle*.

Some considerable time later he became aware that he was being closely scrutinized. Three women were standing in a bunch a little further along the narrow street, all wearing their headscarves tied in turbans and carrying shopping bags or vegetable sacks. They were discussing something with obvious distaste.

'Shouldn't be allowed,' one of them said in a loud voice when she noticed that Frankie was now looking in her direction.

'Disgusting!' exclaimed another. 'I've a good mind to walk back to the Town Hall and tell a policeman. *He'd* soon get the thing shifted.'

'Aye, and lock up the bugger what owns it, if there's any justice left in this world.'

Frankie lowered his comic and sat up straight, looking all about him to see what the fuss was about. Only then did it dawn on him that they were talking about The Duke. Women were always a bit funny about the swill-bins. It was just as Buddie always said; they were quick to turn their noses up and start complaining about smells, but they soon shut up if there was a cheap bit of pork or a couple of slices of *buckshee* bacon in it for them. Frankie looked hard at all the women in turn so that he would remember their faces, then sniffed, wiped his nose on the cuff of his shirt and went back to his comic.

'Who owns it, that's what *I'd* like to know?' one of the women asked.

'Can't you guess?' asked her sour-faced companion. 'I reckon it belongs to that little foreign chap with the big dogs and the gold earrings. You know the one, Annie. Keeps a farm somewhere up Great Horton. He used to keep that barmy Great Dane dog that ran amock in John Street Market. Bit Freddie Bailey's bad leg, it did, and put the fear of God in poor old Mrs Hardcastle from over West Bowling way.'

The one called Annie nodded and made tut-tutting noises with her tongue. Then the smallest and fattest of the three set down her vegetable sack and shrugged her shoulders several times as if trying to redistribute the inside padding of her overcoat. She narrowed her eyes and nodded, knowingly.

'Oh, aye, I know *him*, right enough. Wears earrings, he does, just like a bloody Gypsy. I hear his mam's one of them funny *Jews* what isn't supposed to eat pork, and him a *pig-farmer*, of all things. They say she runs a boarding house for *black men.*'

'Aye,' her friend agreed. 'Black Africans and travelling performers and such like. Funny goings on, if you ask me, and her with all them grown-up half-caste kids and no husband living these last twenty-odd years or more.'

'Aye, an *American* they say *he* was. Black as the ace of spades and just as sooty, and who would have thought he'd drop dead at fifty-five, a big strapping chap like him?'

The woman called Annie made even louder tut-tutting noises with her tongue and muttered something about never wanting to look a black man in the eye, let alone *marry* one. Frankie turned the pages of his comic and pretended not to hear their remarks.

'Well, my Alf says yon little chap what owns that truck is a famous band-leader what does the pubs and travels abroad, singing and such like.'

'Aye, and they say he does all the local dance halls and socials, and all.'

'Does he, now?' the first woman interjected. 'Well, he should be made to take his mucky old slop-wagon with him. It shouldn't be allowed, that's what I say, dumping it like that in the middle of town where decent folk have to walk by without daring to draw breath. Mucky, smelly article.'

The three women now proceeded to gather up their sacks and shopping bags and, still muttering their complaints, edged reluctantly past the truck on their way to the nearest trolley bus stop on the far side of Thornton Road. When the one with the loudest voice drew level with the open window, she hoisted her bags under one arm, gave Frankie a withering stare and pinched her nostrils tightly between her finger and thumb.

'Mucky, smelly article,' she repeated in a voice rendered comically nasal by the pincer-like grip of her fingers. 'Should be a bloody law against it, if you want *my* opinion.'

Frankie read his comic twice more from cover to cover before he began to look around for something else to do to help pass the time until Buddie got back from the pub. He was growing bored. His humbugs were all stuck together in a sticky lump and there was nothing much for him to do but sit there and wait. There were plenty of pencil stubs in the dashboard compartment, including one that was short and fat and looked as if it might be a copying-ink pencil. If so, all he had to do was wet its pointed end with spit and it would write like a real pen dipped in ink. He thought about drawing a picture of Dan Dare and the Mekon, but had to abandon the idea after rummaging right to the very bottom of the compartment without finding a single scrap of paper that did not look too important to draw pictures on. What he *did* find was quite a fair amount of money, all in coppers. It was typical of Buddie to toss all his spare money in there and just forget about it. In the best room back at Old Ashfield was a folding table with slender carved legs that were inlaid here and there with pieces of mother-of-pearl. It came all the way from Morocco, and its top was a circular plate of brass etched all over with Arabic writing so artistically done that it resembled intricate floral patterns instead of proper written words. That was where Buddie kept his *real* money. The table-top was littered with every manner of coin from little tanners to great thick half-crowns, from shillings to two-bob pieces. There must have been thirty or more three-penny bits, many of them bronze with flat edges, some small and smooth and made of old-fashioned silver, but worth exactly the same

163

amount. There they all were, casually scattered across the table-top like so much chicken feed. As likely as not, Buddie would not even be aware of how much it all amounted to. It seemed to him that his parents must be very wealthy indeed to own a sitting room even better than Aladdin's Cave and a table full of money as well as having Old Ashfield and everything in it, all to themselves.

He fished out four pennies and turned them over and over in his fingers. Only two bore the head of the King. The other two showed a picture of his mother, Queen Victoria, who had lived until she was really, really ancient. When she dropped dead in her palace, everyone in the country had either been invited to her funeral or been made to wear black arm-bands as a mark of respect. He peered at her profile closely. He rather liked the Old Queen. She looked such a nice lady, with her sad face and droopy eyelids, and he did not think it fair that she had been made to wear black mourning clothes and stop smiling forever, just because her husband had died too early.

He wondered if Buddie would miss the four pennies if they were not returned to the space in the dashboard alongside the other coins. He had remembered that there was a telephone kiosk just around the corner in the next street. He could run there very quickly and, providing he could get the heavily sprung door open, telephone his mam to make sure she was all right. He had only ever telephoned her once before, and then the sound of his voice had made her laugh, and the fact that he had rung her at all made him feel very grown-up and important. He was not supposed to leave the truck without permission, but thought the risk worth taking. He was sure to spot Buddie in plenty of time to get back to the truck and pretend that he had just been stretching his legs for a minute on the pavement nearby.

Only after a struggle did he manage to open the heavy, sprung door of the telephone box. Inside it smelled of urine and stale cigarette smoke because the door was such a tight fit that no fresh air could get in to clear the bad air away. He knew that people got drunk in the town pubs and were often sick in telephone boxes, or the drink confused them into thinking they were in a lavatory. This one was not too bad. Frankie stood on tip-toe until he was at his tallest, lifted the receiver free and inserted his four stolen pennies in the slot. Then he rotated the metal dial, using his strongest middle finger and saying the numbers out loud so he would get them in the correct order.

'Two. Eight. Oh. Four. Seven.'

He heard it ring five times before a loud click told him he was through and a woman's voice rang in his ear. He did not recognize the voice, but he knew every word of the Vera Lynn song that was playing very loudly in the same room.

'Hello? Who is it?'

Frankie was not certain if he should press the button marked with an A and proceed with the call, or press button B and get his money back and forget the whole thing.

'Hello? Hello? Who is it?'

The woman's voice sounded irritable.

A number of people began to shriek with laughter in the background, their voices so loud that the woman who had taken his call had to scream at the very top of her voice for a bit of peace and quiet. Frankie pressed button A but said nothing. He wanted Smallfry to come to the phone. He was worried that strangers were having a rowdy party in Buddie's best room and his poor mam, left in sole charge of the house, was unable to control all the noisy goings-on.

'Well?' the woman yelled into the mouthpiece. 'Cat got your tongue, or what?'

Frankie winced but made no comment. The Vera Lynn song came to an end and was replaced by a record of the Andrews Sisters played just as loudly. He found himself muttering with his hand covering the heavy black bowl of the mouthpiece:

'Please let Smallfry come to the phone. Please let Smallfry come to the phone.'

'Well, I'll be . . . ' the woman began, then broke off to yell right into Frankie's ear: 'Hey, Ethel, come here a minute. You as well, Mary. Come and have a listen to this. By bloody Hell, I reckon we've got one of them cheeky *heavy breathers* ringing us up!'

Frankie did not wait to hear any more. He slammed the receiver back into its cradle and banged the palm of his hand several times against button B, hoping that by some freak chance the big black machine would return his money. When no coins were forthcoming he pushed his way from the kiosk and dashed back to the truck, rounding the corner of the street at such breakneck speed that he was forced to hop awkwardly on one leg in order to maintain his balance. He had only just managed to re-establish himself in the passenger seat of The Duke when his father came dancing around another corner some distance away, body swaying, fingers snapping and feet tapping to a rhythm only he could hear playing away inside his own head. It looked for all the world as if the great Sammy Davis Junior himself had decided to abandon the gaudy tinsel of Hollywood for a chance to try out his talents in the shabby, cobbled streets of down-town Bradford.

'Hiya, cowboy. How're ya doin'?'

'Great, just great,' Frankie beamed. 'How's yourself?'

'Bright as a button, Frankie, my boy. Bright as a big brass button.'

He brought a strong whiff of dark rum and Capstan Full Strength into the cab with him as he swung lightly into the driver's seat and nudged the noisy engine into life. The big truck lurched forward, protesting loudly. As they rounded the corner, its nearside front wheel mounted the kerb and dropped down again with such force that one of the swill-bin lids fell off with a clatter and Frankie had to scramble into the back to retrieve it. Something unspeakable had

166

slopped out of the bin and was seeping across the floor of the truck with the swarm of bluebottles in hot pursuit. Frankie rammed the lid home and clambered back into his seat as Buddie went into the second verse of Nellie Lutcher's 'Fine Brown Frame'.

Very soon they were chugging laboriously up Godwin Street towards the markets, the truck tipping backwards at such a steep angle that the bins were gradually shunting down-hill towards the tailboard. Frankie leaned forward in his seat and grabbed the edge of the dashboard to compensate for the feeling of being slowly tipped over, seat and all, into the back of the truck. He grinned out from beneath the rim of his Stetson in time to return Buddie's wink. There was a sudden, sickening jolt as the swill-bins came to rest against the juddering tailboard, and he wondered what horrors were leaking into the road through all the generous gaps in The Duke's rear end.

THIRTEEN

It was shortly after five o'clock when The Duke bounced its full load of bins and buckets down the steep dirt track and through the secluded rear gates of Old Ashfield. A sharp left turn brought them on to the rear drive, where Buddie drove between the yard walls and the turkey-pens with only a couple of feet to spare on either side. At the far end of the drive where the tall, rather narrow iron gate led up the side of Brooke Parker's to the top of Thorpe Street, they turned right and headed down to the pigsties situated on that side of the house. Jack Fish, the big Irishman's brother, was already there. He was perched halfway up a ladder that was propped against the front wall of the bottom sty, and with a narrow trowel he was forcing wet cement between the bricks where the old stuff had crumbled away. Two other men who often came to help with the pigs were also there, lounging around with cigarettes in their mouths and a half-empty beer bottle standing on the wall between them. They both grinned and came forward to help with the unloading.

'Get yourself indoors and let your mam know we're back,' Buddie told Frankie. 'Tell her the liver's probably good for another couple of days but the fish needs a damn good wash and should be cooked today. The other parcel is for Nader. Don't you go getting the two mixed up.'

'OK, Buddie. Do you want me to come back and lend a hand with the bins?'

'Nope. Just get yourself out of your best duds. And don't get fish juices on your waistcoat.'

Before Frankie could think of anything to say that might change his mind, Buddie strode to the rear of the truck and dropped the tail-flap with a crash, turned his back on the bins and reached over his shoulder to grab one of the metal handles. With one mighty heave, the first of the bins was on his back and on its way to the boilers. Frankie noticed with some satisfaction that the helpers took hold of a handle each and carried only a single bin between them. He had never seen a man lift and carry heavy loads the way Buddie was able to do. Short as he was compared to all the men who worked for him, he could put every last one of them to shame when it came to pulling his weight around the small-holding.

Frankie grinned and made his way backwards up the slope so that he could watch Buddie man-handle another bin from truck to boiler. It had been a good day. Father and son had attracted attention wherever they went, with people calling out greetings or tipping their hats because they knew Buddie, or just staring after them because they looked so different. In the open market at John Street, Frankie had pushed himself right to the front of a small crowd to stare in wide-eyed amazement while a man removed cataracts from people's eyes with the tip of his tongue. The man was an Indian who sold all sorts of exotic potions and mixtures in mysterious bottles with coloured corks. He had long, big-knuckled hands and a silver bracelet and a dark coat that reached almost to the ground. He seated each of his customers on a rickety, high-backed dining chair, tilted their heads at what seemed a very uncomfortable angle, stretched their eyelids with his long brown fingers and *licked* the blinding cataracts away. Then he spat the cataract into a scrap of white muslin and handed it back to its owner as a memento.

'Marvellous! Bloody marvellous!' The crowd clapped their hands and nodded their heads in agreement.

169

One very old man broke down and cried like a baby because it was the first time he had been able to see clearly in *donkey's years*. Another customer, a Pole who limped and spoke very little English, insisted on handing over a large bundle of money in exchange for his wife's restored vision. And all the time the Indian neither spoke nor smiled, merely put his hands together as if in prayer and bowed his head politely. It was all very dramatic and quite the most entertaining thing anyone had witnessed in the market since *Mad Hannah* had one of her queer turns and charged about turning all the stalls over and ripping all the tarpaulins down. It was such a fascinating event that Frankie had been disappointed when Buddie eventually grabbed him by the collar and dragged him off to view the rows of cat baskets and pigeon cages at the top end of the market.

The best part of the whole day had been when a man Frankie had never seen before pressed ninepence into his hand just for looking so much like a genuine Wild West cowboy. The man wanted to take his photograph there and then, but Buddie said there was no film in his camera and it was all a crafty trick to get folk to go along to his studio and spend a lot of money on pictures. He said the man had no right to try to swindle people like that, and if he thought he was getting his ninepence back he could damn well think again because a gift was a gift and now it belonged to Frankie. It made Frankie feel proud when his father got niggly in public and spoke out to show everyone how tough he could be. Later on he was allowed to wander by himself from stall to stall, looking for something to spend his money on. It took him a long time to find the thing he really wanted, but eventually he handed over his coins and became the proud owner of a rainbow-coloured pencil and a crisp, new, shiny red exercise book with the times-tables neatly printed in black letters across the back cover. Here was the perfect finishing touch to a great

170

day. From the instant he took possession of that book, the dreaded eleven-plus examinations, still a whole year away, loomed less significantly on the horizon of his life.

Now the Saturday swill-round was over, but he knew the thrill of it would remain with him for as long as he could recall the day's events and relive them in his imagination. As he strode towards the rear yard with his burden of parcels held away from his body to prevent drips from staining his clothes, he watched his shadow marching along the wall beside him, keeping pace like a ghostly companion. The bright red exercise book, rolled into a neat tube and held in place by one of Buddie's thick rubber bands, jutted from his back pocket like the handle of a six-shooter. Billy the Kid might well have carried his pistol at such an angle to fool people into thinking he was unarmed. That way he could have walked right up to his enemy and shot him dead when he least expected it. The rolled-up book made a good-looking gun for his shadow, and the turned-down wellingtons into which his pant-legs were stuffed might well have been mistaken for the same fancy cowboy boots worn by the mysterious masked hero in *The vengeance of Jake Brody*.

His arms ached and his wellingtons had rubbed blisters on his heels, but he was feeling quite pleased with himself when he strode through the rear gate and down the back yard. A surreptitious glance as he passed the window told him that Smallfry was sitting in her usual chair, her china tea-cup and saucer close at hand and her head bent over the pages of a magazine spread open on the table in front of her. She had forbidden him to look through the kitchen window because she hated to be stared at and spied on, but when he was wearing his Stetson he could manage a swift squint without her even noticing. At the bottom of the yard he stopped and lifted one knee to help support his parcels while he knocked at the door with his free hand. There was no answer. He knocked again, this time a little louder, and cocked his head to one side, listening.

'Yes?'

'It's me, Smallfry,' he called out. 'It's Frankie.'

'You may come in.'

Something in her tone warned him that all was not well, some subtle nuance hinting at tight lips and set features. His heart sank. She was not in a good mood.

There was no sign of either the glossy magazine or the pretty china tea-cup and saucer when he entered the kitchen and closed the door quietly behind him. The table was completely clear and his mother was just sitting there, her hands folded in her lap and her eyes staring into space. He must have done something bad, because she seemed to be trying very hard not to be cross.

Nader got to her feet and sniffed the air, then started to wag her tail and drool at the mouth as she tugged at the length of rope holding her fast in the alcove by the stove. He could tell by her urgent whining that she had not been fed all day.

'Over-feeding makes a working animal fat and lazy,' Buddie had often told him. 'Keep 'em lean, hungry and alert, that's the only way to rear a decent dog. Lean, hungry and alert.'

Nader was certainly all those things. She was ravenously hungry most of the time and so lean her ribs were showing and so alert to the presence of food that she could sniff out an egg before it was even out of its shell. He felt sorry for her because the strong aroma of fish-bits and raw liver would probably drive her to distraction before her once-a-day meal was cooked and ready to eat.

His mother moved her eyes to fix him with a chilly stare.

'That smells disgusting. What is it?'

He dared to place the parcels on the kitchen table without asking permission, glad to be relieved of their weight

and the possibility of staining his clothes with blood or
fish-juices.

'Liver and fish for us, fish heads and skins for Nader,
and a pound of best beef dripping from Mr Hahn,' Frankie
told her. 'Buddie says our fish has to be cooked straight
away because it's going off and won't be fit to eat by
tomorrow.'

'Oh, is that so? I'm just expected to drop everything, am
I? I'm supposed to jump to attention and start cooking this
load of stinking rubbish, am I?'

' . . . er no, Smallfry. I mean . . . er . . . Buddie said I was
to tell you . . . '

'Well in with him today, are you?' she asked with a smile
that was cruel and not at all nice. 'Thick as thieves, are you?
Best of friends?'

Suddenly he knew without doubt that he was in serious
trouble. He could tell by the way she spoke to him, with
her lip curling up at one side and her voice strident with
derision. The chill of her sarcasm stung him like a slap in
the face. He must have done something wrong and now she
would have to work herself up into the right frame of mind
to punish him for it.

' . . . er . . . no, Smallfry,' he offered.

'Oh, no? Come off it, you *liar*. You've been out with him
all day. *All day! And* he let you wear your *full* cowboy
outfit. Thick as bloody thieves, that's what you are. And
I don't suppose either of you gave so much as a *thought* for
me, stuck here by myself all day with nothing to do and
nobody to talk to?'

He chewed his bottom lip. His scalp was pulling itself
tight over his skull and a feeling like sweat was beginning
to tickle his armpits. He remembered the telephone call,
the strange voices, the laughter and the loud music. She
had been alone in the house all day, so he must have dialled
the wrong number, after all. If only he had not made that
mistake. If only he could have spoken to her and told her

173

about the beef dripping from Mr Hahn, just to stop her from getting lonely and upset. It was all his fault. He should have been more careful.

'I'm s-sorry, Smallfry,' he began, not knowing what else to say.

'Sorry? *Sorry?* You bloody-well *should* be sorry, you self-ish, ungrateful . . . ' Here she paused dramatically, staring at the rectangle of tiles surrounding the feet of the stove. 'What the . . . ? What on *earth* is this? Who left this . . . this *thing* in my kitchen?'

Her gaze had come to rest on the small pile of dirty clothes Frankie had left on the hearth that morning. It was only a few feet away from her chair, yet she was obviously seeing it for the first time. Incredible as it seemed, the shabby pile had remained on the hearth the entire day without coming to her notice until that very moment. Frowning and touching her cheeks with her fingertips, she nudged it with her foot, then started nervously as if half expecting something hidden inside it to jump out and attack her. She nudged it again, then turned to Frankie with a bewildered expression and asked:

'Frankie? Do you know anything about this?'

'Y-Yes, Smallfry.' He swallowed hard and felt a sudden urge to empty his bladder. He had dropped into one of those nightmare situations where every word he uttered would be like taking a step through a minefield, fraught with unimaginable danger. 'It's my d-dirty w-washing.'

'Your what?' she asked, blinking rapidly, clearly puzzled.

'My d-dirty washing, Smallfry. B-Buddie said I was to . . . '

'*Dirty washing?*' she echoed, her eyes beginning to widen in amazement. 'Dirty washing? But what do you mean? I'm afraid I don't understand. Why is it here?'

The nervous stammer hooked itself around his tongue so that each word of his reply came out fragmented.

'F-For . . . f-for . . . w-washing, S-Smallfry.'

'*For washing?*'

'Yes, S-Smallfry.'

'Whatever do you mean, child? For washing? For washing by *whom?*'

He swallowed again, dreading the sound of the words
he knew he must say.

'Y-You, S-Smallfry,' he muttered.

'Me? *Me?*'

'Y-Yes, S-Smallfry.'

The expression on her face told him that the awful truth
of the matter was only now beginning to dawn on her. She
seemed shocked, then disbelieving, then mortified and,
finally, very angry.

'How dare you?' she demanded in a strangled whisper.
'How *dare* you?'

'I-I'm s-sorry . . . I . . . '

'How *dare* you treat me like a common lackey? What
right have you to bring your filthy laundry down here
and simply dump it on the hearth for *me* . . . *me* to attend
to?'

'B-But B-Buddie s-said . . . I mean . . . I th-thought . . . '

'I know what you *thought*, you ungrateful little swine.
You thought you could just leave it where it fell and I, the
servant, the slave, the common bloody housewife, would
come along and wait on you *hand and foot.*'

'N-No, I d-didn't . . . it wasn't like that . . . I . . . '

He broke off in terror as she began to rise from her chair
and move towards him, her lips twisted into a snarl and
her hands reaching out like painted talons. The force of
her anger seemed to suck all the air from the room so
there was nothing left for him to breathe.

'What do *you* do in this house?' she demanded, looming
over him. 'Do you contribute anything? Do you pay your
way? Answer me, damn you! Do you earn your keep?'

He shook his head, flinching.

'N-No, S-Smallfry.'

175

'No! *No!* You just sponge off the rest of us, yet you seem to think you're entitled to everything for free, including a personal valet service. And who the hell has to do the donkey-work around here?' She pointed to her own chest, her face ugly with fury. '*Me,*' she screamed in his face. '*Me!* Day in and day out I work my fingers to the bone for you, and what thanks do I get? *Nothing!* I'm expected to cook meals, wash, sew, clean, do all the shopping by myself, run this enormous house, help with the livestock, see to everyone else's needs, and all for what? For *what?* For *what?*'

'I-I d-don't k-know, S-Smallfry.'

She kicked out at the little pile of clothes, sending shirt, socks and pants flying across the room. Then she grabbed Frankie by the shoulder and dragged him towards her. She stooped to spit words into his face, poking him savagely in the chest with her knuckles and yanking him back to the same spot each time her blows drove him backwards and away from her.

'*You* pay for *nothing* in this house,' she reminded him, with a jab of her bent knuckle to emphasize every word. 'You are nothing more than a *parasite*, a lousy little *sponger*, do you hear me?'

'Y-Yes, Smallfry.' Pain and fright brought hot tears flooding down his cheeks. He had begun to twitch so badly that he feared he might wet his pants.

'What are you? What are you?'

'A s-sponger, S-Smallfry.'

'What? *What* did I say?'

'I'm a p-parasite . . . and a l-lousy l-little s-sponger,' he sobbed.

'That's right, and I'll tell you something else, *sponger.*'

She grabbed him by the shoulder and pulled him closer, then jabbed his chest over and over as she told him in a cold, sneering voice:

'*You* are entitled to *nothing.*'

176

'N-No, S-Smallfry.'

'Do you hear me? Do you hear me, you snivelling little brat? *You are entitled to nothing!*'

She shoved him away from her so abruptly that he lost his balance and fell to the floor with a thud that forced the air from his lungs and made his senses reel. For a while he could do no more than sit there, winded and weeping and clutching his bruised chest.

'*Get up!*' she screamed. 'Get up on your feet and stop that bloody snivelling. Just look at you! All dressed up like a stupid cowboy and whimpering and whining like a big soft sissy. You *disgust* me! You *sicken* me! You make me want to *vomit*, do you know that?'

He nodded miserably. Each breath he took became a ragged sob and he could not prevent the crying noises from escaping his throat. Suddenly his mother issued a long, tortured sigh, staggered across the room and sank back into her chair with her arms thrown out across the table and her eyes closed. Slowly, her shoulders sagged and her head fell forward as if she had collapsed in a faint. She remained in that position for so long that Frankie began to fear he had made her ill. He wanted to run for his dad but did not dare move a muscle in case it made her mad all over again. When at last she raised her head it was to issue another long sigh and pass a hand across her brow the way poor Rita Hayworth had done in the scene where she was brutally questioned by the Gestapo to the point of mental and physical collapse.

'I'm v-very s-sorry,' he sobbed, desperate to make amends. 'I d-didn't m-mean t-to upset y-you . . . '

'Just go away,' she replied in a tired voice. 'Get out of my sight and take those filthy rags with you. Go on, get out of my sight.'

Still weeping noisily, Frankie scooped up his scattered clothes and made for the door.

'Just a moment, *you!*'

He stopped and turned, his face caught in a violent spasm of twitching that drew one shoulder up close to his ear and caused his lower lip to quiver.

'What is that thing sticking out of your back pocket.'

'M-My b-book,' he stammered.

'Book? Book? What book? Let me see.'

He pulled it from his pocket and handed it to her. She removed the rubber band, examined the rainbow-coloured pencil, opened the book and flicked her thumb nail over the clean, neatly ruled pages.

'Where did you get this?' she demanded.

'F-From the m-market,' he said, the words broken by sobs. 'A m-man g-gave me n-ninepence . . . Buddie s-said I c-could b-buy anything I w-wanted. It's f-for s-school . . . it's . . . '

He watched, dismayed, as she lifted the lid of the stove and dropped the book and pencil into the flames.

'Let the school provide its own books,' she said, and dismissed him from her presence with an elegant wave of her fingers.

He left the room clutching his dirty laundry against his chest and weeping with great, noisy sobs that refused to come under his control. It was all his fault. She could not possibly have guessed how much the book had meant to him. He had done it again. He had upset his mam so much that she had gone into one of her rages and now he would not be able to learn his times-tables, after all. He had done the wrong thing that morning with his dirty clothes, but he did not know what else he could have done when Buddie told him to bring his laundry downstairs. Perhaps he should have *asked* her. Perhaps he should have shown her the shirt and socks and pants and said:

'Please, Smallfry, please will you wash these for me?'

Instead he had dropped them by the fireplace in a minor panic and left them there, and by doing that he had insulted her and made her feel like a servant. That

178

was an unforgivable thing to do to someone special, like his mam. It was too late, now, to think about what he *should* have done, and what made it even worse was that he would have to get dressed in the same dirty, creased-up things again because he had nothing else to wear. His father was sure to get mad about that and start calling him names for being so scruffy and not knowing when it was time to put on something clean and decent. He sometimes despaired of ever learning to please his parents both together instead of dithering between the two, knowing he could not hope to remain on good terms with both.

He changed his clothes on the steps and returned his cowboy outfit to the chest in the playroom, making sure that everything was properly folded and placed so that it would neither get creased when the lid was lowered nor crush the things already stored in the box. Then he went upstairs and climbed on to the windowsill in his room, wrapping the blackout curtain around him.

'I needed that book,' he told Mr Ted. 'I really needed that book.'

He remained in that spot, staring out into the trees until the light began to fade away and rob them of their colour. It was a long time before his father's voice boomed out to shatter the silence in which he crouched.

'*Frankie!* Get the hell down here, *at the double!*'

With a cry of alarm he jumped down from the windowsill and stuffed his teddy back under the bed. Buddie sounded blazing mad. Smallfry must have told him that Frankie was in disgrace again and had been twitching his face and snivelling like a big sissy. He tried to rub the twitches away from his eyes as he scuttled along the corridor and down the main staircase. Buddie was standing in the open doorway of the playroom, holding the blue denim pants and the cattle-man's shirt and the soft leather waistcoat in his hand.

179

'What the hell is this supposed to be,' he demanded.

'Er . . . I d-don't know, B-Buddie.'

'You ungrateful little bastard. You know damn well I don't expect you to put your suit away in this state. *Fold it*, lazy-bones. Don't just roll it up and stuff it in the box like it doesn't mean anything. *Fold it!*'

'B-But I d-did,' Frankie protested. 'Honest, I *d-did* . . .'

'Don't you dare lie to me, boy,' his father growled.

'B-But B-Buddie, I really d-did, I . . .'

At that moment Smallfry appeared from the best room. She was smiling. The rage had passed, leaving her face soft again and beautiful. She stroked Frankie's untidy hair very gently and began to ease him towards her until his face was pressed against her side and he could feel the warmth of her body through the fabric of her skirt.

'Don't bully the boy, Buddie,' she said in a sweet voice. 'After all, he's only nine years old. Surely he can't be expected to remember *every* important thing you tell him? And you know it makes him nervous when you bully him, and when he's nervous he tells silly little fibs in the hope of avoiding trouble.'

'B-But S-Smallfry, it's true, I *did* fold my cowboy outfit. I *did*, I *did!*' Frankie persisted.

Buddie growled once more and raised his fist as if to strike his son. 'What the hell, boy, if you dare lie to me again . . .'

'Now, now, my dear,' Smallfry interceded softly. 'You mustn't let a small thing like this ruin your entire day. Come now, Frankie, apologize to your father for telling fibs.'

'But Smallf . . .'

Her smile did not falter, but her fingernails suddenly bit into his scalp like sharp spikes, silencing his protests.

'Hush now, my dear,' she cooed. 'You are not in trouble, so you don't need to tell any more childish untruths. You know perfectly well how much we hate and despise liars.

Now, apologize to your father and we'll forget all about it, *just this once.*'

Frankie looked from Buddie's furious face to the crumpled garments so recently stored away in a neatly folded pile. There had been a mistake, a terrible, unfair mistake.

'I-I'm S-sorry, B-Buddie,' he stuttered, defeated by the injustice of the situation.

'Yeah, sure,' his father sneered. 'Trust you to go and spoil yourself, *Mammy's Boy.* Now get back in that room and put those things away *properly.*'

It was a long time before he dared venture along the corridor to the kitchen door for his evening meal. There was a strong scent of fish in the room, not the sharp, pungent stink of the parcels but the appetizing aroma of haddock and cod and finny haddock fried in batter and deep fat. Smallfry responded in friendly tones to his soft knock at the kitchen door, but as he entered the room Buddie looked up from his newspaper and scowled darkly.

'What's all this I hear about you not wanting anything to eat?'

Dismayed, Frankie glanced at his mother. She had wrapped a towel around her hair to keep the fatty smells away, and she was smiling and humming to herself as she piled portions of fried fish on to a big plate and placed it in the oven to keep hot.

'Oh, he's feeling just a wee bit out of sorts,' she explained. 'Isn't that so, Frankie? It always upsets his stomach when he has to ride around in the truck all day with those *awful* bins.'

'Is that so? You feeling too queasy to eat your food?'

Frankie lowered his head and nodded miserably.

'Yes, Buddie.'

'How about if your mam makes you up a fish sandwich with lots of butter? Do you think you could manage that?'

181

Frankie brightened immediately, but then Smallfry turned her loving smile on him and said:

'Oh yes, Frankie. Why not try a nice fish sandwich? Oh *do* try to eat something, my dear, if only to please *me*. You know how I worry when you go to bed without a good meal inside you. Will you try your best to eat a fish sandwich? Will you, dear, just to please me?'

At that moment he would have given anything to be able to nod his head and claim his share of the fish. By now he had finished all his sticky humbugs, and had eaten nothing else since his tripe and flat-cake lunch at noon. That had been more than six hours ago, but no matter how hungry he now was, he was alert to the subtle changes in his mam's voice and he knew her eyes and he knew that particular sweetness in her smile. If he said the wrong thing now, she would hold it against him until later, when he could be punished properly, in private.

'No, th-thank you,' he said. 'I'm n-not hungry.'

He could tell by the look on her face that he had said the right thing. She had no reason to be angry with him any more.

'Suit yourself, boy,' Buddie snapped, exasperation evident in his voice. 'But no meal, no cocoa, that understood?'

'Yes, Buddie.'

'And don't think you'll be coming out with me again in a hurry, not if it turns your stomach so much it puts you off your food.'

'No, Buddie.'

'There's many a kid would give *anything* to be in your shoes, and yet you're so damn short on gratitude that you can turn your nose up at good, wholesome food, just because travelling makes you queasy.'

'Yes, B-Buddie.' His voice had faded to an unhappy whisper.

'Christ, but you're a soft kid. Shit soft. Shit bloody soft! When the hell are you going to start growing up, eh? When are you going to cut loose from your mam's apron strings and start acting like the kind of son a man can be *proud* of?'

Frankie hung his head in shame and muttered:

'I d-don't know, B-Buddie.'

'You're a big disappointment to me, boy,' Buddie sighed in exasperation. 'A *big* disappointment.'

'I'm s-sorry . . .'

'Yeah, sure. Well, there's not much point in you hanging round here while we're eating. Better get yourself an early night, and for Christ's sake, boy, *quit that damn twitching!*'

FOURTEEN

It was late when he heard them leave the house. Smallfry's high-heeled shoes made a crisp, sharp sound as she crossed the tiled hall and stepped out on to the dark terrace. The big key turned in the lock, then two shapes moved along the terrace, their progress marked by the beam of a torch and the echoes of their footsteps overlapping. In the distance a man laughed heartily and a woman's voice responded with lady-like amusement. A moment later the engine of the little green jeep coughed into life and roared briefly before fading away into the distance beyond the main gates. Frankie screwed up his eyes and pressed his cheek against the window, willing his ears to become super-sensitive like those of the old blind man who had heard the deadly spiders coming to get him in *Terror by Night*. But the jeep was gone. All he could hear was the rustling of a breeze in the trees outside his window, and the creaks and groans and sighs ever-present in the big old house when darkness came.

Frankie shivered. He was wearing his bomber jacket over his crumpled shirt and pants, but his feet were bare and beginning to feel the chill, and a knife-edge draught slashed across his neck and right ear from a gap in the wood down one side of the window frame. He was cold and hungry, and he was beginning to fret about the best way of keeping Mr Ted safe now there was a fifty-fifty chance he had been spotted. Buddie might decide to tell Smallfry, especially now he was in such a bad mood, and then Smallfry would be furious because she had ordered the bear to be thrown on the bonfire and burned. It had happened a long time ago, but she was sure to remember the incident as if it were only yesterday. Smallfry never forgot a bad thing done against her. She believed in an eye for an eye and a tooth for a tooth, just like it said in the Holy Bible, so she made it her business to remember *everything*, from big lie to little fib, from the greatest transgression right down to the tiniest slip-up. Sometimes she even accused Frankie of evils he could not recall doing, and then he would deserve extra punishments because upsetting his mam was no trivial thing to be so easily dismissed from his mind. And this time his offence was *really* serious. He had defied his mam and then lied to her, knowing full well that she despised liars as worse than thieves because you could always cure a thief by chopping off his fingers but you could never get to the bottom of a liar. He had kept Mr Ted from being burned on the fire and then hidden him away for months and months in his room. She might even decide that such an offence was wicked enough to be counted in *days*, with a punishment for every single one of those days until the debt was repaid in full. And at the end of it all he would lose the friend he had risked so much to protect. With his mind's eye he saw again the bright red exercise book and the rainbow-coloured pencil swallowed up by the flames, and he knew that part of him would die for ever and never come alive again if she put Mr Ted in the stove.

'Once nine is nine. Two nines are eighteen. Please, God, don't let Buddie tell on Mr Ted. Three nines are twenty-seven. Four nines are . . . thirty-six. Don't let Buddie tell. Don't let Buddie tell.'

He shivered again and lifted aside the blackout blanket so he could stare back into the darkened room. If he screwed up his eyes and looked really hard he could just make out the hulk of the bed and the humped shapes of old furniture stacked in corners. The wardrobe loomed into view against the far wall. It seemed to swell and become more substantial as he watched, and although he told himself it was only his eyes becoming more accustomed to the dark, the impression of increasing size made him nervous. The house was ominously quiet. He tried his best to work out how long he had been crouching there on the windowsill, but in the end he had to abandon his calculations and settle instead for the certain knowledge that it was very late. It was a pity about his watch, his big, gold-plated watch with the loud tick and the sweeping second hand. It had been a fine watch and a perfect time-keeper in spite of all the scratches on its face. He had kept it pinned to the inside of his pocket with a big safety pin, partly because the damaged leather strap would not fasten around his wrist, but mainly because he could not risk being caught in possession of such a splendid object.

'Oh, I wish I still had my watch,' he sighed. 'I wish I had my watch so I could know what time it is and be better than Wally Watmough because his dad won't buy him one.'

There had been a party at the house and some of the guests had done too much dancing and drinking and then tried to use the Tarzan swing when it was much too dark to see what they were doing. Buddie's swing was perfect because he was the Champ and could have done it just as well with his eyes shut, but the others came to grief when they tried to follow his example. Tom Fish's brother burned all the skin off his hands and fingers because he was too drunk to hold the rope tightly enough. He bounced and slithered down the hillside and eventually came to rest in a bloody heap amongst the rubbish near the bottom wall. Blossom's friend had been even more unlucky. He was one of those different types of black men who lived in Bradford but had never been to America. He was not like any of the others. He had a peculiar way of dancing, and nobody could understand a word he was saying because he came from a place called Jamaica in the West Indies and spoke with a funny accent. He had been drinking a mixture of dark rum and white wine when he tried to be Tarzan in the darkness, and Frankie, looking on from a safe hiding place among the trees, had *known* that he was doing it all wrong. A real novice when it came to Tarzan swings, he grabbed the rope too low down, lost his balance completely and crashed *bang smack* into several trees as he hurtled down the pitch-dark hillside like a thrown brick. Buddie and some of the others had needed ropes and tarpaulins to rescue both men, who were then rushed to the Royal Infirmary in the back of the jeep. Jack Fish was allowed home the following afternoon when he was sober, with his hands bandaged, his cuts stitched up and his bruises made even more colourful with a coating of iodine. Blossom's boy-friend had been kept in a special side ward for a long time before some people came to fetch him and he sailed back to Jamaica with one leg still encased in plaster of Paris and two of his front teeth snapped off.

'Daft buggers,' Frankie muttered at the memory. 'I only wish it could have been Tom Fish instead of his brother Jack. And I wish he had hit a tree and landed in the burned-out car-wreck and broken his neck and got blood-poisoning from cutting himself all over on the rusty bits of metal.'

The gold watch had become one of Frankie's most prized possessions from the moment he lifted it out of the dirt on the morning after the accident. He had hoped to keep it forever, but then the police had come around making their enquiries, plain-clothes men whose eyes seemed to be every-where at once. Frankie had got so scared of being arrested and charged with either theft or receiving stolen property that he had rushed down the hillside and tossed the watch into the mouth of the Mucky Beck tunnel. And there it remained, lying somewhere in the filth and slime where nobody would ever dare look for it because of the rats.

Frankie sighed deeply and felt a left-over sob come shud-dering up from his insides. He was hungry. Tomorrow was Sunday, so tonight his parents might stay out late and then make up for it by sleeping in for most of the day. Right now was probably the safest time for him to creep downstairs in search of something to eat. He groped amongst the shadows for his Oxo tin, selected two stubs of candle and struck a match on the bare floorboards by the door. A large part of his room was suddenly bathed in light as the two flames pushed the shadows back into their corners and sent a host of eerie figures dancing over the ceiling. Frankie's own shadow was that of a monstrous hunchback duplicated across two walls. Candlelight was strange, uncertain stuff. It agitated the darkness. It made the shadows beyond its reach seem extra dense and filled with seething, living things. At the same time it served to demonstrate how easily innocent things could be twisted and stretched into fearsome creatures of the night. A candle could be a safe or a scary thing, depending on what was easiest to bear at the time; the solid blackness with its hint of still darker things left unrevealed, or the shifting, flickering shapes so open to misinterpretation.

Tonight Frankie needed the extra light, but that did not mean he was a yellow-belly and a coward. He had often sneaked down to the kitchen, even in the middle of winter, when the nights were so dark he felt he would choke to death on the suffocating blackness. He had even slept in the house all alone for two nights in December when his father was away and his mam had somewhere special to go. Then he had been *really* scared, especially after he heard noises up in the attic, then the Bogeyman's door creak open and shuffling footsteps move along the corridor and down the steps to the kitchen. He had wedged the bit of wood under his bedroom door and not dared open it again until his mam came home, not even to go to the bathroom to do his number two. He had been so hungry it made him ill and so scared he thought he was going to die, but he had known all along that it was not his mam's fault. His other nanny had accidentally let him down by not coming to look after him when she should have done. Word had been sent to her house in Park Road, but later she was very cross and said it was a bloody fairy-tale because no message ever got there, and she *would* have come, if only she had known that Frankie was to be left alone in that big old house for two whole days and nights with the telephone out of order. She had made herself terribly upset about it, and Frankie had been able to forgive her without even trying, because his nanny was a nice lady who had not really *intended* to leave him alone all that time. Smallfry had forgiven her, too, because she told Frankie not to mention a word about it to his father in case he went into a rage and had Nanny locked up by the police for child neglect.

'It's all right. It doesn't matter. I didn't really mind being on my own,' Frankie had insisted, trying to please both his mam and his nanny by making light of the whole thing. And all the time he had been scared that he was damning himself with his own words, because if he really *was* all right in the house alone, nobody would bother about leaving him in future.

This was one of those times when Frankie was nervous again, and though he tried very hard to be brave, he just could not summon up the courage to go groping his way like a blind man through the dark when the kitchen was such a long way from his room. He used both candles to light his way along the corridor, pausing briefly at each door in turn, then hurrying on to the next until he had reached the half-landing. There he left one of the candles carefully balanced on the top step, where its meagre light agitated the shadows and its small flame was reflected in the murky depths of the mirror in the corner. He carried the remaining candle ahead of him as he descended the main staircase, shielding the flame with his cupped hand, comforted by the presence of two extra matches gripped in his teeth and only to be used in case of emergency. He walked slowly, taking care that his school socks, pulled on to keep out the cold, did not cause him to slip and hurt himself on the stone steps. At times he held his breath and felt his heart pounding against his ribs, especially when he passed between the cellar door and the row of coat-hooks in the hall, because then he could not keep his mind from imagining all the horrible things that might be lurking in the folds and crevices beyond the candle's outer limits.

The kitchen was warm. Some small measure of light from the lamp above the turkey-pens seeped across the yard and through the uncovered window to bring the furniture into pale relief. Here and there a small gap in the stove glowed hot crimson with confined heat. Those items of clothing left to hang too long on the chimney-pipes gave out a faint whiff of scorch, like the scraps of towelling Nanny used to wrap up hot bricks in winter-time for warming the boarders' beds. Nader stirred sleepily and tried to clear some irritation from her throat. Frankie hoped she was not going to be sick. His parents would be furious if they returned home after a good night out to find vomit all over the kitchen floor. He could smell fish, especially the strong stuff that had been boiled on the back burner in a tin bucket, heads and tails and fins and all, for Nader's supper. Even that horrid concoction caused his stomach to growl in anticipation of a meal, and as he spoke softly to the dog he was wondering if he dare reheat the fat-pan and fry any fish that was left over from tea-time.

'Easy, Nader. Good girl. There's a good girl. Lie down, Nader. Down, girl. Down.'

The leftovers had all been cooked and stacked on a big plate in the pantry. Frankie set down his candle, found a smaller plate, polished it with the sleeve of his bomber jacket, then proceeded to help himself. He picked bits from here and there in case the larger pieces had been counted, pulled away portions of crispy batter and rolls of skin that had become separated in the pan. There were lots of slices of bread in the crock, brown bread and white just tossed in as if the table had been cleared in a hurry. He selected two slices, one much smaller than the other, and redistributed the remainder so it would not be obvious that the contents of the crock had been disturbed. The only milk he could find was in a single bottle on the stone shelf, so he poured only a small amount into his cup and topped it up to the brim with cold water from the tap. He had already decided to eat his meal in the warm kitchen rather than risk an accident by trying to carry cup, plate and candle back upstairs to his room. His last task before sitting down at the big table was to scrape sufficient butter from the slab to cover his bread generously. He could see Nader's eyes glowing a pinkish silver in the stove's light, watching him, staring at his face as if their owner could see in the dark. He paid her little attention as he tucked into his stolen meal. He was thinking about his middle auntie, the one who spoke with a London accent now that she was courting a genuine Cockney. She had refused to give so much as a penny-piece to the old beggar-woman on Ashgrove who walked the streets all day and slept in dark corners at night.

'God helps them that help themselves,' she had pronounced, tossing her head grandly and pushing her purse right to the bottom of her coat pocket.

He was wondering if the same thing applied to him when he stole food from the kitchen. No matter how often or how deeply he thought about it, he could not figure out if God Almighty was helping him to help himself or looking down from heaven and calling him a rotten little thief.

Boy and dog came alert to the sound of danger at the same instant. There was very little warning; a footfall on rough ground, the rear gate opening, the sound of heavy boots marching purposefully down the yard towards the back door. Nader leaped to her feet and began to growl. Frankie blew out his candle and sat motionless in the semi-darkness, his mouth full of bread and butter and his nostrils filled with the tell-tale scent of hot wax. At the turn of a key the back door opened with a crash and Buddie, muttering loudly under his breath, stamped into the kitchen and then through into the lower corridor without pausing to remove his jacket or boots. He was clearly in a bad temper. The slightest turn of his head would have shown him that Frankie was sitting there at the kitchen table, bold as brass and cheeky as hell, eating a supper of stolen fish and bread and butter. For a moment all Frankie could think about was the baseball accident that had robbed Buddie of nearly all the sight in his left eye so that he could not join the Royal Navy and had to settle instead for the Army or the Merchant Navy, or even the fishing trawlers in Scandinavia. How different Frankie's life might have been if the baseball had fractured the *right* eye-brow instead of the left, or if Buddie had simply flicked on the light as he came indoors. The narrowness of his escape made his head ring and galvanized him into action. He scooped up his plate, cup and candle, slid from the table and hurried into the corridor. By now Buddie was pacing backwards and forwards across the thick carpet in the best room. The lights were turned full on, and just as Frankie drew almost level with the door, the big angry voice began to bellow into the mouthpiece of the telephone in a way that caused Nader to whine in alarm before curling herself up in her corner in absolute silence.

'Well, where the hell is she? She was supposed to be visiting her mother while I did that job for Norman Slater at Thorpe Edge and then went on to do a few deliveries. I got back early because the damn jeep broke down in a back street at Clayton Heights. No, she didn't. Her mother hasn't seen her for *weeks*. Jesus Christ, if I don't get that damn load shifted before somebody spots it . . . '

Buddie paused to draw heavily on his cigarette. He exhaled with a long hiss through his teeth before saying:

'All right, you do that. There'll be the Devil to pay if I don't get that load shifted.'

Frankie's heart thumped as he crept past the door and back up the main staircase, keeping well over towards the far wall so that he would not be visible if Buddie turned his head. He hoped his mam was safe. He would never forgive Buddie if she had been allowed to get lost out there on the dark streets where bad things might happen to her. At the top of the stairs he snuffed out the second candle and crept to the angle near the attic door, from where he could see and hear what was going on downstairs.

Buddie made two more telephone calls, each of which made him shout even louder and grow more and more angry. Frankie bent his head against the banister rails, unable to make much sense of what was happening until he overheard the words:

'All right, you can send someone round for him first thing in the morning. I want him out of the way as soon as possible.'

He felt the colour drain from his face and an icy chill suddenly attach itself to his spine.

'Sure, sure,' Buddie said impatiently. 'He can pack his bag before breakfast. Come for him whenever you're ready.'

Frankie's supper began to congeal into a painful lump in his gut. Buddie was talking about *him*, about packing his bags and sending him away. This was *it*. Somebody was coming to fetch him in the morning. The worst was about to happen, just as Smallfry always threatened it would. *They were sending him away!*

He sat on the steps for a long time after the door of the best room had been shut on his father's anger. He was quite calm. He did not even cry when the words kept coming back into his mind as if they were being shouted at him over and over again by a voice so loud it made him flinch. He just sat there hugging his arms across his legs, one cheek resting on his bent knees, rocking to and fro in the darkness, staring at the sliver of light that was always visible under the Bogeyman's door.

Frankie had never actually *seen* the Bogeyman, but he knew it was there. One night he had been sitting in the dark on the half-landing when he heard it scratching to unfasten the bolts on the inside of its door. He had seen its hideous, skeletal shadow on the wall as the door opened, and he had raced downstairs and out through the front door in a panic. What had puzzled him, later, was the way the Bogeyman had acted as if it, too, had been startled. Its door had shut with a loud crash and the bolts had been rammed into place and a key turned in the lock. It was almost as if it was afraid of being caught in the open, even at night. One of his aunties had laughed at his fears and told him his 'Bogeyman' was just a sick, emaciated old Polish refugee who did not speak English and was terrified of strangers and spent all his time brooding in private since his family was butchered during the war. She said he was a harmless recluse who deserved more sympathy than he was getting, but Frankie knew better. Smallfry had never mentioned a poor, depressed old man with nobody to talk to, but she had often sensed something evil lurking on the top corridor, something that prowled at night in search of the blood of ungrateful little boys. There were nights when she would call him back just as he was on his way up to bed, especially in winter when Buddie was away and the house was so horribly cold and forbidding. She would clutch at him with both hands and stare up at the ceiling, listening, and she would plead with him to be extra careful up there. There were even times when she feared for his life and her feelings of menace and impending death were so powerful that he became rooted to the spot, too terrified to put one foot in front of the other.

'My God, it's loose,' she would say in a frightened voice, 'The Thing is loose.' And she would tremble and her eyes would go all wide and glassy, and when she saw how terrified he was she would make him sleep in her bed, and that always made him feel relieved but guilty in the eyes of God, both at the same time.

He hugged his knees, shivering even as a flush crept over his cheeks and down around his ears. He was halfway

194

convinced that it was a mortal sin to sleep in his mam's bed. He always said his prayers afterwards and begged God to forgive him for thinking evil things. He wanted to touch her when her nightdress came open accidentally and her breasts fell out with the ends so pink and stiff and rough that he could not keep from staring at them. He had seen the way the hair grew in a neat brown triangle between her legs and that, too, made him feel like a sinner who should go straight to Hell and burn there for all eternity. He was no better than dirty Tom Fish when he had to sleep in his mam's bed. It shamed him to remember all the times he had got those pictures in his mind of climbing on top of her and grunting and wiggling his bum the way the Irishman had done. His mam's bed was soft and clean and warm and sweet-smelling, with smooth white sheets and pillows that his head sank right into, and covers that were silky and soft and kept him warm the whole night. It was a beautiful bed, but he always prayed to God to make him brave, or to take the Bogeyman away so that he would never be forced to sleep in his mam's bed ever again.

It was a long time before he left the dark corner and tip-toed to his room with his legs stiff with cramp and his feet turned icy cold from sitting too long in one spot on the draughty linoleum. He curled up fully clothed beneath the army greatcoat and pulled the stiff woollen collar over his head. His body was weary right to the bone and his thoughts were an untidy jumble scattered about the inside of his head. He wondered if he would be allowed to keep Mr Ted with him in a Children's Home. He did not think so. One of the criminals and perverts might steal him and rip him into little pieces, or cut him up and eat him for breakfast because the people in Homes were sick in their minds and were allowed to do terrible things to each other. He knew all about the horrors of the Homes. Smallfry had warned him of the dangers, time and time again, in her efforts to keep him from going there. And now Frankie had proved himself undeserving of her protection. He had failed her. He had let her down. He was being sent away to a Children's Home, after all.

As he began to doze he seemed to hear people arguing and slamming doors, but he thought they might be part of his dreams along with the screaming, insane people and the instruments of torture locked away inside the prison-like building that would soon become his home. Even in sleep he twitched like a puppet on jerky strings, or started up suddenly as if a hand had pinched him or jabbed a pin into his flesh while he slept. And each time the noises disturbed him he mumbled in an urgent whisper:

'Please don't let it be my fault. Please God, don't let it be my fault.'

Morning woke him with a sense of dread. He thought he heard his nanny's voice, shrill and very loud, and his father's thunderous response. Someone was moaning, 'Oh, stop it, stop it, *stop it!*' He heard a slap and a loud cry followed by a series of wailing sobs. Then a door slammed and the voices became muffled and distant. For several minutes Frankie lay quite still in his warm cocoon beneath the army greatcoat, his knees drawn up to his chest and Mr Ted clutched protectively against his belly. In the night he had been troubled by dreams, noisy, scary dreams in which a man yelled at the top of his voice and a woman wept as if in pain or desperately upset. Part of him had wanted to creep out to the curve of the banister to see if the commotion was real or imaginary, but his room had been chilly and dark and his body so weary that the bigger part of him just wanted to drift away from the intrusion. He had opened his eyes several times in the darkness to find apprehension plucking at the edges of his consciousness, but on each occasion sheer exhaustion had been like a lead weight pulling him down and down until he slept again.

196

Now it was full daylight and Frankie was wide awake with his instincts warning him that there was trouble in the house.

'Smallfry!'

He spoke her name out loud as a wave of foreboding swept over him. It occurred to him that he had not really been dreaming at all, and that the anguished voice crying out in the small hours had belonged to *her*. While he had spent the whole night curled up in selfish comfort, his poor mam had been downstairs, weeping and sobbing because something terrible had happened. She might be hurt or in trouble, or distraught because of Buddie's decision to send her boy, her only son, away to a Children's Home.

He threw back his army greatcoat and scrambled out of bed, wiggled the makeshift door-stop from the gap beneath the door, then crept to the curve of the banister and peered down at the rooms on the ground floor. The kitchen door was not properly closed. He could see the hot, red mouth of the stove gaping open so that its fiery breath could fill the room with warmth, and the cloud of steam drifting up from the kettle left simmering on one of the gas burners. Nader was barking, her voice still so hoarse that no stranger, hearing it for the first time, would ever suspect it belonged to such a big animal. A moment later the back door was thrown open and the Great Dane raced off, still rasping, to relieve herself after too many hours spent chained to the kitchen water-pipe.

Frankie eased his face through the banister-rails. He could see his mam's mustard-coloured swing-backed coat slung carelessly over the seat of a chair, one sleeve trailing on the dirty floor and the brooch shaped like a big bunch of fruit pushed awkwardly against the hard wood. One of her patent leather shoes was lying on the floor on its side. It was not shiny any more. It looked dirty and scuffed and not like one of *her* shoes at all. He knew something was very wrong. He could hear a woman sobbing and wailing

197

in one of the downstairs rooms. He did not know if it was his mam, but the sound made him feel cold inside.

'Smallfry! Smallfry!'

Crouched on the draughty landing, Frankie worried the end of his thumb until at last his teeth fastened upon a tiny sliver of nail emerging from the ravages of previous gnawings. He tore at the fragment, deliberately dragging it right across his thumb and into the corner so that it really hurt when he yanked it free. His mounting anxiety showed itself in other ways. His lips pursed and then jerked first to one side and then the other. His eyes began to blink more rapidly, opening and closing with such force that his whole face had to screw itself up in order to accommodate the movement. He was scared. He was filled with a sickening fear that his mam, his Smallfry, had met with some kind of misfortune from going out late and coming home alone at night. A woman called Eileen Robertshaw who lived over the Co-op in Little Horton Lane had once done that, and when they found her the next day she had been robbed and battered to death and all her clothes stolen.

'Body of Naked Woman Found in Local Park.'

He recalled the big black headline printed right across the front page of the *Telegraph and Argus* and he remembered how some people said she deserved everything she got and must have been up to no good to get herself attacked and killed like that in a dark place where she had no business being at that time of night.

Then there was Jimmy Akroyd's big sister, Mabel, who got home late one night and received a terrible good hiding from her father when he found out she had been to a dance at the army barracks where only loose women would ever think of going. Mabel had her bags packed and was gone first thing in the morning, and now she lived in a boarding house somewhere in Manchester and Jimmy never heard from her except for a card on his birthday and at Christmas. It was as easy as that. A late night out, a blazing row at home, and someone was gone from the family just as completely as if they had never really belonged. If that was about to happen to his mam, Frankie knew he would find himself locked away in a Children's Home by the time the first birthday card arrived from Manchester.

He blinked violently and struggled to make sense of everything he had heard during the night. It made him feel guilty and sick with dread, yet for Smallfry's sake he hoped and prayed that Buddie had given her a good hiding for being late home. Better that than an accident, or even a *murder*. Buddie would not go so far as to take his big-buckled belt to her. He would never do that to Smallfry, but he might slap her around a few times if he thought she had done something really bad, like putting herself in danger by staying out too late, or dancing with the soldiers at the army barracks. Frankie wiped the back of his hand across his nose and was surprised by the wetness he found there. He was crying. He was frightened for his mam and for himself and he was crying because he did not understand what was going on.

He hated himself for being a cry-baby, even when he reminded himself that he was a lot tougher and braver than some of the boys at school. He was no softy in the playground. Sometimes he got tears in his eyes when something was really painful, like when the big kids from Princeville gave him the Indian burn, or when Wally Watmough nipped his arm, but that did not count, not *really*. Even Buddie had got tears in his eyes that time he ripped his hand open on a faulty rotor blade and had to go to the Infirmary to get it all stitched up and injected, and it was common knowledge that Buddie was tougher than *anyone*. Frankie only ever cried over his mam. He was afraid of her quicksilver moods, afraid of provoking her rage, of upsetting her, letting her down, disgusting her with his faults. And more than anything else in the world he was afraid of losing her. Perhaps Buddie was right to sneer at him and call him '*Mammy's Boy*'. Right now he was snivelling like a big baby when he did not even know what was going on that he should be so worried about. He only knew he felt sick inside, and that he had not felt this bad since the night he sneaked downstairs and opened the door of the best room just a crack and peeked inside to see the Irishman with his pants down doing dirty things to his mam in her bed.

FIFTEEN

Although the house gradually became quiet, an atmosphere remained that was charged with tension. It reminded him of the space between the lightning and the thunder on a wild winter night, when he would count the passing seconds and try to judge if the storm was coming closer or moving away to a safer distance. He was convinced that whatever bad thing had happened in the house was in some way his fault. Whenever there was any kind of friction between his parents, he was the one who shouldered most of the blame. Even when quarrels began over things that had nothing at all to do with him, at some stage or another he would be sucked in and tangled up until he felt personally responsible for it all. Then he would have to be punished, and the more trouble he had caused for his mam, the more she would need to chastise him. And the awful thing was that he never *meant* to do it. He had never dared provoke his mam and dad or back-talk them the way some of his friends did with *their* parents. He always tried his best to do what was right and be grateful for the good life they had given him. He wanted to make up for all the sacrifices Smallfry had been forced to make because of him, and for all the disappointments his father suffered through having a puny kid who was growing too slowly and did not measure up to what a *real* son was supposed to be like. He tried his best, yet still he seemed to do things that made his parents disgusted with him or unhappy with each other. It was not fair. He would never understand why God had made him such a skinny, all-round failure and then handed him over to unique parents who deserved so much better in a son.

He sniffed and wiped the back of his hand across his nostrils. By now the Saturday swill-round, the markets and the cowboy suit were a hundred million light-years away. It was as if the pleasures of yesterday had happened to some other kid instead of him.

'I'm sorry, I'm sorry, I'm sorry,' he muttered. 'I'm really sorry. I'm really *really* sorry.'

His eldest auntie, who was already turned thirty and therefore quite old, was sitting at the kitchen table with her legs placed neatly together and her hands clasped in her lap. She always sat correctly because she was a professional dancer and knew how to avoid bad circulation and varicose veins, and poor posture such as slouching and lolling over on one hip. She was beautiful. She had long, wavy hair that shone like polished coal and the softest, smoothest, prettiest skin the colour of home-made butter toffee. Her eyes were huge and black, with neatly arched brows and long, shiny lashes. She was as stern as a school teacher and very prim and proper in her behaviour, but when she smiled she looked just like Topsie in the American comics who was not born like other kids but *just growed an' growed* as if by magic. She travelled everywhere as a professional dancer, wearing really exotic costumes and performing in places Frankie had never even heard of. On her photographs she looked so lovely she almost took his breath away, but she was sometimes very bossy and acted as if she knew best about *everything*. Frankie suspected she did. She certainly knew all about vitamins and olive oil and natural medicines, and she was so healthy she could practise her steps all day and then go out and dance all night long.

By contrast, his 'Little Auntie' was the youngest and smallest of Buddie's three sisters. She was perched now on a high stool with one leg crossed over the other, chewing gum as she filed her fingernails with a long pointed file. She was Frankie's favourite because she was always making him laugh and sometimes slipped money into his pocket when nobody was looking. Her hair was jet black and as Chinaman-straight as his own, and she could wiggle her hips in time to the music exactly like a real African jungle-dancer. This auntie was tiny and brown and very, very clever because she had been promoted from a star pupil to one of the dancing teachers at Ostap Buriak's famous dancing school in Morley Street.

Their mam, his fat nanny, was standing in front of the gas oven, stirring the porridge-pan with a long wooden spoon and nipping her lips together in a thin, tight line that showed her bad mood. Nobody was speaking. There was an air of vexation in the kitchen that had Nader, who had skulked back indoors in the hope of begging something to eat, cringing in her corner with her flanks twitching and the whites of her eyes showing.

Bent almost double in a crouch, Frankie inched his way along the top corridor and down the seven steps to the half-landing. Then he shuffled on his backside down several of the main steps until he could look through the banister rails into the best room. The door was wide open and he could see one edge of the big, brass-ended bed that was set into the arched alcove. Buddie was sitting at the bottom of the bed, plucking at the strings of his guitar in a way that said his bad temper was still there, simmering quietly away beneath the surface. There was no sign of Smallfry, just a mound of anonymous humps and hillocks beneath the colourful, gold-fringed bed cover. A log fire and a single ornate table-lamp joined forces to cast a rich, burnished glow over everything in the room. It was a wonderful place, with swirls of shiny maroon plaster and strips of ornamental tree-bark on the walls, against which were displayed plates and plaques, paintings, swords, brasses and pewter items. Hanging from the ceiling was an enormous hand-painted paper lantern that came all the way from China and turned in the warm air with an elegant shimmer of silken tassels. From his place on the steps Frankie could see firelight twinkling on the engraved brass inlays of an Oriental cabinet that was taller than himself and had dozens of tiny secret drawers behind doors that locked with fancy brass keys. Here dainty compartments housed gold-coloured dragons and fat brass Buddhas, ebony elephants with tusks of real ivory, carved Javanese dancers with jointed heads and limbs that could be set in different positions. He could also see a cluster of pale ivory that at first glance resembled a chunk of natural coral, except that this was more breathtaking than anything a mere ocean could produce. Frankie had seen it for himself, had stared in wonder at all the perfect, miniature figures of people and animals scrambling around a hillside full of minuscule fruits and flowers. It was a magical carving, because every examination revealed a new face or a different expression, a bird, animal or insect, a bush or a flower freshly discovered. Buddie called it a priceless little piece, but Frankie knew it *must* have a price. He reckoned it was worth at least a million pounds of *anybody's* money.

'My husband and I have a magnificent collection of antiques and curios,' Smallfry liked to inform suitable acquaintances, those who would appreciate such information. 'Together we own items of great value from virtually every country in the world.'

And sometimes she would proudly show off pictures of her dear son, and it would always surprise her when people gasped at the wonderful things to be seen in the backgrounds.

He remembered being made ready one sunny afternoon with his hair neatly brushed and his hands and face scrubbed clean, and being called into the best room to have his photograph taken amongst those wonderful exhibits. It had all been done by a friendly Polish man called Bez who had a studio in Bradford where he did photography for a living. He took pictures of Frankie leaning against the furniture, perching on a sideboard with his hand on a bronze statue of Jonah and the whale, posing in the fireplace with a fancy sword in his hand and dozens of carefully placed objects in the background, sitting cross-legged on the vast dining table with a huge brass bowl held elegantly in his lap. In that one session Bez had taken dozens of pictures from every possible angle, each one meticulously arranged so that it showed a particular part of Buddie's collection to best advantage. It had been a long, difficult afternoon, and Frankie had grown bored with sitting still and keeping his face solemn the way he was supposed to, but the photographs had all turned out to be treasures in themselves. On every single picture Bez had managed to make him resemble a young eastern prince, the son and heir of some exotic Sultan right out of the fabulous Arabian Nights.

He felt a sudden stinging sensation in his eyes as he realized that this might be the very last time in all his life when he was able to look into the colourful Aladdin's Cave that was his parents' best room.

The sound of a knock at the back door caused him to jump back in alarm and brace himself in readiness for a frantic dash to the very top of the house. If this was the man from the Homes come to take him away, Frankie would make sure he was not taken without a fight. Rather than go meekly to his terrible fate, he had made up his mind to grab Mr Ted and his savings and make a desperate bid for freedom via the attics and the roof-spaces leading to one of the empty houses. That was the way the sick young soldier had gone when the police came to search the house, and not even the plain-clothes detectives with their all-seeing eyes had been able to discover where he had been hiding for all those weeks. Frankie had the soldier to thank for his precious army greatcoat. It had fallen unnoticed on to the dark landing during the scuffle to get the man upstairs on the night of his arrival, and eager, opportunist fingers had quietly slid the garment into the nearest bedroom before anyone was even aware that it was missing. Since then it had kept Frankie warm and safe during the longest and coldest winter nights, and in all that time he had not been required to explain to anyone how he had come by it. He was loath to leave it behind, but if he was forced to make a run for it, the cumbersome overcoat would only hold him back and probably lead to his capture. His first priority was to avoid being locked away with perverts and criminals in a Children's Home, and for that he may be forced to make many such sacrifices.

Nanny's voice reached him from the kitchen:

' . . . good of you to come . . . take your coat . . . cup of tea . . . ?'

Frankie relaxed and crept further down the stairs when it became apparent that the tall man who had entered the kitchen was not, after all, the official child-catcher for the Children's Home. The visitor was wearing a dark hat and overcoat and carrying a stout leather bag just like the one Dr Thambi had brought to the house when Frankie was sick after almost drowning himself in the Mucky Beck. This man was also a doctor, only he was an ordinary Englishman, with a grim face and white whiskers and hands that looked as if they would be dry and cold to the touch. He had brought a woman with him. She was dressed in what appeared to be men's shoes and the same kind of long, belted gabardine coat worn by the nit-nurses from the clinic who came periodically to examine all the kids' heads at school. They spoke in whispers, then Nanny led them along the lower corridor, showed them into the best room and closed the door firmly behind them. For a moment she leaned her ear against the wood as if trying to listen to what was being said in the room, then she shook her head irritably and turned away. When she paused to shout up into the dimly lit staircase, the top of her head

206

was almost level with the very step on which Frankie stood. She yelled so loudly that he almost jumped out of his skin and she was so close to him he was amazed she did not see him crouching there in the shadows.

'*Frankie! Frankie!* Get yourself shifted, lazy bones. *Breakfast!*'

She immediately turned on her heels and waddled back towards the kitchen, allowing him time to scramble to the top of the main stairs and call out from the landing:

'I'm coming, Nanny.'

Now he could feel the anxiety building up in his chest and pressing itself against the inside of his ribs. Someone had sent for a strange doctor and he had come to the house with a proper nurse, so the visit must be serious, which meant his mam had been taken badly. It was terrible that on this, of all days, her son was to be taken away from her. The anxiety rose into his throat in a hard ball. He might even find himself trapped in the kitchen when the child-catcher arrived to pluck him bodily from the bosom of his family. He could only hope that at the opening of the rear gate, or at the first small hint of a footfall on the paving stones in the yard, he would have the presence of mind, and the courage, to race for the inner door and make his bid for freedom.

The kitchen door stood open, but still he rapped his knuckles softly against the wood and hesitated before stepping into the room. His eldest auntie moved her head to stare at him for a long, hard moment before closing her eyes and sighing as if she just could not bear to look at him any longer. Still perched on an upright chair with one leg swinging, the other auntie stopped filing her nails and chewing her gum just long enough to roll her eyes upward and give a long, low whistle through her teeth. His nanny turned from the stove and glared at him with her hands fisted on each hip. Her gaze swept over him, taking in his badly crumpled jacket, grubby pants and skinned knees, his wrinkled socks and scuffed shoes, and then his hair, still uncombed, which he guessed was sticking out in all directions. The way she looked him over made him feel ashamed.

'Jesus, Frankie,' she said. 'You look like you were put together by a lunatic. I've seen *scarecrows* better turned out than this.'

'I'm sorry, Nanny,' he offered, trying to smooth the creases from the front of his jacket and praying she would not notice the stains on his school shirt.

'Have you been *sleeping* in those clothes?'

'No, Nanny,' he lied. 'But I forgot to fold them and they got all crumpled in the night.'

She looked him over again, her eyes small and dark and critical, her mouth thin and disapproving. He might have known she would start right off by picking on him. She always did. She could be kind when it suited her, but most of the time she was looking out for faults and hoping to get him and his mam into trouble with Buddie. Smallfry said it was because she hated all little boys just for being boys, and she hated Frankie worst of all because he was good for nothing and far too small and skinny for his age.

'Did you ever see anything like this before in your life?' Nanny demanded of her daughters. 'He looks no better than a bloody tramp off the streets.'

The elegant elder auntie came to his rescue. With a sigh of exasperation she waved him to his seat, her neat black brows arched like bows over her eyes to give her face a permanently bemused expression.

'Just give the boy his porridge, Ma. He can't help the way he looks.'

'Oh me, oh my,' Little Auntie said in a sing-song voice. 'I can just see my sister's face when she gets a look at the state of that jacket she made for him.' She stretched her chewing-gum right out to arm's length before gathering it back into her mouth with a practised movement of her lips. 'I *told* her it was a waste of time and money to send him

208

anything decent. Well, didn't I? Didn't I tell her it was a waste of time?'

'I might have known there'd be a cock-up,' Nanny said. *'Now don't you worry about a thing, Ma*, his father says to me on the phone last night. *I'll have him ready for you first thing in the morning, bag packed and all.* Ready my arse! Just *look* at him! I'm not taking him home with me looking like *that*.'

Frankie crept to his seat and sat perfectly still, staring at the stack of corned beef tins crammed haphazardly into a shopping bag in the corner. He hardly dared breathe. If Buddie had said all that to Nanny on the telephone, he could not possibly have been talking to the authorities at the Children's Home to arrange for Frankie to be locked up. It was all a mistake. Nobody was sending him away forever. He was only going as far as Nanny's house. It had all been a sickening mistake and now everything was going to be all right again. His shoulders sagged as gratitude flooded hotly into his cheeks and caused a tightness to creep right over his scalp. He was so relieved he could have thrown up right there at the breakfast table in front of his nanny and his aunties and he would not have cared one bit, even if it meant getting a good hiding for being disgusting and having no manners.

'Sit up straight, Frankie!'

His eldest auntie snapped the words so sharply they made him start. 'Come on! Head up! Stomach in! Shoulders back! How many times do I have to tell you that slouching is bad for the spine and poor posture stunts the growth?'

'Yes, Auntie.'

She measured him with her big brown eyes and her face seemed to soften a little. 'You'll be staying with us at Nanny's house for a few days until your mam gets better, and if you know what's good for you, young man, you'll keep your head up and your back straight and start paying attention to what your aunties say.'

209

'Yes, Auntie . . . er . . . I won't be going . . . er . . . anywhere else, will I?'

'Anywhere else?' she asked, arching her bowed brows even higher. 'What do you mean by that? Where else were you *expecting* to go?'

' . . . er . . . nowhere . . . I mean . . . I just thought . . . '

His auntie sighed, leaned across the table and looked very deeply into his eyes. She smelled nice, and she had a look on her face that said she was trying her best to be patient with him. When she spoke again she pronounced each word so clearly and precisely that she might have been speaking to a foreigner or a deaf person.

'Young man, you are simply going to stay at your Grandmother's house for a few days while your mother is too poorly to look after you. Do you understand that?'

'Yes, Auntie.'

'And when your mother is feeling better, you will be brought back home. Do you understand *that?*'

'Yes, Auntie. Can I see her? Is she *very* poorly? She won't have to go into hospital, will she?'

Auntie sighed again and closed her eyes. Across the room, her younger sister made a small *huffing* sound down her nose without breaking the twin rhythms of chewing and filing. Nanny set down a huge dish of porridge with a clatter and said:

'She'll be as right as rain, if I know that one. Always manages to fall on her feet, she does. Always has and always will. She has the luck of the devil, if you ask me. The luck of the bloody devil.'

'Is Buddie in a bad mood?'

'Aye, lad, and who the hell can blame him, with that lot in there to contend with and only half the sense he was born with where *she's* concerned?'

'Ma!'

The eldest auntie gave Nanny a warning look while the other wriggled in her seat and began to chuckle quietly to

210

herself. Frankie looked from one to the other and felt bad because they did not seem to care very much that his mam was ill in bed, with Buddie and the doctor and a nurse from Edmund Street Clinic in attendance.

He did not want to think about breakfast. Even his recent reprieve from the Children's Home was far out-weighed by his concern for his mam's safety. The treacle made him feel better. Nanny had made that special thick, creamy porridge with milk cooked inside it and a dash of cinnamon to give it spice and not a single lump anywhere to be found. She had ladled it into a soup plate in big, smooth dollops and now she was sticking a tablespoon in the treacle tin and twisting it round and round until it was too full to hold any more. She held it high above the dish so that the syrup fell off and rushed all over the surface of the porridge in quick, squiggly, golden dribbles. Then she jabbed the spoon at his face so abruptly that, but for his presence of mind, her generosity might have cost him a tooth. On a reflex his mouth shot open to receive the spoon and his throat was filled with a delicious sweetness. She pushed his plate towards him and lifted a big white jug from the top of the stove where it had been standing to keep warm. The milk was hot and bubbly, with melted butter floating on top because that was the way Nanny liked it best.

'Thank you, Nanny.'

He hunched himself over his plate and sank his spoon into the porridge with enthusiasm. He gave not a second thought to his auntie's instructions to sit up straight, nor did he recall for a moment the dark, ridged poison bottle that may or may not be concealed in the big front pocket of Nanny's wrap-over pinny.

There was a big pile of dirty washing in the far corner of the middle kitchen, an untidy mound of clothes and blankets and towels reaching almost as high as the tiny square window where cobwebs grew in woolly grey strands

211

across the glass. Nanny used up a lot of swear-words without putting anything in the box while she knelt on the stone floor with her bottom sticking grandly into the air behind her. Each time she bent forward to rummage elbow-deep in the heap of clothes, Frankie caught sight of her frilled under-slip and baggy cotton knickers. Her stockings were thick and brown, stitched in some places and neatly darned in others. Above their elasticated tops the pale flesh bulged, dappled and blue-veined, unevenly sectioned by bulky rubber suspenders.

'By, bloody hell,' she exclaimed at last, having already used up her extensive store of stronger words. As she huffed and puffed and hoisted herself to her feet with the effort turning her cheeks from pale pink to brightest red, she pronounced again:

'By, bloody *hell!*'

Frankie sat in silence while his shoes were cleaned with black polish and a crumpled shirt was spread across folded towels and pressed with a hot iron until it looked decently laundered. He surrendered his jacket and watched the same old-fashioned flat-iron, heated against the hot coals in the stove, smooth away the night-time creases. Nanny spat on her hands and wiped them down the dark fabric until all the bits of fluff and dog-hairs were removed. Then she made him climb on to the seat of a chair and hang his head over the sink while she doused his hair with cold water before brushing it flat and sleek, with a proper parting on one side. It would not remain so for very long. Sooner or later it would dry into straight, coarse tufts and look just as untidy as ever. This was but a temporary improvement, but at least it left the women satisfied, if only grudgingly so, with his appearance. He was feeling rather pleased with himself by the time Nanny declared him fit to accompany her and her smartly-turned-out daughters to Lansdowne Place.

He was ushered into the playroom to wait while Nanny helped the doctor and his nurse tidy up the sickroom and make the patient more comfortable. It took a long time. There was bedding to change and a white enamel bucket to be emptied and washed out and covered with a clean cloth. Smallfry was a picture of wilting beauty in her best, peach-coloured nightgown when at last he was pushed into the sickroom to see her. He was shocked by her appearance. There were dark rings beneath her eyes and her hair was spread out across the pillows in a wild tangle. She looked terribly ill. He could see she was totally unaware of her surroundings as she turned her face fitfully from side to side, moaning and muttering in her delirium.

'Smallfry?' His voice came out as a whisper. 'Smallfry?'

She responded with a weak moan. Her eyes flickered as if she wanted to open them and look at him, but she simply did not possess the strength to raise her lids. Her right hand lifted towards him, reached out briefly, fingers fluttering in a frail and pretty gesture, only to fall into a collapse and hang, quite still and lifeless, over the edge of the bed.

'Oh, Smallfry . . . '

He heard the door close with a click behind him as his father carried an untouched breakfast tray from the room. At that instant his mother's eyes snapped open.

'Has he gone?' she mouthed.

'Y-Yes, Smallfry . . . ' he stammered, startled.

'The others?'

' . . . er . . . in the kitchen.'

She sat up quite suddenly and grabbed him by the shoulders, her grip so firm and her face so clear that she might not have been poorly at all.

'What have that lot been saying about me?' she demanded. 'Tell me, and I want the *truth*. Quickly now, before your father comes back. What have they been saying about me?'

'They . . . they haven't . . . they haven't said anything, Smallfry.'

'Liar!' she hissed. 'Bloody liar!'

She grabbed the upper lobe of his ear and twisted. He felt tears spring to his eyes as her fingernails bit into his flesh.

'Honest, S-Smallfry. Honest. They d-didn't s-say anything.'

'You're lying!'

'No. N-No. It's the t-truth . . . '

'Swear to God?'

'Yes, S-Smallfry . . . Ouch! I swear. Honest . . . I swear to G-G-God.'

'Why are you all dressed up like that? Where the hell are you going?'

'W-With Nanny,' he stammered.

'Why? What for?' Her eyes were fiery. She looked very angry, and with every word her grip seemed to tighten on the lobe of his ear until his neck was twisted round at a painful angle.

'I'm to s-stay with her for a d-day or two,' he told her, wincing. 'J-Just until you get b-better.'

'And what are you going to tell them, eh? What are you going to tell them about *me*?'

'What? I d-don't know . . . I . . . '

'Well, my lad, you'll tell them nothing, do you hear?'

'Yes . . . I mean . . . no . . . I mean . . . '

'*Nothing! What* will you tell them?'

'Nothing . . . n-nothing . . . honest . . . '

'Not a word! Don't you dare go running to those jealous bitches with nasty lies they can use against me. I want no tale-telling, do you hear me? No lies. If you *dare* cause trouble for me, I'll . . . '

'I won't, Smallfry. I-I won't . . . I swear . . . '

'You'll tell them *nothing*, do you hear me? *Nothing*, or so help me God, I'll make you wish you'd never been *born!*'

At the sound of footsteps in the hall she promptly released her grip on his ear and collapsed back against

214

the pillows in what appeared to be a dead faint. Shocked, he stared down at her closed lids and pale, drawn face, at the limp arms and softly bent fingers. She looked terribly ill. He might have doubted that she had rallied so briefly from her sickbed, were it not for the burning pain in his left ear and the fact that he was still trembling from the force of her sudden anger.

'Did she speak to you, Frankie?'

'... er ... n-no ... I m-mean ... she's asleep, I think ...'

Buddie nudged him towards the door and lowered his voice to a friendly whisper. 'Well, never you mind about that, young fella. She's pretty weak at the moment and doesn't understand what's going on around her, but the doctor says she'll be all right again in a couple of days.'

Frankie looked back as the door began to close on the best room. His mam was lying limply against the pillows with her eyes closed and her hair spread out like a delicate auburn fan. She was very still. One slender arm was hanging over the side of the bed, its fingers pale against a silken fringing of gold, crimson and silver. She reminded him of the doomed Russian Princess on her royal deathbed, fading silently into long-shot as the music swelled and THE END loomed large across the screen at the New Victoria cinema. The comparison frightened him. The possibility that he might lose his mam was a worry that sometimes gave him the most awful nightmares. She was forever warning him that one of these days she would take to her bed and simply pine away of a broken heart until she died. Then everyone would blame themselves and shed buckets of tears and turn out in their thousands in the pouring rain to give her the biggest, finest funeral Bradford had ever seen or was ever likely to see. And Frankie, of course, would have to be put in a Children's Home because his father would only make his life a misery if she were not there to protect him.

215

Frankie cupped his hand over his burning ear and shuffled unhappily into the kitchen. He knew he would have to say his prayers especially hard if he was to prevent his mam from slipping away peacefully in her sleep the way she always feared she would, one of these days.

SIXTEEN

Nanny's house was on the corner of Lansdowne Place and Claremont Terrace, opposite the walled grounds of the church and just a short walk up the road from Edmund Street Clinic. It was a very large house, with steps up to the front door and a hidden back yard that led out through narrow passageways to a row of shops and warehouses in Morley Street. There were big rooms on either side of the hall, and at the far end of the corridor four steps led down into a huge kitchen with several doors leading off to other rooms. Here an enormous, black-iron cooking range did everything from heating the water to airing the laundry, from cooking meals to warming bricks for the lodgers' beds. A coal fire was kept burning in the grate to heat the oven, water-tank and hot-plates, and here and there a long metal hook or a stout trivet could be swung out across the flames or lowered to bring some soot-blackened cooking utensil into closer contact with the heat. Here were chrome-coloured handles and knobs that seemed to do a dozen different jobs, dampers that slid open to adjust the draught in the big chimney, pans that could be lifted out full of soot or fine ash that glowed crimson with pools of trapped heat and a scent that tweaked the nostrils like the smoke of steam-train engines. On rainy days all the wet laundry was hung above the range to dry. On fine days it was dried outdoors, then folded into piles and stacked on every available surface to air properly before going back in the big blanket-chests in Nanny's bedroom. And every day the vast black cooking-range was laden with clothes for ironing, plates warming, loaves proving, pans simmering or meals keeping hot for later, and not one bit of heat was ever wasted.

'Waste not, want not,' Nanny would tell them all. 'Look after your pennies and your pounds will take care of themselves.'

Nanny always practised what she preached. Even though her sacks of fuel came either *buckshee* or dirt-cheap because some of her boarders worked at the Gas Works, she always made the most of every lump because she hated waste. At night she made up the fire with fresh coal, then damped it down with dust from the bottom of the sacks, or with a thick layer of cold ash, or with tea-leaves that had to be scrupulously collected after every mashing, or even with piles of potato-peelings to blanket the fire and keep it smouldering like a sleepy volcano all through the night. In the morning she would prod it awake with her poker, open the damper and set the draw-tin in place so that air rushed up the chimney with a busy roar, dragging the fire back to life. There were winter nights when Frankie dreamed of that great cooking range. It was to him the focus of all their lives, the very heart and soul of Nanny's house.

To the right of the kitchen door were the main window and the back door, both situated a whole storey above the lower level of the yard. To the left two deep steps led down to the lesser kitchen with its walk-in pantries and sloping cold-stores, and the big, low window that looked out on to the quietest corner of the front garden. Nanny's house was a fascinating place. It was tall and gloomy but seldom really dark in spite of its narrow panelled staircases. Every door had a number and a piece of matting outside, and all the upstairs lights stayed lit for a count of thirty-two after their buttons were pressed, then switched themselves off automatically so as not to waste electricity. Lots of people turned their noses up at Nanny because her husband was dead and she took in lodgers, but Frankie reckoned there was nobody else in the whole of Bradford who would *dare* run a house like the one in Lansdowne Place. In Nanny's house there were jugglers and actors, musicians, painters, dancers, singers and explorers. And what made her house so scary and exciting was the fact that every one of her lodgers, every man, woman and child, was as black as the ace of spades.

'It's nothing but a gin-house for whores, freaks and niggers,' Smallfry had told him in the strictest secrecy. 'You mark my words, Frankie. One of these days the police will close that place down and throw them all on to the streets, bag and baggage, right where they belong.'

While the house was quiet, Frankie was allowed to sit at the table in the smaller kitchen, drinking milk from a pint mug and watching Nanny open up all the tins of corned beef at both ends and push the meat out on to a plate in one big lump with fatty bits around the edges. She used her special opener for the job, the one that hung by a loop of string from the nail above one of the pantry shelves. It was a strange-looking gadget with a wooden handle that used to be painted yellow until years of use wore all but a few spots of colour away. Fixed into the handle was a ten-inch metal spike with a point shaped into a z-bend, and sliding freely along the spike was a small piece of curved metal with two pointed bits like the twin legs of a clothes peg. Nanny stabbed the end of the spike into the very centre of the lid, pulled the handle down and adjusted the little legs until they were slotted over the edge of the tin. Then she yanked sideways, turning the tin with her free hand until the lid was sliced free and could be lifted clean off. The whole process took no more than a few seconds and worked to perfection every time. Nanny was very proud of her opener. It had come from an expensive shop in Leeds and it was special because it could open any tin can that was ever made, be it round, square or oblong, triangular or oval, large or small.

He was put to work beating the batter really smooth for the Yorkshire puddings and cutting up pieces of Mr Hahn's best beef dripping for the big roasting tins. Then he had to pick the eyes out of a whole bucketful of potatoes and carrots before Nanny could chop them into even-sized lumps for the vegetable pans. He was really enjoying himself until his cousin Marlene arrived home from church and made him feel as if it was *her* house and he did not belong there, even on a visit, and he had absolutely no business helping with the food. She was all dressed up in her Sunday best, with ribbons in her hair and milky-white ankle-socks and black patent shoes that squeaked when she walked.

He was disappointed when Nanny said they should sit outside in the sunshine and remember to keep clean and not touch the dustbins or open the back gate or bicker with each other as they usually did. While Marlene busied herself with the task of setting cushions on the top step, Frankie was sent into one of the front rooms to speak to his auntie. This was the room where all the sisters slept. It was crammed full of furniture and had mirrors everywhere and a strong smell of perfume in the air. He was greeted by his middle auntie, the thinnest one with the small breasts and frizzy hair, the one with the explosive temper, who smoked foreign cigarettes and made big money posing for the artists at the Bradford School of Art. She always seemed to be sewing things for other people, like the real American bomber jacket she had sent for Frankie only a few weeks ago, and the pretty patchwork cover she had made for Nanny's bed when she was still at school and just as clever with her hands as any grown-up person. He had heard that she was courting seriously with a Londoner called Spencer who was likely to get himself in trouble with the police before very long because of his careless mouth and his interest in politics. If she married him she would have her work cut out and no mistake, according to Nanny, and she would have to live in a prefab in Brixton, where people spoke with funny accents and would not want to be bothered with a Yorkshire lass like her.

'Hello there, Frankie.'

'Hello, Auntie. Thank you for the jacket.'

She nodded and picked something pink from between her front teeth. 'I hear your mam's badly again.'

'Yes, Auntie, but only for a few days.'

She nodded again and sucked the bit of pink stuff from beneath her fingernail. 'Yes, until the next time, I don't doubt. What happened to your knees?'

'I slipped and fell down the hill.'

This time she shook her head rather sadly from side to side and rummaged in her handbag for a small parcel wrapped in coloured tissue paper. She unwrapped it very carefully to reveal several uneven chunks of Turkish Delight all dusted with fine white sugar. With a dainty movement she popped a piece into her own mouth and offered the rest to Frankie. Hoping to impress her with his manners, he took the smallest one he could find and thanked her very politely. For several minutes they chewed and sucked in silence, surveying each other from time to time with smiles made awkward by sticky lips.

'Is she good to you, Frankie, your mam?'

'Oh *yes*, Auntie.'

'Looks after you really well, does she?'

'Oh *yes*, Auntie.'

'And what about your dad? Is *he* good to you?'

Frankie sensed the minefield opening up before him, the questions and answers that would make him say things he did not mean and had never intended to say. His auntie did not like Smallfry, and Smallfry said he must be on his guard at all times because the entire family was crafty and sneaky and could easily make him say out loud something he should not even *mention*. He felt trapped. She might be asking which of his parents he loved the best, or which one he would rather live with, or who should be shouted at for not looking after him properly. His face became blank as his mind leaped off in all directions in search of a suitable reply. Then his features creased all over in a broad smile as inspiration came to him in a flash.

'Mrs Ramsbottom tells everyone I live like a *proper little prince,*' he proudly announced.

'And who the hell is Mrs Ramsbottom, when she's at home?'

'. . . er . . . well, I don't know *exactly*, but she goes to church every Sunday and she saw me riding Trigger on the day I got my picture in the *Telegraph and Argus*. And when she came with the church pamphlets, Buddie caught her looking through the best room window and her eyes were as round as *saucers.*' He paused to catch his breath, then beamed and added: 'She said the house was just like a palace and I had everything a boy could ever wish for and I'm the luckiest kid in all the whole wide world.'

He was disappointed by her lack of response. At first she just stared at him with a peculiar expression on her face, then she pursed her lips and closed her eyes the way Buddie sometimes did when he was not quite cross but pretty exasperated.

'Mrs Ramsbottom, huh?'

'That's right,' Frankie confirmed.

'And did she look all around the house? Did she see the kitchens? Did she go upstairs?'

'No, Auntie. I just *told* you, she looked through the window and saw the best room and her eyes were as round as *saucers.*'

'And she saw you riding the horse?'

Frankie nodded, smiling. '*And* she cut out my picture and stuck it on her pantry wall for everyone to see.'

'And then she had a look through the window and went away to tell everyone what a *fantastic* house my brother and his family are living in?'

'Well, yes . . . I *think* that's what she did.'

222

Auntie pursed up her lips again and peered at him through narrowed eyes, looking at him from head to toe and back again, inspecting him in much the same way Nanny had done at breakfast time.

'A *proper little prince*, huh?'

He nodded, wishing her eyes did not make him feel so shabby.

'Ah, I can see it now,' she said then. 'Here we have the pampered only son who has already been given absolutely *everything* a boy of his age could ever want to make him happy.' She paused to gather up a deep breath and expel it in a sigh, then added: 'Well now, Frankie, and who am I to argue with that? I'm sure this Mrs Ramsbottom knows the truth of it better than anyone else possibly could, so if *she* says you live like a proper little prince, then a proper little prince you must surely be. Now, does His Royal Highness have such a thing as a nice big kiss for his auntie?'

He left the room feeling good, his cheeks pink with pleasure and embarrassment because she had hugged him so tightly and kissed him full on the mouth. She had smelled of a flowery perfume and tasted of Turkish Delight and icing sugar, so that each time he licked his lips it was just like kissing her again and he felt fresh colour rushing up into his cheeks. It was a stroke of luck that he had remembered to tell her about Mrs Ramsbottom. He was always nervous around his middle auntie because she was the one with the quickest temper and he did not see her often enough to learn how to relax in her company. Smallfry hated her like poison and said it would be good riddance when she married her snobbish Londoner and took herself off the two hundred miles to Brixton. In his heart of hearts, Frankie was not sure how he felt about her going away. He just wished his aunties and uncles and cousins and grandmas could be ordinary, everyday, common-as-muck people like all the other folk in Bradford. Then he would not need to be constantly on his guard and he could stop feeling like the cowboy who strayed into the hostile Indian camp every time he came to Nanny's house.

He was given two ginger biscuits and sent out into the yard where his cousin Marlene was waiting for him on the top step. Nanny had insisted on cushions so the cold from the stone would not strike up through their clothes to give them piles in later life. Frankie pulled his cushion to one side so that he could lean his shoulder against the wall. He had no wish to sit too close to Marlene. He had to be careful of her because she nipped him whenever she was feeling peevish; tiny, spiteful little nips with her long finger-nails that hurt like hell and raised purple blood-blisters on his skin.

'Boys are not supposed to fight with girls,' he was constantly being reminded. 'Boys are rough and tough and must never be so cruel as to fight with young ladies.'

Frankie found it difficult to follow those instructions. He did not like girls, young or otherwise. They might look all soft and sweet and innocent on the surface, but in his experience they were sneaky, and much tougher and nastier than they pretended to be.

He was particularly wary of his cousin Marlene. She was Little Auntie's daughter, but she had always lived as the only child at Lansdowne Place, so she acted as if *all* the aunties were her mothers and Nanny was *her* grandma *exclusively*. Marlene was bigger and taller and plumper and much more self-assured than Frankie. She was fair-skinned, with light eyes and pale golden freckles and soft brown hair that fell in natural curls and never seemed to get all tangled up of its own accord. Marlene always managed to keep her socks in the right place and her pretty dresses spotlessly clean. She did not bite her nails or scuff her shoes, and the skin over her knees was pinky-smooth and free from scars and was never, ever stained with patches of ingrained dirt. Her colouring had always puzzled Frankie. Auntie was Buddie's sister and

224

her skin was quite a lot darker than his, yet *she* was the mother of a light-skinned daughter while Buddie's son was black-eyed and gypsy-dark. It did not seem a fair deal at all, especially when Smallfry was so often made to feel really angry that *her* child was born the wrong colour. He bit into one of his ginger biscuits and scowled as he tried to push the word *nigger* from his mind. When Smallfry screamed that word at him it was even worse than getting the big belt or the leather shoe. *Nigger* was the very worst word in all the world. It was a hurting word. Every time his mam called him a nigger it hurt Frankie on the *inside* where nothing ever seemed to make it better.

'Are you listening to me?'

'What? Oh, I'm sorry, what did you say?'

Marlene smiled at him and tossed her head so that her golden-brown hair danced about her face. She had been nibbling a biscuit all around the outside with dozens of tiny bites, making it smaller and smaller until now it was just a minute piece held between her finger and thumb.

'I was asking you about your mam.'

'She's been taken badly,' he told her. 'We had to send for the doctor and I'll be going back home soon and I don't want to talk about it, so shut up, Marlene.'

'Oh well, suit yourself and see if *I* care. Anyway, *I've* been to the new Sunday School with Auntie, and I got a gold star in my book for knowing the whole lesson all the way through without a *single* mistake.'

'Good for you. I got a gold star once, except that . . . '

'Why are you not wearing your Sunday best clothes?' she cut in, frowning at him with measured distaste. 'Surely *that* can't be your Sunday best. Why are you always so scruffy?'

She lifted her nose in a haughty expression and went through the motions of moving further away from him, though the row of metal railings enclosing the steps reduced the drama of the gesture to a mere shuffle. This done, she popped the remaining fragment of ginger biscuit into her mouth and chewed it with her lips pressed neatly together and her hands clasped in her lap in a very lady-like manner.

Frankie watched her in silence. Over her frilly, blue and white dress she was wearing a knitted cardigan with a row of brightly coloured animals around the bottom. He had once owned a jumper exactly like it, knitted by Little Auntie at the same time from the same special pattern. He had liked his jumper, but after a while it became so filthy and stained that Buddie made him put it amongst the dirty washing in the corner. By the time he saw it again it had gone all shrunken and matted, and the hot water pipes above the stove had dried it to a horrible hardness. He had not really minded very much when Rosie pulled it down with a lot of other things and savaged it into little pieces just because she was bored with being chained up in the corner all day.

'Stop staring! I hate it when people stare at me like that. Didn't anyone ever teach you it's *rude* to stare?'

He shrugged and looked away, then concentrated all his attention on eating his second ginger biscuit without dropping a single crumb on the steps. Marlene was always bossing him about, just because he was the youngest. Her tenth birthday had been in June, which made her exactly thirty-two days older than him. That was only a month, one measly, short little month, and yet there was such a difference in their sizes that he was often taken for only eight years old while *she* made everyone believe she was *at least* eleven.

'*Your* mam's expecting,' she suddenly announced, smoothing her dress with clean hands and setting her face in a know-it-all expression.

'She's what?'

'You can't deny it. I overheard the others talking about it last night and again this morning, so you can't deny it. She's expecting. That's why the doctor was sent for and that's why there's all this bother and that's why they don't

226

want a stupid boy hanging around the place, so there!'

Frankie scowled. He had not the slightest idea what she was talking about, but something in her attitude and her voice concerned him. It was not right that a mere cousin should know something about his mam that he did not know. After a lengthy silence he found himself forced to confess that he did not understand what she meant by *expecting*.

'What? Oh, you big soppy kid,' she said in a very superior tone. She was clearly delighted by his ignorance. 'Don't you know *anything* about the facts of life?'

'Of course I do,' he answered defensively. 'Me and my dad are *always* chatting about them.'

He could say that much with confidence. Buddie had a seemingly endless store of *facts of life* that he revealed to Frankie from time to time. There was the one that said small boys should be seen and not heard, and another that said a slice of jam and bread would always land face-down if it was dropped on the floor. There was even one to say that only good girls got into trouble because all the *bad* ones knew how to keep from getting caught. He was sure he knew a great deal more than most kids about the so-called *facts of life*, but this knowledge did not give him any clues as to what his cousin was talking about when she said his mam was *expecting*. He shrugged his shoulders and tried a more subtle tack.

'I don't believe you. You're telling lies.'

She rounded on him with her eyes flashing and her fingernails at the ready.

'I am *not* telling lies,' she hissed.

'Oh, yes you are.'

'No I'm not, *stupid*. I'm bigger than you, and I'm older, so I *know* a lot more, so *there*.'

'Oh, get lost, Marlene. You're just a daft girl. You haven't even got a *dad*.'

'And I don't *want* one, so *there!*'

She nipped him spitefully, catching a fold of skin on the back of his hand and pinching it with her nails. Then she jumped up to stand on the top step, towering above him with her hands on her hips and looking just the way Nanny must have looked when *she* was ten years old.

'Ouch!' He sucked hard on the pinched skin. 'Now you're in trouble. I'll tell Nanny you did that. I'll tell.'

'Well, you're a scruff, and you're always dirty.'

'And you're too fat.'

'I'm not fat.' She stamped her foot and pouted. 'I am *not* fat.'

'Yes you are, and nobody likes you even one little bit because you're a spoilt brat and your voice is too loud and you've got too many freckles and you're *fat.*'

He sprang away just as she lashed out with one shiny, patent leather shoe. He grinned up at her from the bottom of the steps, confident in his victory. His sense of triumph was to be painfully short-lived.

'Well, *your* mam's expecting, and when it's born she won't want a scruffy little runt like *you* any more.' She stuck out her tongue and screwed up her face, then began to chant:

'*Ner, ner, ner! Frankie's mam's expecting a baby, Frankie's mam's expecting a baby, Frankie's mam's expecting a baby.*'

Satisfied that she had now won the contest, she tossed her skirt to reveal the frills of her petticoat and strode back into the house with her nose in the air. Her words rang in his ears and seemed to jangle right the way down to his bones.

' . . . *expecting a baby . . . expecting a baby . . . a baby.*'

He was still standing alone in the yard when Nanny bustled out to sharpen her big carving knife on the top step. Because she always used the same spot, the stone had gradually worn away into a smooth depression which allowed the knife to slide to and fro so easily that she could sharpen her knives to a perfect edge without even needing to watch what she was doing. Once again Frankie was given a clear view of suspenders and hefty thighs as she stooped to her task. He waited until she had gone back inside, then climbed the steps and seated himself on the much plumper cushion close to the railings. He allowed his shoulders to slouch and his head to hang forward until a thick tendril of hair fell down over his eyes. He could hear a heavy vehicle labouring up Morley Street and a dog yapping in one of the other yards. Marlene's words had left a hollowness in his body that seemed too big for him to keep contained. It was like being turned to ice and gradually melting away from the inside.

'She's expecting a baby, a baby, a baby,' he whispered, and the words, said out loud, frightened him.

Trevor Murgatroyd's mam had been expecting a baby all through the winter of last year. It swelled up in her belly and made her fat and ugly and bad-tempered, with lots of lumpy blue veins on her legs. When it came she could not get her washing done or look after her steps properly, and it screamed and screamed, day and night until everyone wished they could send it back where it came from. Trevor complained it was nothing but noise and nuisance and smelly nappies. Frankie had seen as much for himself when he went there one dinner-time to swap marbles and count the dead mice in Trevor's traps. And one day he had been horrified to see the new baby feeding at Mrs Murgatroyd's breasts just like the piglets did with the sows after littering. He hated that particular memory. He did not want to think of some strange child sucking on his mam's breasts and touching her with its hands and being her favourite. It would probably grow up to be a girl who could help with the housework and be a God-send in the kitchen. Or it might be a boy that grew taller and more clever and much braver than Frankie ever knew how to be, and then everyone would be so well satisfied with it that they would scowl at him and shake their heads and say:

'Oh, Frankie, why can't you be more like your little brother?'

It might be a big, pale-skinned baby with fair hair, or a chubby blue-eyed baby that did not stammer or bite its nails or wet its bed or twitch its face whenever something made it nervous. His mam had suffered enough disappointments in her life since Frankie was born, so this time God and all His Angels would be good to her. This time she would be given the son or daughter she really deserved and really wanted.

'Frankie's mam's expecting a baby!'

Marlene had been right to jeer at him and call him stupid, because when the new baby came he would surely lose all the special privileges that came from being his parents' only son. He might even be sent away to a Children's Home because his room and his bed and his place at the table were needed for the new arrival. Frankie had no illusions about his own personal worth. His mam was expecting a baby, so whatever happened now, he knew for certain that nobody was going to want *him* any more.

They all had corned beef and Yorkshire puddings and crispy roast potatoes and cabbage for Sunday lunch, with stewed rhubarb and thick custard for pudding. His eldest auntie was worried about him. She thought he was looking a bit peaky and wondered if he might have worms or be sickening for something serious. Nanny did not think so because his appetite was so good and she had never in her life seen *anyone*, man or boy, shift as much food as he could shift at a sitting. He pretended not to be listening when they talked about him or his mam. Their words were deliberately chosen to exclude him, and on one occasion when he thought they had finished speaking and were just getting on with their dinners, he looked up to find them mouthing words at each other like deaf people over the top of his head. Even later, when he was made to sit quietly in an armchair while his meal was digesting in his stomach, he pretended not to hear snatches of their conversation as they did the washing up in the big pot sink in the other kitchen.

' ... heavy bleeding ... four months gone ... went down to see that Mucky Mary in Cobden Street ... Oh, she *never!* ... Oh, yes she did ... well, would you credit that? ... silly cow ... deserves everything she gets ... '

Their words meant little to him. It was the other words that kept repeating themselves inside his head with added sting, the words about his mam expecting a baby.

There were corned beef sandwiches with tomato sauce for tea and a dish of corned beef scraps to eat with his bread and butter at supper-time. Nanny let him lock the bathroom door from the inside and get bathed in private if he promised to scrub every inch of his body and not splash the water all over the floor. He was glad the hot-water tank was noisy and took a long time to fill up again once the taps were turned off. It gave him a chance to cry the way he had wanted to do all day. All he had to do was lock himself in and the crying came of its own accord, pouring out of him in deep sobs. He felt safer there. Nobody could hear him through the locked door with the cistern filling. Nobody would make fun of him for being a sissy and a cry-baby, and nobody would ever guess how scared he was that his mam was going to have a baby.

He slept in a man's shirt with the sleeves rolled up, in a small bed in Nanny's room that had stiff white sheets and two feather pillows inside real cotton cases. His right knee was bandaged up where the scab had come off when he rubbed it with scouring powder and a scrubbing brush to get all the dirt out of his skin. Nanny had been pleased with him for not getting blood-stains on the towel when

231

his knee started bleeding again, and in the middle of the night she woke him up with a drink of warm milk and wiped his face with a handkerchief and told him not to worry because everything would be all right very soon.

On Monday morning he had porridge and a corned beef sandwich and a big cup of sweet tea before Little Auntie put on her best green coat and walked with him all the way to school, right to the playground gates. Nobody had said a word to him about wetting Nanny's spare bed in the night. He was sporting a fine big bandage on his knee, he had tuppence to spend, a piece of Auntie's forbidden chewing-gum stuck under his tongue and two bits of knicker elastic sewn into garters to hold his socks up. Everyone was being very kind to him and somehow that just made him feel worse. It was as if they knew, all of them, that he would be going away soon, that some other kid was coming along to take his place as the *proper little prince* of Old Ashfield.

SEVENTEEN

Frankie had to stay at his nanny's house for a whole week. Marlene took great delight in tormenting him with her persistent nips and her snide, whispered comparisons between adorable new babies and grubby little boys with spiky hair. For most of his stay she treated him like the poor relation barely to be tolerated, but she left him alone when he told her he had nits in his head. Nanny confirmed that he was mistaken, but to Marlene the possibility that one tiny insect had missed the head inspection and might suddenly jump from him to her in order to lay its eggs was a prospect too horrible to contemplate. From that moment onwards she kept a safe distance between Frankie and herself, choosing to pull snooty faces or stick out her tongue and cross her eyes from as far away as she could get without actually leaving the room.

It was by far the worst school week he could remember having in a long time, especially when Wally Watmough started making fun of him for having an auntie to bring him to school every morning and take him home again each night. On Monday he was sick after dinner and had to sit in Nurse's room with a damp flannel on his forehead. On Tuesday he developed a horrible spot on his chin just below his bottom lip, and Nurse dyed it bright purple with a dollop of Gentian Violet so that everyone thought he had contagious impetigo when he hadn't. Then he had a fight with two kids in the yard who demanded to know why he looked like a Gypsy and where all the darkies in his family had come from. On Wednesday he was made to stand on a chair all through morning assembly after Miss Richardson caught him muttering urgently to himself and quite naturally assumed him to be deep in conversation with a spotty little girl in the next row. Twice on Thursday his school milk was stolen by Wally Watmough and his gang of big lads, and on Friday he was smacked over the back of the head with a geography book and told to stay behind after school for being lazy and not paying attention in class. It was all because he could not concentrate properly on his lessons. Sometimes he forgot for a while about his mam and the new baby, but then the memory would return in a sudden thump that made his stomach ache, and his mind would start to fret and worry about what would happen to him when the baby arrived. That was how he found himself standing on a chair in the hall with his hands on his head while the entire school filed out into the sunshine on Friday afternoon.

When his youngest auntie realized that Frankie was neither in the noisy main flow nor among the late stragglers pushing and shoving each other down the porch steps, she marched into the assembly hall as if she owned the place and ordered him to get down off the chair and collect his jacket from the cloakroom. Fixing Sir with one of her especially withering scowls, the ones Buddie said could curdle milk at fifteen paces, she politely informed him that no petty headmaster in a greasy suit was going to make *her* stand waiting in the school yard like a plum for the next twenty-five minutes when all the other kids were already halfway home and school was officially over for the week.

'My dear *madam*,' Sir said with measured emphasis. 'Let me inform you that here at St Andrew's Junior School, Listerhills, the rules of everyday discipline must be observed at all times.'

'Not in *my* time,' she countered.

Still standing with his hands clasped on the top of his head, Frankie stared from one to the other, from the tall, blustering headmaster to the small brown woman who stood with her hands on her hips and her mouth working rhythmically upon a portion of chewing-gum. She glared steadily up at Sir as if nobody in the whole world could have authority over her.

'Young woman, I must protest most strongly . . . '

'You can protest all you like,' she shrugged, 'but I'm taking my nephew home right this minute. Come on, kid, grab your coat and let's go.'

Frankie dithered, caught between the two forces like a bone placed between two hungry dogs. Sir had given him a half-hour's detention and Auntie was ordering him to leave right now. He found himself incapable of decisive movement until Auntie grabbed him by the collar and shoved him in the direction of the door. The steady drumming of her high heels on the polished wooden floor kept him moving. He did not look back to see if Sir's face was beetroot-red and shiny with perspiration above his faded shirt collar. It was not until they were halfway down St Andrew's Place that aunt and nephew glanced sideways at each other, smiled sheepishly, then burst into happy laughter. They both knew there would be an awful lot of mileage in the story of her bare-faced cheek and Sir's blustering disbelief as one of his small charges was unceremoniously snatched from his control.

There was a big dish of deep-fried corned beef fritters already cooked and keeping warm in the oven when he got back to Nanny's house. They were served up with mashed potatoes and thick onion gravy, and a big serving of spicy chutney as a special treat. His eldest auntie insisted on feeling his forehead as if he had a temperature, then prodding about at the back of his neck to see if his glands were swollen up.

'He looks peaky,' she announced, not for the first time.

'Oh, stop your fussing,' Nanny said. 'There isn't much ailing him if he can eat three fritters and still come back for a second helping of spuds.'

'I don't like the look of him. Perhaps he's sickening for something.'

'Nonsense. He's as right as he ever was. Isn't that so, Frankie?'

'Yes, Nanny.'

'And you don't feel sick or feverish?'

'No, Auntie.'

He wondered only briefly if it would do any good to tell them the truth. He decided against it because he was sure no pill or medicine would stop him feeling sick and hurt in all those secret places where it did not show.

He was alone in the kitchen with Nanny when she wrapped her hands in an old towel, pulled a covered dinner plate from the depths of the cooking range and set it on a tray with several slices of bread and butter. One of the boarders had arrived back from his work and come directly to the kitchen for his evening meal. He stood on the inside steps with the corridor at his back, his dark bulk all but filling the door-frame. Frankie recognized him as Lame Joe Suleman, the one-time professional dancer who now worked at the same foundry in West Bowling where Frankie's grandfather, the American, had once worked. That had been during the depression years when Bradford folk did not like foreigners taking their jobs and sooner or later all the black men had to be laid off. After that, Grandfather had made his living singing songs at the clubs and theatres and charging people for music lessons in his spare time. It must have been better than working in a smelly old foundry, except that when he was only fifty-five he dropped dead on stage and left Nanny to fend for herself with six half-caste children and a house in Lumby Street that was only rented.

Frankie stared at the man who stood cap-in-hand in the kitchen doorway with dirt smudged in iron-grey stains on his coal-black skin. Perhaps his grandfather had looked like Lame Joe, with tight grey woolly hair and beautiful teeth, a man all shiny black from head to toe, like a negative before the photographs were made up. He did not think it right that Nanny had been married to someone like that. Smallfry had warned him about the black men. She said they were only decent on the outside, and secretly they all had disgusting habits like eating raw food and drinking blood and doing dirty things with girls who were only twelve years old and sometimes even with *boys* who were only twelve years old.

'Hi there, young fella.'

Frankie looked away in sudden embarrassment as Nanny finished pouring tea into a big white pint pot before lifting the tea-tray from the table. He fidgeted in his seat and pretended to be reading his comic until the boarder had thanked Nanny in his deep, low voice and limped away to eat his corned beef fritters and mashed potatoes all alone in his room. Frankie was not allowed to speak to black men, not even to a nice one like poor Mr Suleman, who sometimes got tears in his eyes because he used to be a big-shot entertainer but now had to work in a foundry up West Bowling because one of his legs had let him down and he would never be able to dance on stage again. He was not allowed to speak to the man, but he found himself hoping that Nanny had put a really big portion of spicy chutney on the side of Lame Joe's plate and plenty of extra sugar in his tea.

It was long turned five o'clock on Sunday when the rattle of swill-bins and the distinctive roar of The Duke's engine announced Buddie's arrival to the entire neighbourhood. Nanny was busy baking downstairs in the smaller kitchen, using the big gas oven to cook trays of corned beef pasties with onions and potatoes and herbs mixed up inside. Frankie watched his father warily, looking for signs that might betray what was going on in his mind.

'Hiya, Frankie. You been behaving yourself?'

Frankie glanced at Nanny for confirmation, then nodded

proudly with a relieved smile. Only he and Nanny knew that he had wet the bed every night for a whole week. She had brought a thin rubber sheet to protect the mattress and promised not to say a word to his parents about it, and now he could tell by her smile that she was going to keep her word. Some of his tension began to ease, but several minutes were to pass before he plucked up enough courage to ask:

'How is she? Is she better?'

'She sure is, kiddio. Not quite herself yet, but up and about for most of the day and a whole lot better than when you saw her last.'

'Oh, that's good.'

Frankie was comforted by the news. He watched his father's dark, sternly handsome face and knew he would not dare ask the question now uppermost in his mind. It would never do for a small boy to speak to an adult about babies, especially when the adult was his dad and the baby was not born yet and the whole subject revolved around his own mam. Instead he hovered awkwardly in the background with his shoes polished and his socks held neatly in place by his new garters, watching Buddie help himself to a cup of bitterly strong tea and one of Nanny's hot, spicy, fresh-out-of-the-oven corned beef pasties.

At five forty-five he followed Buddie out to the truck. In one hand he carried a brown paper bag with looped string handles into which Nanny had packed a few presents, including a parcel of pasties that had warmed right through their wrappings to make little grease-stains on the carrier. He did not know what Smallfry was going to say about the three pairs of cotton underpants his Auntie had bought from the Jewish draper's shop in Westgate. Smallfry did not believe in underpants. She did not even believe in knickers for little girls, and if she had her way they would all be sent to school with bare bums so that the air could circulate freely the way Nature intended. Some of the boys at Frankie's school wore underpants all the time, every day, winter and summer alike, with a clean pair every other Sunday, even though they did not show and nobody could ever see if they were dirty or clean. There were also three pairs of socks in the carrier bag, long and fawn in colour, with elasticated tops that did not need garters and two thin red lines around the tops for decoration. And right on the top, in a square, flat box wrapped up in dark blue tissue paper, was Frankie's pride and joy, the special present from him to his mam.

Although it was Sunday and supposedly a day of rest, Nanny's boarders were as lively as ever. The sounds of music and laughter and chattering voices spilled out from behind every door and window. Groups of noisy, flamboyant individuals were gathered on the landings and stairs to exchange news and let off a little steam after the pressures of the working week. Mr Suleman was sitting at his open window, puffing on a cigarette and blowing the smoke outside so that it would not make the room smell bad. Frankie felt sorry for him, and now that he was going home and could not be in any danger, he thought it might be all right to speak to him, even if he *was* jet black.

'Be seeing you, Mr Suleman,' he called out, smiling and waving his free hand.

The man's face immediately opened in a big white smile. He leaned out of the high window and waved his arm, showing a pale, desert-toned palm criss-crossed all over with foundry-blackened lines.

'Hey, be seein' you, young fella. Mind how you go now, you hear?'

'You too, Mr Suleman.'

He had to say goodbye to Marlene as if they were great friends, then kiss all his aunties in turn and give Nanny a big hug. She kissed him right over his ear so that it rang inside his head, then winked and nipped his cheek between her podgy finger and thumb. His Nanny had been good to

239

him all week. He knew Smallfry would be relieved to hear that she had not tried to poison him, not even once, and she had not made him go into one of the dark upstairs rooms with a black man.

Frankie was glad to be going home, yet he left Nanny's house with a twinge of regret and felt a familiar apprehension closing in on him as The Duke made its perilous way down the rocky dirt track to the gates of Old Ashfield. There was a sense of dread in coming home, a fear that things had changed and nothing would ever be the same again. He wondered if going away for a whole week left a definite space behind where he was supposed to be, or if such a long absence was like lifting the whisk out of the Yorkshire pudding batter and watching the stuff slowly close up and smooth out until it looked as if no whisk had ever been there at all.

'There's someone I think you should meet before we go inside,' Buddie said as they approached the yard gate.

Frankie's heart sank. Here was the first change, even before he had stepped inside the back yard. He heard the rattle of a heavy chain and a strange, ominous snorting sound that reminded him of the savage wild boars that chased Tarzan through the jungle and killed the cruel white hunter with the big gun and the leather patch over one eye. He wondered if Nader was ill, or if Buddie had kicked her in a spot that made her breathe as if her nostrils were blocked. Buddie opened the gate and held it while Frankie ducked under his arm.

'Not so fast, now. Take it easy. There now, Frankie, I'd like you to meet the newest member of the team. This is Bebop.'

Frankie stopped dead in his tracks. He felt the chilly fingers of fear plucking at his nerve-ends and causing the saliva to dry up in his mouth. Facing him from the middle of the yard, standing like a bulky tank at the very end of its chain, was the biggest, ugliest, most ferocious-looking

240

bulldog he had ever set eyes on. This animal bore little resemblance to Lady, the old bulldog who had to be put down after Rosie died because she fretted and lost her appetite. This animal was *huge*. It had a massive head and a face that might have been pieced together after a serious road accident. Looking not unlike the wild boars of Tarzan's acquaintance, it had two long, protruding lower tusks that jabbed upwards from its lower jaw as if to hold in check the untidy folds of its face. Its immense, barrel-shaped chest heaved precariously over bowed front legs that seemed inadequate for their purpose. While Frankie stared in horror, a growl began as a low, menacing rumble in the back of the dog's throat and increased in intensity until the sound of it turned his blood to ice.

'*Relax*, Bebop,' Buddie snapped. 'This here's Frankie. You'll be seeing a lot of him, so you might just as well start getting used to each other right off.'

The bulldog lowered its head and glared, snorting through its flattened nostrils and slavering streams of saliva. It looked for all the world like an enraged bull preparing to charge. Frankie jumped back in alarm, stumbled into his father's big boots, staggered to one side clutching his precious brown paper carrier bag, then felt himself yanked upright by the scruff of his neck.

'Simmer down, boy. Don't let him see you're nervous of him, not if you know what's good for you. Jesus, didn't you learn *anything* from Rosie?'

Frankie nodded miserably. He had learned a great deal from Rosie, mainly that a dog was not to be trusted under any circumstances, and least of all when it was put on guard duty in the back yard. He was praying that Buddie had not done his usual trick to fool would-be burglars by fastening the heavy chain to the wall bracket with a flimsy bit of parcel string. At the back of his mind was a growing suspicion that this monstrous thing, this great wheezing Bebop, was quite capable of snapping open the

241

links of the strongest, thickest chain ever known to man.

Frankie suddenly found himself swinging through the air and being brought to rest with both legs straddling his father's shoulders. Thus elevated to temporary safety, he was carried down the yard to the back door while the bulldog leaped against its chain and issued a series of savagely asthmatic barks, convinced that its master was holding a favourite titbit just out of its reach.

Bebop was a thoroughbred bulldog selected by Buddie for his size, his strength, and the meanness of his temper. He had already been installed as guard dog for six days, a whole week in which to establish his new position as number one dog. He was stubborn and single-minded to the point of lunacy, and in this place of much lesser beasts he considered himself to be second only to the hot-tempered master of the house. As far as Bebop was capable of understanding, this undersized, nervous newcomer represented a test of his ability to guard both his master's property and his own place within the pecking order. In that first brief confrontation a pattern was firmly established and Frankie marked down as the never-to-be-accepted intruder upon Bebop's personal territory.

The kitchen was hot and stuffy and wonderfully familiar. Two long wooden trays containing dozens of pale and fluffy day-old chicks had been placed across the water pipes in the alcove to keep warm. Their squeaks made a piping chorus of sound and their movements blew a fine, pale dandruff into the air. There were chicken giblets in a bucket in the sink, covered by an old newspaper to keep the flies off. The kettle was simmering above a low light on the gas stove and his mam's crimson cushion and fringed silk shawl were right there in her favourite chair, just as they had always been. While Buddie went into the best room to check on her, Frankie looked around with a strange tightness in his chest and in his throat. It was good to be home. He did not really belong anywhere else. God had

242

put him in Old Ashfield on the day he was born and God intended him to stay there forever, of that he was certain.

Nader thumped her tail against the wall in greeting. She seemed thinner and sadder than when Frankie had seen her last, and could not curl up in her corner because someone had placed a cardboard box there. It contained a bundle of old rags and something small and pink and twitchy.

'One of Dora's piglets,' Buddie explained, closing the door quietly behind him. He scooped the tiny animal up in his big brown palm and dropped it into Frankie's arms. 'Name's Toto. I don't reckon he'll ever be able to walk too well on account of his back legs don't bend in the middle the way they should, but it could have been those legs that saved his life. Dora rolled over on three little ones while they were feeding and chewed up all the rest, one by one. If this little chap had been strong enough to get to the teat he'd have been a gonner too, just like all the rest.'

'What, *all* of them?' Frankie asked, aware of the fragile bones and feeble heartbeat that made his own small hands seem large by comparison. 'The whole litter?'

'Yep! Every last one,' Buddie told him. 'So much for giving her a second chance, eh? It's the knife for her this time, I'm afraid. If she can't do a simple thing like breeding without turning gangster on her own piglets, then she's only fit for the dinner table, right boy?'

'Right,' Frankie agreed. He stared down at the tiny transparent ears and eye-lids, at the soft snout and wrinkled, petal-pink skin, at the sleepy, mysterious smile so peculiar to pigs of all ages. 'Poor little Toto. Do you think he'll survive without his mam to take care of him?'

'Maybe, if I can find someone willing to keep him warm and feed him from a bottle every few hours and make sure he doesn't get himself eaten by one of the dogs. Got any ideas, kid?'

'Who? *Me?* Can *I* do it? Can I? Can I?' Frankie stared up at his father with wide eyes, suddenly quite breathless with excitement.

'Well now, I reckon the job's yours if you want it.'

'Honest? Do you really mean it? Does that mean he's mine? *Really* mine?'

'Reckon so.'

'Oh thanks, Buddie, thanks. I won't let you down. I promise I'll take good care of him.'

'Right, then. He's your sole responsibility from now on. You'll find plenty of dried milk in the big tins at the back of the top kitchen. I've written out the mixing instructions on the label. You're to keep his bottle and teats washed out after every feed, and you're not to let him go running around the house, pissing and shitting everywhere. You got that?'

'Yes, Buddie.'

'And you can only take him upstairs to sleep while he's still too small to get out of his box by himself. That clearly understood?'

'Yes, Buddie.'

'Now, how's about a plate of corned beef hash and a cup of tea before your mam wakes up?'

'Oh . . . corned beef hash?'

'Yep! What's the matter, did you have corned beef at your Nanny's?'

'Well, yes . . . *sometimes* . . . and she sent a whole bag of pasties . . . ' He gazed down at the plump pink bundle of bald skin and spindly legs curled untidily in his lap and he wondered if his piglet, his very own Toto, might grow to be the handsomest little pig in Yorkshire. Then he grinned up at his father and said, imitating his cowboy drawl:

'Yep, I reckon corned beef hash and a cup of tea will be just fine and dandy.'

They had finished eating and Buddie was rinsing the dishes under the hot water tap when the forbidden words slipped out of Frankie's mouth of their own accord.

'Is Smallfry expecting a baby?'

The words rang in the quiet room. One moment they were trapped in his mind as any secret should be, the next they were said, spoken out loud.

Buddie stopped what he was doing and turned off the tap. Then he turned around very slowly and leaned back against the sink with his arms folded across his body and his brows knitted into a frown. Outside in the yard, Bebop had managed to climb on to an up-ended milk crate and set his front paws on the windowsill. His big face, glaring and slavering, looked even more monstrous pressed against the glass and viewed through a veil of condensation.

'Who told you this, boy?'

Frankie bit his lower lip and made no reply.

'Come on, speak up. I want to know who told you that your mam's expecting.'

Frankie wanted to tell, but for a long time he could not get his mouth to work. He kept thinking of the disgrace of being the subject of that taunting playground chant:

'Tell-tale tit
Your tongue will split
And all the little doggies in the town
Will have a bit.'

'You'd best answer me, boy.'

'It was Marlene,' he blurted at last. 'Marlene told me last Sunday. She was listening in and she heard the others talking about it.'

'Your cousin Marlene has big ears and an even bigger mouth. What else did she tell you?'

'Nothing.'

'And you didn't hear anything about it from any of the others?'

'No, Buddie. Is it true? Is there going to be a baby?'

Buddie started grinding his teeth the way he always did when he was deep in thought, taking so long to answer that Frankie began to fear the worst. The boy stared at

245

the ghostly apparition at the window and resolved to shift that old milk crate as soon as he had the opportunity. It was not nice for decent folk to look up and find something so ugly it might have escaped from a horror movie staring back at them from the yard.

At last his father cleared his throat with a growl, spat into the plug-hole and ran the cold tap briefly.

'Are you sure nobody else has spoken to you about this?'

'Yes, Buddie, I'm sure.' He was beginning to feel as if the whole world was holding its breath, waiting to hear the answer to his question. The sensation made his heart pound in his ears.

'Well, Frankie, it seems your cousin Marlene may have made a bit of a mistake. Maybe they were talking about some other lady, huh? Or maybe she just heard the story wrong. That's what you get for listening in where you've no business to be.'

Frankie still did not dare breathe.

'It isn't true, then?'

'Nope.'

'No baby?'

'No baby.'

'Not even later, when it's had time to grow?'

'Nope. Your mam had a belly ache that wouldn't go away and the doctor had to be called to take a look at her. That's all.'

Frankie let the air from his lungs in a long, long sigh as his world began to shift back into place, the way it was before he went away to Nanny's house.

'Feeling better now?' Buddie asked.

He nodded, grinning sheepishly.

'You're a rum kid, Frankie. It wouldn't do for *Mammy's boy* to have his nose pushed out by a new baby, would it?'

This time the words did not hurt because they were said without malice. Buddie was smiling, but he was still scowling and he looked troubled, as if he was secretly upset by what had been said.

'Buddie . . . ?'

'What is it now?'

'There won't be any trouble at Nanny's, will there? I mean . . . they didn't know anything about it, *honest*. Marlene told me in secret. It wasn't Nanny's fault.'

'We'll have to see what your mam says about that.'

'Will she be cross?'

Buddie took out his tobacco tin and rummaged around in it until he found a narrow, hand-rolled cigarette already flattened at one end and scorched at the other from a previous smoking. When he placed it between his lips and touched it with a lighted match it flared, threatening to scorch his moustache. He shifted what remained of the cigarette to one corner of his mouth, squinted through a thin spiral of smoke and gripped Frankie by the shoulder.

'I got a good idea,' he said, pushing the boy towards the door. 'Let's you and me just go in there and find out, shall we?'

EIGHTEEN

The best room smelled wonderful. A heady combination of scents met Frankie's nostrils as the door swished open and a delicate glass mobile began to turn, tinkling its fairy-soft song in the sudden draught. Here was woodsmoke, sandalwood, essence of rose and jasmine, all drifting in lazy curls of smoke from ornate incense burners, giving the atmosphere a hint of the mysterious Orient. And somewhere in the background, elusive and yet quite unmistakable, was the scent of Californian Poppy that marked his mother's presence in the room.

Smallfry was sitting up in the big, brass-ended bed, her nightgown as snowy white as were the marshmallow pillows at her back, her hair as rich a shade of burgundy as were the heavy velvet drapes that framed the arched alcove with their luxurious folds. Even the top cover on the bed was white, with an intricate all-over pattern of embroidery that shimmered like threads of pure silver in the light. It reminded Frankie of the delicate tracery left behind by Jack Frost on the insides of windows on chilly nights, those beautiful frost-sketches of winter tree-scapes, skeletal leaves and ferns, perfect snowflakes. Against this paleness Smallfry reclined like the legendary Snow Queen herself, her white shoulders and bosom barely concealed by a neckline of ivory lace, even her long crystal earrings flashing with reflected light to imitate real icicles melting slowly in the heat.

'Smallfry!'

He spoke her name like a shout inside his head. She was

just as beautiful as he had pictured her during all the days of his absence, when he had found comfort and a sense of security in remembering details of her, those many tiny things that made her *his* mam instead of someone else's. She had pale green eyes and long lashes that were brushed and brushed until they looked jet black and seemed to hold her eyes wide open and touch her cheeks each time she blinked. Her lips were full and coloured the same vibrant red that fired her long fingernails with tongues of flame. To emphasize her high cheekbones she had dusted a rosy blush of rouge over her cheeks, and for the perfect finishing touch a neat black beauty-spot had been placed close to her lower lip, just like the ones all the most stunning beauties were wearing in Paris, France.

'*Smallfry!*'

Her arms opened and he rushed to embrace her, sinking his face into the soft, perfumed warmth of her bosom. Her arms encircled him, pressing him so close that he could feel the heartbeat pulsing in her breasts as his face was cushioned against their plumpness. Love rose up inside him as a great wave that threatened to drown him with its sweetness.

'There, there, my darling,' she cooed, rocking him to and fro in her arms and stroking his hair tenderly, lovingly. 'Everything is all right, now. The worst is over. You're home, now. There, there, Frankie. Hush now, hush, my dear.'

Frankie was not crying. His heart was full to bursting and his eyes prickled, but the need to cry was safely under his control. He would not shame himself before his father by crying like a big sissy just because he was home at last and his mam was well again.

'There, there. Hush . . . hush . . . it's all right, my darling.'

He wanted to tell her that she had made a mistake because he was not crying, but despite their seemingly gentle pressure, the hands that held him and stroked his hair were so firmly placed that he could not raise his head, even to show Buddie that he was dry-eyed. His face was pressed into the lacy bodice of her nightdress so that every breath he took was hot and perfumed. Face powder was tickling his nose, forcing a sneeze to form at the very top of his nostrils. He was sprawled face down across the bed with one foot on the floor and the other tucked beneath his body in such a way that his circulation was impaired and his toes were beginning to go all prickly. He wanted to move but found himself pinned against his mam like a dying bluebottle to a fly-paper. He wanted to stand up and prove to them both that he was no soppy *Mammy's boy*, but the possessive hands held him fast and the voice above his head poured out its soothing, misguided words:

'There, there, there. Oh, hush now, my poor darling. It's all over. You're home. You're safely home, and I promise you will never have to stay there ever again. Hush, now. Hush, my darling.'

'Marlene told him you were expecting.'

Buddie spoke with a disembodied voice that seemed to come from everywhere in the room at once. Frankie felt his mam stiffen. Her grip on him tightened. He was beginning to sweat.

'I already told him the *truth*,' Buddie was saying very slowly, as if choosing every word with extra care. 'I told him you had a belly ache that wouldn't go away. That kid Marlene should learn to keep her mouth shut and her nose out of other people's business. I told him she made a mistake. She got it all wrong, got hold of the wrong end of the stick through ear-wigging on adult conversations. I told him it was just a plain, old-fashioned *belly ache*.'

'And does he accept your explanation?'

'Sure he does. Why the hell shouldn't he? I'm his father, damn it, and what I say *goes*.'

While they spoke about him as if he had left the room, Frankie tried to snatch the opportunity to raise his head.

The soft hands with their deceptively strong grip immediately drew him back to his original position. He sucked air through the side of his mouth because his nostrils were squashed shut against one of her breasts. He heard her ask for a glass of water with a slice of fresh lemon inside, then the door opened and closed, jangling the glass mobile, and he and his mam were alone in the room. In an instant she had shoved him to his feet and gripped him by the shoulders. Her eyes flashed cold fires of anger.

'What did I tell you?' she demanded in a hissing voice. 'What did I tell you about those bitches at Lansdowne Place? Didn't I warn you they were all liars and trouble-makers? Didn't I tell you they'd run me down if they had the chance?' She began to shake him by the shoulders so violently that his teeth rattled. 'Well, didn't I? *Didn't I?*'

'Y-Yes, Sm-Smallfry . . . '

'They're all jealous of me. *Jealous*, that's what they are, but I'll show them. I'll show the bad-mouthed cows. They couldn't wait to start spreading the dirt, could they? *Expecting*, am I? *Expecting!* Well, we'll soon see about *that!*'

' . . . er . . . yes, Smallfry . . . '

The door opened and Buddie re-entered the room with a tall glass of cold water in which floated a large wedge of lemon. He found Smallfry kneeling on the bed and wiping a lace-trimmed handkerchief over Frankie's face, her eyes soft with concern as she smiled at her young son.

'Hush, darling,' she soothed. 'No more weeping, or you'll make yourself ill. We should never have left him there so long, Buddie. I told you he'd suffer. I *knew* he'd come back in a state of distress. Didn't I tell you so?'

'Yes, you did, but he'll never learn to toughen up if you keep on fussing over him like that. What the hell has he got to cry about, anyway?'

'But Buddie, I'm not . . . oh . . . !'

Frankie's words were stifled amid folds of cotton lace as his nose was savagely pinched and twisted to one side

251

beneath the handkerchief. He knew he deserved the pinch for attempting to contradict his mam, even if she *had* made a mistake. The sudden pain caused tears to spring to his eyes.

'Oh, stop your snivelling and pull yourself together, *Mammy's boy*,' Buddie growled.

Smallfry smiled again. 'Now, Buddie. Please don't spoil his homecoming by losing your temper. Come, Frankie, kick off your shoes and climb up on the bed so you can lie beside me. There, isn't that cosy? Oh, my poor darling, you look so *thin*. Has Nanny been neglecting you? But then, I don't suppose you had much of an appetite in that house, did you?'

' . . . er . . . well . . . er . . . ' Frankie stammered, then a stream of words fell from his lips in an untidy tumble. ' . . . oh . . . did you see my pig? Did you see Toto? That's a Swahili name, from Africa. It's for children and babies and small animals. Isn't he a fine pig? Dora killed all the others, and now she has to go for slaughter. Did you know that?'

'Yes, darling, I know all about that.'

'And Buddie says Toto can be *my* pig, just mine and nobody else's, *forever*.'

'Yes, darling, that's very nice. Now, rest your head back against the pillows. There, that's better. Now you relax while I stroke your brow, and no more tears. Will you promise? No more tears?'

He glanced at Buddie, met his glare of disapproval head-on.

'Yes, I promise,' he muttered, wishing the mistake could have been avoided. 'No more tears.'

After a while he became so relaxed and comfortable that he was loath to move a muscle lest it mar the pleasure of his homecoming. He watched Buddie remove a broken string from his guitar and replace it with a new one, an expression of intense concentration on his face as he twisted the little knobs that set the instrument in perfect tune. For

Frankie time seemed to hang suspended. Only when his bladder was so full that it hurt did he dare excuse himself and dash upstairs to the bathroom.

'Can I come back down?' he asked eagerly.

'Of course you can, my dear. We might even persuade your father to play his guitar for us. Now wouldn't that be nice?'

'Oh, yes. Will you, Buddie? Will you?'

'Well, now . . . ' Buddie flicked his fingers and a Spanish Flamenco danced briefly across the strings. ' . . . I reckon I just might do that.'

Frankie ran from the room with his eyes bright. The linoleum was cold beneath his bare feet, and after the heat of the best room the rest of the house had a damp chill about it that made him shiver. He ran silently upstairs to the bathroom, did what he had to do, then groped his way along the gloomy corridor to his own room. He found it dark and unwelcoming, and because it had been shut up tight for a whole week, the familiar smells of mould and damp had become offensive, especially after the perfumed atmosphere of the best room. He rummaged amongst the bits of carpet beneath the bed, pulled out his precious parcel and, without opening its newspaper wrappings, hugged it to him in a fierce embrace. He was laughing. Buddie had not snitched on him, after all. Mr Ted was still safe.

'See you later, Mr Ted,' he promised, then stuffed the parcel back into its hiding place and hurried downstairs to the kitchen. He had no sooner entered the room than the huge, ugly, wheezing face of the new bulldog appeared at the window to slaver all over the glass and fix Frankie with its mean, wild-boar stare. He shuddered and turned away. Nader bared her teeth as he tip-toed to the cardboard box, crouched nervously and reached out a hand to stroke the back of the sleeping piglet. Then he lifted the special gift from his brown paper carrier bag and returned with it to the best room.

253

'Come in, my darling,' Smallfry called in answer to his knock. Her green eyes widened and she threw up her hands in surprise when he handed her the flat, square box with its wrapping of deep blue tissue paper. 'A present? My goodness, is this for me? Oh, Frankie, how *wonderful*.'

He stood with his hands clasped behind his back and his face wreathed in smiles as she opened the box with care, so as not to damage her lovely nails, and lifted out the dazzling white handkerchief with its pretty lace trim and beautifully embroidered corner. His auntie had chosen well. Every penny of his spending money from Nanny had gone into buying that gift. He had not bought a penny loaf or a stick of Spanish for himself all week, just so that Smallfry could have something special that came from him and would really please her and would last for ever.

'Oh, Frankie, it's *beautiful*,' she said. 'Look, Buddie. Look at the roses and violets and forget-me-nots. And just see what it says here, among the flowers . . . *To Mother* . . . Oh, isn't that sweet?'

Buddie nodded and winked an eye to show his approval of the gift. Frankie beamed. He wondered if he would dare tell his father, when he caught him in a really good mood, that Smallfry had made a mistake and he had not really been crying at all while she was holding him so tightly.

'Come here and give your favourite lady a big kiss.'

He wiped the back of his hand across his mouth and pressed his lips against her turned cheek. He was not allowed to kiss his mam on the mouth because it would smudge her lipstick and spread nasty germs. This was just one of the many reasons why he hated Tom Fish. Every time he saw the big Irishman kissing his mam's mouth it made him feel sick inside, with a feeling like shame that he could not really describe, even to himself.

'Oh Frankie, Frankie.' Smallfry tossed her beautiful hair and her laughter was even prettier than the tinkling

254

sound of the glass mobile. 'You look *exactly* like your father when you scowl like that.'

A sense of pride brought the smile back to his face and dispelled the sudden dark cloud created by memories of the Irishman. When she patted the bed beside her he climbed up and settled himself comfortably in the crook of her arm. She reached for his hand, her own soft and white with neatly painted crimson nails, his small and dark, with long brown fingers and nails so badly bitten that they resembled unsightly scabs growing on the ends of each finger. She seemed not to notice their ugliness. She was smiling. He closed his eyes and breathed the warm fragrance that was so distinctly his mam's own, and he wondered when he had last felt so good, so *loved*.

Buddie's nut-brown fingers plucked at the strings of his guitar, coaxing a melody from polished wood and taut wire and mother-of-pearl trim. He hummed a husky accompaniment, at first merely hinting at the tune with short phrases, but soon singing the words in his deep, almost-Fats Waller, almost-Louis Armstrong voice.

'To spend one night with you . . .
In our old rendezvous . . .
. . . za . . . za . . . za . . . za . . . '

Frankie lolled back against his mam's shoulder with one leg crossed casually over the other, feeling sleepy now in that hot room with its gleaming *objets d'art*, flickering firelight and piquant blend of perfumes. He was Aladdin reclining on a bed of swan's down in his spectacular cave, or Kublai Kahn resplendent in his tent of many treasures, or the King of England ruling over his fabulous collection of jewels.

'And reminisce with you . . .
. . . za . . . za . . . za . . . za . . .
. . . that's my desire . . . '

Frankie could see himself reflected in the dusty mirror of a sideboard whose wood was black as ebony and carved all over with fruits and ferns and bare-breasted women and the faces of grinning gods from faraway places. He saw himself, skinny and small and swarthy, lounging in aristocratic comfort upon a golden brass bed with snowy white covers. How he wished his nanny and his aunties could see him now. This was exactly what Mrs Ramsbottom had meant when she told everyone he lived like a young prince in the very lap of luxury.

'*To hear you whisper low . . .*
Darling, I love you so . . .
. . . za . . . za . . . za . . . za . . .'

He smiled sleepily, letting his father's voice and his mam's closeness wash over him in waves of warm contentment. He was safe, now, at least for a little while. Tomorrow he would have to face the ferocious Bebop, and he must remember to chant triple or even quadruple prayers to keep Buddie from going to prison. Then on Monday morning he would no doubt be called into Mr Sunderland's office to be punished for Auntie's bare-faced cheek. In the back of his mind he knew that dangerous shadows still lurked in every corner, but just for tonight they had all been rendered harmless. He was safely home, and tonight he was afraid of nothing.

'*. . . but now it's time to go . . .*
. . . za . . . za . . . za . . . za . . .
. . . that's my des . . . ire . . .
. . . oh yeah!'

As the song ended, Buddie and Smallfry smiled into each others' eyes and blew a silent kiss across the room. Frankie's nervous twitch had deserted him completely, leaving his features relaxed and calm and his mouth curved in a gentle smile. The luckiest boy in all the world, the Little Prince of Old Ashfield, had fallen asleep in his mam's arms.